# Hostile Takeover

The Billionaires' Club Series: Book 1

## AE Moran

The Invisible Publishing Company

# The Billionaires' Club Series

# Contents

# Chapter 1: Lane

I adjust the wide leather seat, tilt it back, and prop my feet up on the footrest. I only have to look out the window of my private jet to see the New York City skyline coming closer.

I'll have to sit up pretty soon, button my shirt collar and tie my tie, and go out there and show everyone what a shark I am.

In the meantime, I can just relax here in this seat and enjoy the sight of my hostess, Shirley, coming toward me with my bourbon glass on a small round tray.

She perches the tray on her fingertips with practiced ease. Her tight pencil skirt hugs her hips and she sways when she walks on her high heels.

She sees me checking her out and blushes as she bends over to hand me my drink. "Can I get you anything else, Mr. Prince?" she asks.

I grin up at her. I can think of a lot of things I'd like her to get me, but that can wait. We're too close to landing in New York. We don't have time for all the things I can think to ask her to do.

I reply, "That's all. Thank you, Shirley," and she walks away, which gives me plenty to look at.

I should be paying attention to what's going to be happening on the ground instead of admiring an air hostess's ass, but damn! What an ass!

I take a sip of my drink and turn back to the window. Everything waiting for me on the ground comes rushing back—now that I no longer have Shirley distracting me.

Just in case I might have forgotten, my assistant Stewart comes over and sits down in the chair opposite me.

The chair is another extra wide leather airplane seat, but he doesn't kick back or put his feet up. He holds his tablet in one hand, so he can only be here to talk about business. He wouldn't disturb me if he didn't want to talk about business.

"Do you want to go over the numbers one more time before we land?" he asks.

"Not really, since you ask. We've already been over them enough. I know the numbers. This meeting won't be about the numbers anyway."

He grins at me. "Let me guess. This meeting will be about pure law-of-the-jungle intimidation. Admit it. You eat this stuff for lunch."

I try not to show how pleased his comments make me. "I'll eat them for lunch."

He checks his tablet. "The Titanium Finance executive board is Spencer Holt, Bradley Lenz, Reese McCall, Cesar Pound, and Samantha Mulholland."

"I know who they are, Stewart," I murmur. "You don't have to tell me."

He shifts in his seat. "Right. I guess I'm just nervous."

"Which is why I'm the one who's going to be eating them for lunch. You won't be doing it. Just let me handle it. You've already done an outstanding job of preparing me for this. Just sit back and watch the fireworks."

His eyes dart to the window and he grimaces like he might be about to be sick on the floor. "Maybe I should remove myself to the next county to avoid the explosions."

I laugh, but right then, Shirley comes back. "Mr. Prince, Captain Shortland asked me to tell you we'll be landing in ten minutes."

"Thank you, Shirley." I down the rest of my drink, hand her the empty glass, and fold down my footrest as I sit up. "It's too late to run away now," I tell Stewart. "We're going in and we're going to take this company. No one can stop us."

He only nods, but his eyes keep skipping back to the window.

I can't look at him anymore. I need to get my game face on.

I button my shirt, pick up my tie, and take my jacket off the seat back next to me.

Stewart's reaction doesn't make me nervous for the meeting ahead. It will be hostile and probably downright dangerous, but I was born for this shit.

His reaction makes me deadly calm and coldly determined. I'm going to own Titanium Finance if it's the last thing I do. No one better get in my way.

I stand up, put on my jacket, tie my tie, and then go to the bathroom in the back of the plane. I check my suit, comb my hair, straighten my shirt sleeves for the hundredth time.

I look good enough to meet the Titanium Finance executive board—which is another way of saying I look intimidating enough. They don't want me to acquire their company, but I really don't care what they want.

Titanium Finance is too good to pass up. My company, Apico Acquisitions, has been trying for months to maneuver Titanium into a sale.

Now it's crunch time. If the Titanium Finance executive board doesn't play ball, I'll have to pull a hostile takeover on them. I don't want to do that.

Okay, yes, I do want to do that. Nothing thrills me more than flexing my muscle on people who can't stop me, but I can play nice when I absolutely have to.

I go back out into the plane's main cabin where I meet up with Stewart. Now he looks seriously green, but that only delights me more. I'm the shark here, not him. That's why I get paid the big bucks.

We return to our seats, but we only have to sit there for five minutes before the plane glides in to land at the JFK airport. I stay in my seat and relax while the pilot taxies to a private hangar.

Stewart checks his tablet again. "The chopper is on its way to pick us up."

I only nod. My team is too good to leave any detail of this project to chance. Everything is set up perfectly.

"The executive team from Apico Acquisitions is already on the way to the Titanium Finance building," Stewart tells me. "They'll meet us there."

I don't answer that, either. I already know what's about to happen and what I'm about to do.

I drop down into a dark, silent place inside myself. No one can touch me here. A wall of black ice surrounds me. I barely hear the plane's engines whining or the thump of chopper blades getting closer.

I pretend to look out the window at the chopper touching down on the tarmac outside the hangar, but I don't see anything out there. I only see this dark, silent, internal landscape and the task in front of me.

It's always like this when I go to war against another company. This cold determination it takes to win—it happens to me automatically. I don't even have to try to turn myself into this killer. I already am.

The plane's engines wind down. Stewart and I disembark and head straight for the chopper. I don't even care that the rotor wash messes up my hair. I'll only look more threatening if the Titanium board thinks I don't care about looking perfect.

The chopper lifts off. Now I can see straight down between all the New York skyscrapers to cabs and cars whizzing back and forth through the streets below. Everything down there is so far away from me.

Stewart gets the message that I don't want to talk. He knows me well enough. He recognizes when I need him to leave me alone.

He doesn't say anything all the way to the Titanium Finance building. The chopper sets down on the roof. My executive team from Apico Acquisitions meets us there at the entrance to an elevator leading down inside the Titanium Finance building.

Marshall Weiss, Marco Van Sant, Ricardo Thorn, Russel Shauer, and Ethan Rosch rush over to me and try to talk to me, but I can't hear them over the noise.

We all head for the elevator together where another three young women come toward me. I don't recognize them. "Welcome to Titanium Finance, Mr. Prince," a blonde one tells me. "The Titanium board is all ready for you downstairs. If you follow us, we'll show you where to go."

I only reply, "Thank you."

"Can I get you anything?" she asks. "Anything to eat or drink—or would you like to stop by a private suite before the meeting to prepare?"

"I don't need to prepare. Just take me to the board. I don't need anything else."

She looks away and mumbles, "Yes, Sir."

No one else says anything. I say it as casually as I can, but the rest of my board knows how I get before meetings like this.

An air of danger hangs over the group on our way downstairs. The three Titanium employees ride down with us in silence.

All three wear business suits with their hair done up in neat, sweeping professional arrangements. They all wear class jewelry and each one carries a laptop, device, or business folio.

I can't tell if these girls are officers in the company or just someone's assistants. These three young women could be the most junior employees in the company.

I don't know and I don't care. I just need to find out where the Titanium Finance executive board is. The rest will take care of itself.

The tension spikes to the breaking point when the elevator stops. The three girls step out. "This way, Mr. Prince," the same blonde tells m e.

I follow her. Stewart and my team follow me.

This feeling of iron-clad resolve takes over my whole mind as I walk down the hall. The three girls lead the way to a massive conference room on the next floor down from the roof.

Towering glass windows give an expansive view of the New York skyline. A colossal fireplace built of black stone covers one wall of the room.

The long polished granite table runs down the middle of the room with conference speakers, electronic ports, and power points in front of every huge leather chair.

This has to be the Titanium Finance executive boardroom. Wow. These people really rolled out the red carpet for me.

My reputation must have preceded me, but that's nothing new. I didn't name my company Apico Acquisitions for nothing. I'm in the business of acquiring other people's companies.

That's why I'm here, not to make these people feel better about it.

I slow my approach as I walk into the room. The Titanium Finance executive board all stands up from their seats.

I measure each of them in the blink of an eye. I know all their records, resumes, and reputations as well as they know mine.

Spencer Holt is a weasel in thick glasses. He's the company Chief Information Officer, which is a nice way of saying he's a computer geek who knows how to sweet talk circuit boards and programming software better than he knows how to deal with people.

I like to think of Bradley Lenz as a younger version of myself. He's ambitious, driven, and determined. He's Titanium Finance's Chief of Operations.

Reese McCall is a middle-aged man with a beer gut. He handles the company's marketing and not very well if I do say so. He'll be the first on the chopping block as soon as I take over this company. We can do so much better.

Cesar Pound is the Chief Public Relations officer and I don't have any beef with him. He's a thirty-year-old family man who keeps his nose clean and makes sure the company keeps its nose clean, too. Titanium Finance is as successful as it is because of Cesar.....and because of the only woman at the table.

Samantha Mulholland is also thirty with wavy, chocolate-brown hair and a body that just won't quit. Her tight power suit has been tailored around the chest and sides to make her waist look long and narrow down to full, hourglass hips.

Clear, soft, puppy-dog eyes glow out of her perfectly made-up face. She has a round, almost cherubic facial structure that makes her drop-dead gorgeous.

She's hands down the most intimidating person in the room besides me. In fact, she's the only person on the Titanium side who's intimidating at all.

She's the company Chief Financial Officer, which means she holds this company by the balls. I might be able to snatch the company out from under its shareholders and take it as my own. I wouldn't be able to run it for ten seconds without her.

I've been strategizing on how to win her over, but I still haven't come up with anything yet. Her reputation for being a savage when it comes to anything financial is only slightly overshadowed by her reputation for loyalty to her boss—the last man in the room.

# Chapter 2: Lane

Titanium Finance CEO Derek Salazar stands at the head of the table. He's thirty-five and he built Titanium Finance from the ground up. He's been telling everyone on the Eastern Seaboard that he'll never sell. He just doesn't see the writing on the wall yet.

Derek strides toward me when I walk in and holds out his hand. "Welcome, Mr. Prince. Thank you for meeting us."

He says all the right words, but I could cut the hostility in the room with an axe. He shakes my hand and then waves me and my team toward the table. "Please—take your seats and let's get started."

He sits back down at one end of the table. The rest of his execs sit on either side of him at their end of the table.

That leaves me to sit at the other end of the table with my people around me. Stewart remains standing behind my chair just to give me an extra godfather vibe.

Derek pretends to consult the iPad in front of him. "We've all had a chance to go over your proposal, but our answer is still the same. We aren't prepared to sell Titanium Finance at this time."

"At this time," I repeat. "Does that mean you have some alternate conditions to propose that would make you consider it?"

"I'm afraid not," he replies. "Your offer is very generous...."

"But apparently not generous enough. Let me ask you this. Are there *any* conditions under which you would be willing to consider selling—any conditions at all? Are you so entrenched in keeping this company that you won't see reason?"

He raises his hands for an instant before he puts them back down on the table. "Titanium Finance is not for sale, Mr. Prince. That's the bottom line."

I study him across the table. Is it me or is he just so attached to this company that he'll walk away from a generous offer like mine?

He would never get an offer like this from anyone else. He must realize that.

"Is it me?" I ask and smile at him just to show there are no hard feelings if it is me. "Would you be willing to sell to someone else under these conditions—or do you have some objection to selling out to me in particular?"

A few other people on his board shift in their seats. They must have discussed this between themselves.

Derek tries to shrug it off, but he finally caves with the truth. "I'll be honest with you, Mr. Prince, since that's obviously what you want. I don't believe you're the right man to run Titanium Finance. I don't believe you'll be able to make this company work because you don't understand our culture. I don't believe you'll be able to reproduce my relationship with my employees."

"I disagree. I run a lot of companies, Mr. Salazar. I'm sure I can run this one, too."

"It's precisely because you run a lot of companies that you wouldn't be able to run this one. Titanium Finance is a close-knit community of like-minded individuals all pulling toward a common goal. This company requires a personal touch. It wouldn't work if the man at the top was being pulled in a dozen different directions—let alone dozens of different directions by different company obligations the way you are. You would bring this company down in a matter of months if you took it over."

"That's why I offered to keep you on as Managing Director," I tell him. "You could still run the company the same way you are now. You would be as involved in your employees' everyday business just as much as you are now. You would all keep working toward the same vision. Nothing would change in the company culture. You could make sure of that."

He glares at me for the first time and lowers his voice to a snarl. "I would never agree to be an employee in my own company, Mr. Prince. This company is my heart and soul. You are the last man alive I would ever sell it to."

I expected nothing less than this, either. I glance up and down the table. Reese McCall glares at me. Other than him and Derek, only one person on the Titanium side will even look at me.

Samantha Mulholland leans back in her chair gazing down the table at me. She studies my face extra closely like she's trying to figure me out.

She doesn't display any emotional reaction at all that I'm trying to buy her boss's company. She just sits there removed from the whole proceedings—which is strange considering how uncomfortable everyone else in the room is acting.

I glance at the other Titanium execs. "Does your team all feel the same way? Do they all think I'm the last man alive you should sell the company to?"

Derek starts to say, "What they think doesn't matter...." but at the same time, Spencer Holt glances at him. That confirms it. At least one person on the Titanium side does think selling to me is a good idea.

I check the others. Cesar Pound fiddles with his stylus on the table. Bradley Lenz leans back in his chair like he's relaxed, but he won't look at me, either.

Samantha just sits there. Of everyone here, she's the only one I can truly believe never once considered selling Titanium Finance to me. It never once crosses her mind to betray Derek even by suggesting that he sell his precious company.

She could see all the evidence in the world that Titanium Finance will be better off under me than it will be under Derek. In fact, she has seen that evidence.

None of that matters. Her loyalty to him and the company over-rides everything else. She doesn't let her personal feelings interfere with the job.

I have to convince her. None of these other people matter. She controls Titanium's finances. Once I own this company, I'll rely on her to run it for me as well as she runs it for Derek.

"It looks and sounds to me like you're irrational about this company," I tell Derek. "It looks and sounds to me like you won't take the advice of people who think selling to me is a good idea. You're too emotionally invested in this company."

Derek's features harden even more. He doesn't even try to hide his fury. "You have our answer, Mr. Prince. Titanium Finance is not for sale—to you or anyone else."

"Then you leave me no choice but to go to the shareholders themselves." I lean farther back in my chair and adjust the button of my jacket even though it's already buttoned. "I'm going to own this company one way or the other. If you won't sell, you leave me no choice but to carry out a hostile takeover."

"You bastard!" Reese McCall blurts out. "Are you trying to ruin us? You would ruin this company just to make sure no one else owns it! You're as gutless as they say."

"Who says that?" I ask in as calm a tone as I can.

Reese winds up for another volley, but Derek lays his hand on Reese's arm to silence him. "You won't be able to carry out a hostile takeover of Titanium Finance, Mr. Prince. Our shareholders are as dedicated to our company vision as we are. They believe in the values this company stands for. They won't let you buy them out, either."

"You don't think so?" I extend my hand over the back of my chair without looking. Stewart puts his tablet in my hands with the list of Titanium Finance shareholders already up on the screen.

I read down the list of names. "Apart from you, Mr. Salazar, the majority stake in Titanium Finance is owned by the Silverberg Trust, Labyrinth Enterprises, and Global Intelligence Systems. We've already purchased three hundred units from each of those three stakeholders. As soon as we pass seven hundred units, the price will break through the next resistance level and trigger an automatic selloff among the remaining shareholders. You won't be able to stop us from acquiring this company."

Derek's lips go white and smoke billows out of his ears. "You won't get away with it."

"Did you really think you could stop me?" I stand up, hand Stewart back his tablet, and adjust my jacket one last time just to drive the dagger home. "I'll give you twenty-four hours to reconsider my proposal. If you don't accept it, none of you will get anything."

The rest of my board takes that cue to stand up, too, and we all walk out of the room. Spencer Holt, Bradley Lenz, Reese McCall, and Cesar Pound shoot to their feet at the same time.

Derek stands up more slowly. Samantha doesn't budge. She stays sitting in the same place while my team and I walk out of the conference room.

We leave so suddenly that our three female escorts don't show up in time to lead us out of the building.

"That went exactly the way you expected," Stewart murmurs in my ear once we get into the elevator."

"He's out of his mind," I mutter under my breath. "This company is his baby. He doesn't even recognize when he's about to get cut off at the knees."

"What do you want to do about him? He's going to cause us problems once we do acquire the company."

"He doesn't mean anything. He won't cause us any problems. He's a child. I can handle him."

"So that's it? You're going ahead with the takeover? You aren't going to give him a chance to reconsider?"

"He'll never reconsider and he'll never sell. Forget him. I want you to spend the next twenty-four hours pulling up everything you can find on Samantha Mulholland. No one else matters. We need to concentrate all our efforts on her from now on."

# Chapter 3: Samantha

Derek Salazar walks out of the conference room the minute Lane Prince and his team end the meeting. This was hardly a negotiation the way it was supposed to be. It was more of an ultimatum, but that's Lane Prince's style. He's a hatchet man and everyone knows i t.

He seems to thrive on it. He might even get off on it. That's the really amazing thing. He doesn't care if everyone knows he's a shark. He actually seems to enjoy putting the fear of God into everyone.

Derek stalks out of the conference as soon as the door finishes hitting Lane in his perfectly chiseled ass. The guy has looks. I'll give him that.

He sure knows how to cut a figure when he walks into a corporate executive boardroom. I've never seen a suit cut as well as his.

His short-clipped sandy hair and brilliant blue eyes make him look every inch the savage that he is.

He knew he had the Titanium Finance by the throat before he walked into this room. He had all the shares locked up.

Lane actually did Derek a favor by conducting this negotiation. Derek is just too proud to see that. Lane offered Derek a chance to get out with his dignity and his wealth intact. Now that's gone.

It isn't my job to fix that. The other execs on the Titanium Finance board have already stated their opinions and encouraged Derek to sell.

He loves this company too much to give in. I don't need to repeat what the others already said. That will only hurt his feelings.

He's right about the company culture being something special, but the whole staff works to make it that way.

I'm dedicated to his vision of keeping it that way, but I have nothing to lose if Lane does take over Titanium. I'll still have a job. Derek won't.

The rest of us follow him out into the hall. We have to hurry to keep up with him. He must be really mad and I don't blame him.

"I told you we should have taken his offer," Bradley Lenz insists. "We all could have gotten hefty compensation packages as part of the sale. Now none of us will get anything."

Derek spins around fast. "Go pack up your office, Bradley," Derek snaps. "You don't have a job here anymore."

Bradley stiffens, but he doesn't back down. "You don't have the authority to fire me without the Board of Directors' approval. We all told you it was a terrible idea to stand up to Lane Prince. Now he'll carry out a hostile takeover and we'll all be left out in the cold thanks to your selfish, stupid attitude."

Derek narrows his eyes at Bradley. Derek might be ten years older, but he can't run Titanium Finance without Bradley. Derek can't run this place without all of us.

"You better watch your mouth," Derek snarls. "This is my company. If I don't want to sell it to some crook from the other side of town, I won't. The discussion is over. You all can go back to work."

"You can't go it alone, Derek," Bradley insists. "We're all saying the same thing. You still have twenty-four hours to do the right thing. You talked a good line in there about all the employees being a community and pulling together for a common cause. If you really meant it, you'll do the best thing for all of us and accept Lane's offer. If you don't, you could lose everything—not just for yourself, but for all of us."

Derek glares at him and then waves at the rest of us. "I don't hear all of you saying the same thing—not at all. I hear you blowing a lot of noise out of your mouth. I don't hear anyone else saying it."

"You have to admit it's an incredible offer," Spencer Holt murmurs. "We would never get an offer like that from anyone else."

"We wouldn't get an offer like that from anyone else because we wouldn't sell Titanium to anyone else," Derek fires back. "Jesus, Spencer, you can't be serious about actually wanting to sell it to him."

"I don't have to want to do anything," Spencer chokes. "He'll get the company one way or the other. He always does. The only question is whether any of us will still have a retirement plan when this is finished."

"Oh, please!" Derek spins around and faces Reese McCall. "Will you say something? Talk some sense into these people."

Reese shuffles his feet and looks away, but that only brings him around to looking at the rest of us. This is the first time Reese has shown any uncertainty about this. He acted so smug and hostile in front of Lane.

"You have to admit they're right," Reese stammers. "That offer was out of this world."

"I can't believe I'm hearing this!" Derek barks. I can't, either, because he's heard it from all of them before. We discussed this more than once. The other execs told him exactly the same thing.

He finally turns to me. I haven't said anything, before or since.

"What about you, Samantha?" he asks. "Do you think I should accept Lane Prince's offer? I can't believe you would actually suggest that."

"I won't suggest that, but if you don't accept it, you better work fast and pull a dozen rabbits out of your hat. It looks to me like he's already end-running your stockholders. If he's that far ahead of us, it's gonna be pretty hard to stop him."

"You do that," he tells me. "You can stop him from carrying out this takeover."

"I can't do anything. You need to contact your majority shareholders and find a way to stop the automatic selloff."

"He can't do it, either," Spencer chimes in. "The selloff is computer generated. If Lane really has bought that many shares in Titanium, we may already be too late."

"This is nuts," Derek mutters and turns away toward the elevator. "There has to be a way to stop him and I'm going to find it."

He leaves to go back to his office. The rest of us stand around casting glances at each other before we separate, too.

I go to my office, but I can't work. All our current projects are now up in the air until we know whether Apico Acquisitions will be buying us out.

Lane might want to change everything we do. All the work I'm doing now might be irrelevant once he takes over. How would I know?

I leave early at seven PM and drive uptown. I normally work late, but what's the point?

I walk into a swanky restaurant where I meet my sister Olivia and my brother Casey waiting for me.

Casey kisses me on the cheek. "Hey, baby girl. They finally let you out of your cage. I'm shocked."

I laugh at him. "You're one to talk. Do you wear that tie to hide your shock collar—the one the senior partners use to make sure you don't get too far away from the law stacks?"

He joins in the joke. He looks incredible in a deep blue suit, gold tie tack, gold cuff links, and his hair cut curly on top. His dark eyes match mine and Olivia's. Anyone who looks closely can see we're related. We all have the same coloring and the same facial bone structure.

Olivia looks nice in a tailored business suit, pearl earrings, and her hair twisted into a princess swirl on the back of her head. Two long, looping curls hang in front of her face.

"How's the world of high finance?" I ask her.

"You would know that better than I do," she replies. "I'm not the CFO of a major corporation."

"No, you're just a managing partner of a major investment firm. Don't sell yourself short."

Casey steps up to the bar. "What are you girls drinking tonight? We're here to celebrate."

"I'll have a Bloody Mary," I tell him.

"I'll take a glass of pineapple juices," Olivia replies.

"What—no hangover for you tomorrow?" Casey teases. "It's your birthday. Tie one on. Heaven knows you've been working hard enough lately."

"No hangover for me, thanks. Just the juice."

Casey orders for us and the three of us settle down on stools at the bar. He orders a tumbler of Scotch on the rocks and raises his glass in a toast. "Here's to thirty-two years beautiful years of life on Planet Earth with Olivia. May she someday learn to relax enough to drink booze again so she doesn't make the rest of us feel like such losers."

We all laugh. "Happy birthday," I tell Olivia and we drink the toast.

"Do we want to get food?" Casey asks.

"Sure," I reply. "This place has great seafood. We came here for a work party three weeks ago."

"How come Titanium Finance has all the best parties?" he asks.

"What's wrong? Don't you and the other law zombies have pizza parties in the stacks at Holden & Sons?"

He turns bright red and laughs. "Are you always gonna harp on me for being a law zombie? That's the third time you've mentioned me being stuck in the stacks."

"It was only the second time."

"It turns out that I don't spend any time in the stacks at all. I make my clerks who do that for me."

Now it's my turn to laugh. "So you're a law stacks slum lord. I thought you were more compassionate than that."

He starts to shoot me another snarky remark when Olivia's phone rings in her handbag. She pulls it out, checks the screen, and makes a face. "I gotta take this."

"Hey! It's your birthday!" Casey yells after her. "You're supposed to be taking the night off."

"Nice try, big brother," I tell him after she walks out into the hall. "We're all slaves to the grind."

"I'm a slave to my bladder." He tosses the rest of his drink. "Try not to get too lonely without me."

"Do you want me to order something for you?" I call after him.

He answers over his shoulder, "Surprise me," and walks off toward the bathrooms.

I wave the bartender down, order some appetizers for all three of us, and sip my drink while I wait for my brother and sister to come back. The bar gets noisier as the evening wears on. We should have gotten a table.

I start to look around to see if any are available for us to nab. I face front real quick when I see Lane Prince coming toward me.

He glides right up to my stool and sits down where Olivia was just sitting. "Just the lady I was hoping to run into," he purrs.

"I'm busy here, Mr. Prince. Go back to whatever you were doing before you came over here."

"Call me Lane," he tells me. "We can be on a first-name basis, can't we? We'll be working together all the time once I take over Titanium Finance."

"You haven't taken it over yet. You're the enemy until then."

"I'm not your enemy." He leans a little closer. "Come on. Talk to me. I want to get to know you."

"Why—so you can milk me for information to help you screw over Derek Salazar? Forget it."

"You know I'm not screwing over Derek Salazar or anyone else—and I don't need information from you to do it. He's doing it faster than anyone else could do it for him. You're too smart not to see that."

I take another sip of my drink to hide that I know he's right. Derek is his own worst enemy.

I don't say that out loud, though, Lane doesn't need me to confirm it.

"Can I buy you a drink?" he asks again. "Why are you here all by yourself?"

"What I do in my free time is none of your business—and no, you can't buy me a drink. Are you here with those guys over there? Go back there and leave me alone. I'm not talking to you unless you actually succeed in taking over Titanium Finance and I get into a situation where I get paid to talk to you. Until then, get lost."

He starts to say, "Can't we just talk about this....?" but right then, Casey comes back.

He shoves between me and Lane, turns his back to me, and towers over Lane's stool. "You heard the lady, asshole. She isn't interested in you. Walk away while you still can."

Lane bristles and stands up. "I was trying to be polite to her and she was all alone. Who the hell are you—her boyfriend?"

"I'm her brother, you jackass," Casey snaps. "Now back off before you get hurt."

Lane changes his tune in a heartbeat. He stares at Casey and then Lane's cheeks turn bright red. "Oh. Sorry."

He beats in and vanishes into the crowd. Casey sits down on Olivia's stool and orders another drink. Casey mutters, "Dumbass," under his breath.

I beam at him. "My hero."

"Who the hell does he think he is? He thinks he can just waltz in and take whatever he wants. He's a cocksucker."

"He's Lane Prince, sweetheart," I tell him.

"I know who the hell he is, sweetheart," Casey replies. "That doesn't give him the right to horn in on every woman he lays eyes on. God knows the guy has enough women throwing themselves at him everywhere he goes."

"I know he does." I take another sip of my drink, but just then, Olivia shows up and so does our food.

Casey yells at the bartender and gets us a booth in the back away from the evening bar crowd. We sit down, eat our calamari, and drink a few more toasts to Olivia.

Casey walks us out afterward. "Do I need to take you home to protect you from the Lane Princes of the world?"

I do my best to laugh it off. "He isn't as bad as he seems."

"No, he's worse."

"It isn't like that. We're just on opposite sides of the playing field right now. If he does buy Titanium, I'll have to get on his team real quick and put all this hostility behind me."

He raises his eyebrows. "So you actually think this merger is going to happen?"

"It isn't a merger. It might be a buyout, but it will probably turn into a hostile takeover. Don't tell Derek I said so, but I really don't see how it can end any other way."

# Chapter 4: Lane

I step into The Billionaires' Club and scan the room. I spot Derek Salazar right away, but he's busy talking to Judah Hayes and Dante Helme.

Judah is the club's only African American member. He's tall, muscular, powerful, serious, and quiet in a smoldering, volcanic way. He never loses his cool, though—not ever. He's made of iron inside and out.

Everyone in the club respects him and I've done business with him. I would trust him with my life, and more importantly, with my money. He runs an investment conglomerate with a bunch of different firms that form a cluster of multiple services.

Dante is an older guy with tightly clipped pale grey hair, a lined face, and a short grey beard. He's as tall and powerful as Judah and Dante has the years of experience that make him deadly.

He's the CEO of a mega healthcare company that runs aged-care, rehab, and recovery facilities all over the country.

I don't want to think I feel any discomfort about being in the same room with Derek, so I waltz right in. I go to the bar, get myself a drink, and join Jackson Metcalf and Kevin Drake.

Kevin is a young guy with a lean, light physique and an easy-going nature. He doesn't have the same killer attitude as most of the other club members. He's just too damn nice. That's his superpower.

He runs a personnel service that provides staffing to just about every significant company I can think of. That's how he made his money. He's also The Billionaires' Club's membership officer.

He doesn't have to go out there and thrash everyone else in the industry. He practically runs all our companies by providing all of us with the people we need to run them.

Jackson is a tank. That's the best way I can describe him. He's five-foot-ten, jacked to the limit with big, broad, muscular shoulders that look outstanding in a suit, straight brown hair, and brutal green eyes.

He's a mining tycoon with operations all over the world. He mines everything from gold and silver, oil, titanium, uranium—you name it.

His personality matches his appearance exactly. You only have to look at him to know everything about him. He's forceful, hard-driving, exacting in his standards, and he pushes himself twice as hard as he pushes everyone else. He's uncompromising in every detail.

Half the people I know can't stand him. They either hate him for holding them to the same high standard or they're petrified of him. The other half of the people I know worship the ground he walks on.

Everyone who works for him loves him to the ends of the Earth. They might be a little scared of him, but you can't help but respect the guy.

He has a quiet, forceful kind of seriousness that makes me instantly trust him. He never compromises—on anything—especially not something as important as his integrity.

He would never do anything illegal or even anything less than the best. He doesn't play that way. He considers himself better than that and he backs it up in all his business dealings.

I pretend to scan the club again. It occupies the whole top floor of an enormous complex downtown.

Three-hundred-and-sixty-degree, floor-to-ceiling windows surround the club on all sides. Luxurious leather couches, top-of-the-line modern furniture, and a full buffet fill the area.

Living gardens, a stream and fountain, and a big stone fireplace divide the floor into sections. The club even has a billiards area, its own movie theater, and kitchens where the members can order any food they want.

Jackson clinks his glass against mine. "How's the world domination game coming along?"

I nod. "I took back the Crimea last week. I'm moving into Central Asia making a play for the Far East next. I'll let you know how it goes."

Both Jackson and Kevin laugh. "Just make sure you secure your supply lines," Jackson tells me.

"And don't go in winter," Kevin adds.

I join in the joke. "I'll be sure not to. I won't go in spring, either. Too muddy."

"How's the Titanium acquisition looking?" Kevin asks.

I glance across the club at Derek. He's shifted his position to turn his back to me. I probably shouldn't be talking about that here at all, so I just say, "They're still considering my offer."

"They would be fools not to accept," Jackson points out, but just then, Dante and Judah come over to join us.

Derek comes with them, but he obviously doesn't want to. He hangs back just for a second and then saunters over to join our circle.

"Asher Gottlieb asked me about joining the club," Dante tells Kevin.

He frowns. "Hmm. I'll have to check his net worth. I didn't realize he was that high up the food chain."

"His father is the one who's that high up the food chain," Judah replies. "Asher is nothing without his father."

"He owns three of his own companies independent from the family business," Jackson chimes in. "Asher might not be in the billion-dollar range, but he's on his way there."

"I'll still have to check," Kevin replies. "Anyway, he hasn't applied yet. Tell him to submit his application through the proper channels. I can't do anything until he does that."

Dante nods. "I already told him. He said he would."

"He's kind of a try-hard, isn't he?" I ask. "He was a daddy's boy the last time I talked to him."

"When was that—five years ago?" Kevin asks. "He could have grown up."

I shrug. "Maybe. He doesn't try too hard to be independent of his old man. Asher is—what—thirty-four now? He should have been independent long ago."

Kevin laughs at me. "Not everyone is as cut out for independence as you, man."

"Lane's right," Jackson adds. "Thirty-four is too old to be working for another man, especially your own father."

"Asher got the stake for his first company from a personal loan from his father," Dante tells us. "You gotta wonder if he would have been able to cut it at all without that."

"The club's charter doesn't say anything about how a member made their money," Kevin points out. "The only criterion is that he has a billion-dollar minimum net worth. If he has that, he's in."

"That doesn't mean we have to like it," I point out.

"Give the guy a break," Kevin tells me. "It isn't his fault he's Saul Gottlieb's son. Bad things can happen to the best of us."

The rest of us laugh and Jackson turns to me to change the subject. "Did you meet Wilson Avery earlier like said you were going to?"

"I just left having drinks with him and his partners at Revelation Steakhouse. I saw Samantha Mulholland there, too."

Derek's head whips around fast and he freezes there staring at me. Kevin laughs at me. "You better watch yourself. She'll cut your nuts off."

"I think she's terrific. She's an outstanding CFO. I couldn't ask for anyone better to run Titanium Finance."

Don't ask me why I said that right in front of Derek. Maybe I'm just losing my head after bumping into Samantha at the bar.

"Do you mind?!" Derek snaps. "You don't own Titanium Finance and you aren't going to."

I try to shrug it away. "Maybe not yet, but you know she's awesome. That's all I'm saying. She's your righthand woman—your ace in the hole as it were."

"She won't be yours," he fires back.

I only shrug. We'll see whether Samantha becomes my righthand woman and my ace in the hole the way she's Derek's.

He only glares at me. Judah changes the subject again and starts talking about Miles Reynolds, one of our oldest members who passed away recently.

"They already cremated the body and the family is having a small, private service for his closest relatives," Judah tells us.

"We could send them flowers on behalf of the club," Kevin suggests.

"We should have a memorial for him here," Dante points out. "We could just invite other club members and remember him in our own way. No one outside the club has to know, but we should do something."

"That's a good idea," Kevin replies. "I'll bring it up at our next board meeting."

I stick around for a little more small talk. In a few minutes, Derek leaves. That's my cue to leave, too, so I call my driver Eddie and go outside.

My limo pulls up in front of the club and I get inside. "Where to, Mr. Prince?" the Eddie asks.

I open my mouth to answer when I happen to glance across the street through the limo's opposite window. The windows are tinted so no one outside can see me in here.

My hair stands on end when I see Samantha Mulholland parking her car in front of a luxury apartment tower across the street from The Billionaires' Club.

Samantha sits behind the wheel while another younger woman hugs her from the passenger seat. Then the passenger gets out, exchanges some words with Samantha through the open passenger door, and shuts the door.

Samantha smiles and waves until the woman goes up to the building door. A uniformed doorman lets her in.

The passenger pauses there and turns back to wave again. Samantha waves back. They both smile with the same broad cherubic look on their faces.

I definitely see the resemblance between Samantha, her brother, and this young woman. This must be Samantha's sister.

The doorman holds the door while the sister goes inside. Samantha faces front and puts her car in gear to drive away.

I'm just about to tell Eddie to take me home when some random dude walks up off the street, yanks Samantha's passenger door open, and gets into the seat in her sister's place.

I barely notice at first. The doorman has his back to the car and doesn't see. Everything looks normal from the outside.

I'm the one person in the world strategically positioned to see what's going on inside the car. The guy lunges across the seat, grabs Samantha by the hair, yanks her head back, and shoves a gun in her face.

I start clawing at the door handle to get out of the limo, but before I can move, Samantha takes her foot off the brake and drives off. Holy shit! She just got carjacked. Whoever that guy is, he's holding her at gunpoint and making her take him somewhere else.

I hop back in the limo and slam the door. "Follow that car, Eddie!"

"Yes, Sir," he replies and pulls out into traffic. I get on my phone and call 911.

"911 emergency operator," the operator answers. "Please state the nature of the emergency.

"I'm in a car on Madison Avenue heading north—past 44th Street! I just saw a woman get carjacked in front of the Sentinel Arms apartment building. There's a guy in the passenger seat holding the female driver at gunpoint! We're passing 55th Street now. I'm following them."

"Can you give me the license plate number of the car, Sir?" she asks.

I read it back. "They're turning onto 57th Street—no, now they're turning south on Park Avenue! They're heading back downtown!"

"Are you able to continue following them, Sir?" she asks. "I'm dispatching Police units now."

"Yeah, we're following them." I move the phone away from my mouth. "Stay with them, Eddie. Don't lose them."

"Yes, Sir," he replies.

Samantha's car drives with the flow of traffic down Park Avenue. I try to listen for any sirens, but I don't hear anything.

I'm just about to ask the operator how long it will be before the Police get here when Samantha's car suddenly jerks off the road, veers into an alley, and plunges into a dark underground parking garage.

The alley is too narrow for the limo to follow. I don't want the kidnapper to see the limo, either. The car is too noticeable.

I push my phone over the seat into Eddie's hands. "Stay on the line. Tell the cops where they are."

"Hey—where are you going?!" he yells after me.

"I'm going in there. I have to help her before he does something to her."

# Chapter 5: Samantha

I scream when the gunman yanks my hair again. "Shut the fuck up, bitch!" he roars in my face. "You better shut the fuck up if you know what's good for you!"

I struggle to keep my composure, but it isn't easy when I see his gun pointed right at my eye.

I can't breathe and he doesn't make it easy by yanking me around like this.

He jerks my head toward him. "Get out of the car, you stupid bitch! Come on!"

He slides across the passenger seat and drags me with him, but my seatbelt stops him from taking me anywhere. I scream again when he pulls my hair hard enough to hurt.

I try to follow him and unbuckle the seatbelt at the same time. He loses his temper and punches his gun into my face.

My head swims and I blink stars out of my eyes. I hear him bellowing at me, but I can't hear him until I reel back to consciousness.

"Get the fuck out of the car before I blow your fucking brains out!" He punches me again. "I said get the fuck out of the car!"

I fumble with the seatbelt and finally unclip it, but he doesn't wait for me to take it off.

He climbs all the way out of the car pulling me after him. I get tangled in the seatbelt and almost break my arm before I get the seatbelt off.

He hauls me out of the car by my hair and throws me on the pavement in some dark underground garage. I try to look around, but he kicks me hard in the ribs.

I can't even scream anymore. He's gonna kill me. I know that now.

My phone is in my handbag on the passenger seat floor. I can't get to the phone to call for help. No one knows where I am.

He attacks me again, punches me in the face a third time, and rips me off the pavement by my hair. I'm too dazed to scream.

He yanks me upright and marches me toward a stairwell in the corner. I stumble and he shoves the gun in my face again.

"You better fucking cooperate, bitch," he snarls in my ear. "If you give me any trouble, you'll pay for it."

I can barely see straight from all the blows to my face. I feel my face swelling up, but that doesn't concern me—not as much as my life does.

I don't know what this guy plans to do with me, but it won't be anything good. When he finishes, he'll probably kill me anyway.

I have to find a way out of this, but how? I need help, but I don't even know if anyone could hear me down here.

If I start screaming now, he might just decide to shoot me here. I don't want to risk that.

He kicks open the stairwell and marches me up the stairs. The parking garage and stairwell are made of solid concrete. No one will be able to hear me.

We climb a long way. I really hope he takes me to an apartment in a corridor full of other apartments. Then maybe someone will hear me scream for help.

He doesn't take me anywhere with other apartments. The stairwell ends in a tiny landing with one door on it. He unlocks it with one hand and shoves me inside hard enough to make me stagger and sprawl on my face.

In a fraction of a second, he's on top of me and pins me face down on the carpet under his weight. I feel him start to tug up my skirt.

I freeze in place. This is really happening.

He crams the gun into the side of my head and snarls in my ear. "Make one sound and I'll blow your fucking brains out, you worthless bitch,"

He squashes me flat and his stiffening bulge digs into my ass. I stare straight in front of me. I can't deal with this. I need to go somewhere else—somewhere I won't feel what's about to happen.

Without warning, the guy yanks my head back by my hair and slams me face down into the carpet.

He's just pulling my head back to do it a second time when something flies out of nowhere, connects with his head, and the force of impact tears the attacker off me.

The guy goes flying, but he's holding onto me so tightly that he winds up pulling me over onto my back.

I lie there stunned as I stare up at Lane Prince standing over me. What the holy hell is he doing here?

His normally calm face contorts in brutal rage. His leg is still flying up in the air from kicking the attacker in the head. Before I can move, Lane takes a step and kicks the guy a second time.

The guy goes sprawling, but just as fast, he swipes up his gun to point it at Lane. I blast off the floor and scramble backward to get away from them. I barely have the presence of mind to pull my skirt down before I bump into the wall.

Lane slaps the gun away easily and it flies across the room. He stalks a step forward and the attacker scrambles backward to get away from him, too. I sure as hell wouldn't want Lane looking at me like that.

The attacker stares up at Lane in terrified horror, but just as fast, a bunch of cops kick in the door, storm the apartment, and surround all of us in guns.

"Don't move!" they yell and hold all three of us at gunpoint. "Don't move! Get down on the floor with your hands behind your head!"

Lane raises his hands very slowly. The cops rush him, grab him, and force him down onto his knees. He puts his hands behind his head, but they wrench his arms down to cuff him behind his back.

He falls on his knees right in front of me—right where I can see his brilliant blue eyes looking deep into mine. "Everything's okay now, Samantha," he murmurs. "You're safe. No one is going to hurt you. You're safe now."

They yank him away and drag him out of the room in handcuffs. Before I know what hit me, a million cops surround me all talking at once. I'm too stunned to think straight.

Did that really happen? Some asshole carjacked me downtown and brought me here to assault me. Lane......

I glance around. The cops are dragging the attacker away in handcuffs, too, and the cops put the gun in a plastic bag.

I really need to tell them what happened. I need to tell them that Lane was the one who saved me, but I can't get my voice working. My whole face hurts. The rest of me feels numb. I can't move or even really see or understand anything going on in front of me.

I sit there for a few more minutes before the paramedics show up. They shine lights in my eyes, pat me down all over, and then load me onto a stretcher to take me to the hospital.

The cops don't bother me after I leave the apartment. The medics take me downstairs, load me into the ambulance, and then the world goes quiet on our way down the street.

I go into another trance once we get to the hospital. The doctors X-ray my head and then give me a CT scan. No one asks me about the attack or Lane or anything.

They finally park me in a curtained area of the emergency room. I just lie there trying to think. I can still feel that guy lying on top of me trying to pull up my skirt. I'll never forget that as long as I live.

I'm still lying there feeling totally numb when someone pushes back the curtain to check on me. I expect it to be one of the nurses, but it's Lane instead.

He sits down on the bed next to me. "Oh, my God. Look at your poor face. You poor thing. Did you break anything? Are you okay? I'm sorry I couldn't get here sooner. I had to straighten everything out at the Police station." He raises his hand and very gently uses one finger to move my hair away from my pulverized face. "Poor girl. You were so brave. You did great."

I open my mouth to say something, but no sound comes out. He's the one person in this whole thing I can actually talk to, but my voice won't obey me.

He came for me. I don't know how he found out where I was or what was happening, but he saved my life. He saved me from a terrible fate.

"Lane...." I choke.

"Yeah, sweetie?" he murmurs.

I try to speak again, but the fear and agony of the attack come out of my mouth instead. I give a strangled noise halfway between a scream and a roar.

That sound hurts, and when it does come out, the fear and rage come with it. Tears burst out of my eyes and then, before I can stop myself, I break down crying right in front of him.

"Hey! It's all right!" he murmurs and puts his arms around me. "You're okay now. You're safe. It's over."

I know I'm safe and it's over. That's why this hurts so much. I'm okay because of him.

He hugs me once and then pushes me back. He keeps petting his hands down my hair and rubbing my arms and shoulders.

That touch warms me and comforts me. I can't even think that he's a stranger I only met earlier today.

I barely know him, but the way he's touching me is the only thing in the world that makes this okay.

"That's okay, sweetie," he murmurs. "It's okay to cry. You were so brave. I'm so proud of you. You did everything right."

How does he know that? How does he know what happened during the attack?

I can't ask him any of that, just like I can't ask him how he found me in time.

He doesn't do anything except comfort me. He keeps pushing my hair behind my ears and rubbing my arms. I've never been so grateful to anyone for anything.

Just then, one of the nurses comes in and sees us—as if we're doing something we shouldn't.

Lane stands up and faces her. She can see me bawling my eyes out.

"We're releasing her," the nurse tells Lane and then turns to me. "You can go home now, Ms. Mulholland. Detective Beckett left his card for you to call him when you're ready to answer questions about what happened."

"Is she all clear to leave the hospital?" Lane asks. "How bad are her injuries?"

"She doesn't have any fractures to her head or face or body. All her X-rays came back negative. She's on standard concussion protocol. If she starts becoming difficult to rouse or altered in any other way, she should come back in. Other than that, the bruising to her face will subside on its own. She doesn't have to stay here. I'll be right back with your discharge paperwork, Ms. Mulholland."

The nurse leaves. Lane stays standing for a minute and then sits down on the edge of the bed where he was before. "The Police impounded your car while the Crime Lab goes over it for fingerprints. I'll take you home."

I sniff back the last of my tears. I should ask about him getting arrested. I should ask if he's all right. The Police better not try to pin this on him.

I find it impossible to say anything, even to express my gratitude to him for everything he's doing. I always thought he was some kind of Terminator robot who only cares about stealing other people's companies.

I never would have imagined he could act this caring, especially toward someone he barely knows. We're enemies across the boardroom table, but I can't think of him that way.

He stays with me and keeps murmuring encouragement while I sign myself out of the hospital.

I heave myself off the hospital bed and wrap my arms around myself trying to keep warm. It isn't cold, but I can't stop shivering.

Lane takes off his jacket and puts it around me, but it doesn't do any good. He also puts his arm around my shoulders and guides me out of the building. His presence is the only thing that makes me feel better.

He dials one-handed on his phone on our way down the corridor. "Eddie—I'm on my way out. Meet me at the Emergency Department entrance—not the ambulance bay—the other one."

He hangs up. I don't know what to expect, but when we leave the Emergency Department, a big, sleek black limo meets us at the curb.

The driver opens the door for me and Lane to get in. He sits me on the seat before he climbs in and sits next to me. He switches on the heater and then the limo purrs away into traffic.

# Chapter 6: Samantha

Lane doesn't say anything as his limo glides out into traffic and winds its way across town.

What is he thinking right now? Is he thinking he doesn't want such a basket case as his new CFO?

I stare through the window at the lights passing the car....and start crying again. I just can't seem to stop myself.

I can't stop thinking about the attack....and the fact that I'm falling apart like this. I don't know what's happening to me.

I don't even understand the thoughts going through my head right now—or if there even are any thoughts going through my head right now.

Lane doesn't ask permission. He slides across the seat, leans right against me, puts his arm around my shoulders, and holds me tight. "It's gonna be all right, sweetheart," he murmurs in my ear. "Everything is gonna be all right. You're okay now. You were so brave. You did everything right."

I try one last hopeless time to talk to him—to ask all the questions warring in my head.

I barely managed to say, "Lane...." before I break down again.

His being here and holding me like this gives me permission to break down. I can actually feel how hurt and scared I am.

I'm still scared. I dread going home to my apartment. He'll leave...and I'll be alone. I don't think I can handle that. In fact, I know I can't.

I can't ask him to stay. That would be weird. I want to call Casey to come and stay with me, but then I would have to explain to him what happened. I couldn't do that. I couldn't even face him.

Somehow, Lane has suddenly become closer to me than my own brother. I feel safer with Lane. He already knows. I don't have to explain anything to him.

I would have to be strong for Casey. I wouldn't be able to fall apart like this. Don't even get me started on Olivia. I could never tell her about this.

The limo pulls up in front of my apartment building. Lane gets out first and offers me his hand to help me out. Is he going to leave now? Is he going to make some polite excuse to leave me here and go his own way? I wouldn't blame him.

He tells the driver to drive around the block. Then Lane takes my hand and leads me to the building.

The doorman, Anthony, gives Lane a curious look, but Anthony doesn't say anything before he opens the door for us.

I stop in the lobby and push the elevator button before I realize I don't have my keys to get into my apartment. I don't have my handbag, my phone, or anything else that was in my bag.

I go back over to the doorman. It takes me a few tries before I can find my voice to speak to him. "I'm....I'm sorry....Anthony....I don't have my key...."

"It's right here, Ms. Mulholland," he tells me. "The Police dropped it off for you earlier. They said they missed you at the hospital and they returned it to the building."

He bends behind the lobby counter and pulls out my handbag—my handbag that was lying on the passenger seat of my car when the attacker dragged me out.

The elevator bell dings right then. I get into the elevator and Lane gets in with me. When is he going to leave? Will he make sure I get into my apartment and then excuse himself? I'm sure he has better things to do than babysit me.

I don't want him to leave. I can't handle being alone right now. I don't know if I'll be able to handle being alone ever again.

He follows me out of the elevator to my apartment and stands off to one side while I unlock the door. He doesn't make an excuse to leave nor does he ask permission before he follows me inside.

I squirm out of my skin, now that he's inside my apartment. It's a big, modern, open-plan penthouse with a mezzanine bedroom, a terrace with a garden and a pool, and huge windows looking out over New York.

I always thought this apartment was beautiful. Now it feels cold, industrial, and hollow like a giant hospital ward or maybe a prison. I shiver again even though I'm still wearing Lane's jacket around me.

He comes over to me—again without asking for permission. "Why don't you go upstairs, take a hot shower or a bath, and change into something warm and comfortable? I'll wait for you down here."

I look up into his eyes—those eyes swimming with compassion and understanding. He knows. He knows everything.

He pushes me toward the stairs leading up to my bedroom. I head that way, but at the bottom of the stairs, I look back.

He crosses the room to the thermostat and turns on the heater even though it isn't cold. Then he sits down on the couch, takes out his phone, and does something on it. How long does he plan to stay here?

I go upstairs, strip off my suit, and take the hottest shower I can stand. I stand under the spray letting it scald every inch of my skin.

I want it to burn away the feeling of that guy lying on top of me. I can't tell if it works.

I get out, comb my hair, and put on my pajamas, my big fuzzy bathrobe, and slippers. I throw my suit in the trash and take Lane's jacket to the living room.

He leans back against the couch cushion still working on his phone. I sit down next to him, hand him his jacket, and mutter, "Thanks." God, how pathetic and inadequate that sounds compared to everything he's done.

He lays the jacket over the other arm of the couch—the one on his other side. He puts his phone away, but he doesn't leave. "Do you feel better?" he asks.

I nod at nothing.

"Would you like me to stick around for a while—just so you don't have to be alone?"

I look down at my hands in my lap. They don't seem like they belong to me anymore.

Of course he understands about that. I can't believe he's being so kind to me. I should have been more polite at the bar, but it's too late now.

He reads my mind and rubs my back through my robe. "It's okay," he breathes. "You don't need to get it all together right away. It might take you a while to get over what happened. That's okay."

I don't tell him it isn't okay. I have a job. I won't be able to do it if I don't pull myself together.

I'm one of the few people responsible for running Titanium Finance. Lane wouldn't want to acquire Titanium Finance if not for me. No one has to spell it out for me. I'm the CFO. I'm part of the package.

I'm no good to him the way I am. I'm no good to Derek or anyone else, either.

Lane stands up, walks off, and does something somewhere else in my apartment. He comes back carrying the big, fluffy feather-down bedspread from the guest room. Don't even ask me how he knew about it.

He wraps it around me, sits down, and pulls me toward him. "Lie down here," he tells me.

He steers me to lie down on the couch with my head in his lap. He makes sure the bedspread is tucked around every part of me to keep me extra warm.

He slouches toward the end of the couch, rests his head and shoulders on the arm on top of his jacket, props his feet on the coffee table, and rubs my back and shoulders through the bedspread again.

I don't know what to think about all this. I see him taking such good care of me. I don't think even Casey could do what Lane is doing.

I'm unimaginably grateful to him for this. I don't want to question it in case I accidentally push him away.

I just want to curl up in the feeling that he's here taking care of everything. I don't want to go anywhere or think anything or be responsible for anything. I couldn't right now if I tried.

I curl up on the couch. He keeps tucking in all the corners of the bedspread around me. Then his hand falls on my head and he rakes his fingers through my hair.

My face throbs from all the bruising, but that touch feels unimaginably good. I can't think of anything I need more than this.

I shut my eyes. Those gentle strokes tell me he's still here. He's watching over me. He won't let anything happen to me. I can sleep without worrying about anything else.

# Chapter 7: Lane

I wake up and stare at the ceiling for a while before I remember everything that happened last night. Samantha Mulholland—she got carjacked, assaulted, and wound up in the hospital with bruises all over her face.

Now I'm in her apartment. She lies with her head in my lap and that bedspread wrapped around her in a big down ball. She's sound asleep.

Poor thing. I hate to think what would have happened to her if I hadn't been right there in exactly the right position to see that guy attack her.

She's all right physically. She's still a wreck mentally, but that's understandable considering the circumstances.

Titanium Finance doesn't look nearly as attractive without her as the CFO, but that's a conversation for another day. The important thing is that she's home and on the mend. I'll handle Titanium without her if I absolutely have to.

I pick up my phone and answer a bunch of messages from Stewart.

*Where are you?* he asks. *You missed the executive meeting at nine o'clock.*

*I had an emergency last night,* I tell him. *I'm still dealing with it. I'll let you know when I plan to come back in.*

*Will it be sometime today?* he asks.

*I wish I could tell you. Something happened last night. I can't just drop it. I'll be back as soon as I can. In the meantime, you can relay any messages to me here.*

*Okay,* he replies. *Is everything all right?*

*It is now. I'll be back in the office soon. I promise.*

*Just to remind you, the Titanium deadline is in three hours. What do you want to do about it?*

*Go ahead and start acquiring the remaining available shares,* I tell him. *Get everyone standing by so that, as soon as the auto trigger trips the selloff, we're ready to buy up everything as soon as it comes on the market. You can handle all of that without me.*

*You got it. I'll handle it.*

*Thank you,* tell him.

I spend another hour answering emails before Samantha wakes up.

She stirs, sighs, and then tenses when she remembers where she is and why. She sits up and tightens the bedspread around her shoulders.

Her bruised face looks worse today than it did last night. The swelling looks puffier and she has two black eyes. She's going to get bombarded with questions when she goes back to work.

The bruising makes her eyes look even wilder and more frantically terrified. She just looked stunned and in shock last night. Now she looks petrified.

Her eyes dart around the apartment without seeing anything. She barely looks at me when I rub her back.

"Good morning," I tell her. "Would you like some breakfast? I was just about to make something for myself. What do you say? Are you hungry?"

She doesn't leave the couch or unwrap her bedspread when I go into the kitchen and check the fridge. She stays cocooned there with her back to me.

She takes good care of herself. I find eggs, whole wheat bread, fruit, and cream cheese in the fridge. I make her some scrambled eggs and a plate of fruit with cream cheese on the side.

I make coffee for both of us. I'm just putting our plates on the coffee table in front of her when someone knocks on the apartment door.

She shoots me a crazed look. She's barely holding it together even here in her own apartment.

I put down my coffee cup and go to answer the door. I expect it to be the landlord or a neighbor or something.

Instead, I find myself facing Detective Sergeant Andreas Beckett, the same detective who took my statement last night after I got arrested in that jackass's apartment.

He frowns at me. "Mr. Prince? What are you doing here?"

I jerk my thumb over my shoulder. "I went to check on Ms. Mulholland at the hospital. She had no way to get home after you impounded her car, so I drove her. After that, she didn't feel safe to stay by herself, so I offered. Do you want something?"

"I came by to ask if she felt ready to give us a statement."

I glance behind me. Samantha sits on the couch wrapped in her feather bedspread. She looks like a giant marshmallow with a head of messed up hair sticking out the top.

"Um...." I mumbled. "Just hold on a sec. Let me ask her. She's been a little fragile since last night."

I leave the door open. He stays in the hall waiting while I go back to the couch.

I sit down next to Samantha and try to take her hand, but she's so buried under the bedspread that I can't find her hand. I wind up squeezing her knee instead.

"Do you want to give a statement to the Police now?" I murmur under my breath. "I'll be here with you—but if you do it now, you won't have to do it later. It would probably be better to do it and get it over with—don't you think?"

She gives me another terrified look and then casts her eyes down at the floor. She nods and half-whispers, "I guess so."

I squeeze her knee one more time. "I'll be right with you. I can back up your story. Okay? No one is going to do anything or call you a liar. I was there....and I already gave a statement so they already know what happened. This is just a formality. Okay?"

I look deep into her eyes. My God, she's beautiful! She's a thousand times more beautiful like this because she's vulnerable.

She nods again and whispers, "Thank you."

I squeeze one last time and go back to the door. "Come on in," I tell the detective. "She's ready to give a statement now."

He comes inside, I shut the door, and he crosses the room to the couches. I sit down next to Samantha and wave to another couch across from us.

"Take a seat," I tell him. "We were just about to eat breakfast."

He turns to Samantha. "How are you, Ms. Mulholland?"

She opens her mouth, but no sound comes out. She looks ten times more petrified now than she did last night.

He waits, but when she doesn't reply, he clears his throat and takes a notepad out of his inner jacket pocket.

"Let's start from the beginning," he prompts. "Tell me where you were and what you were doing when the assailant first attacked you."

She gulps, casts one last pathetic look around the apartment, and barely squeaks out, "I....I was.....I was dropping off my....my sister.....in front of her apartment building....."

He nods and scribbles down what she says. "Then what happened?"

She has to work up her nerve before she can make a sound. She keeps faltering over the words. "I.....I waited....until she went inside......and I started to drive off.....and he yanked the passenger door open.....and then he was inside with a gun in my face."

"What did he say?" Detective Beckett asks.

She swallows hard and clamps her eyes shut. I place my hand on her knee again. "It's all right," I murmur. "He already knows everything, remember?"

She looks up at me with her eyes swimming with tears. "How does he know?"

"Because I told him," I tell her.

"Mr. Prince saw you from across the street," Detective Beckett tells her. "He was getting into his car and saw you through his window. He saw the guy get into your car and hold you at gunpoint. Then he followed your car to the assailant's house. That's how he found you in time to intervene—and he called the Police."

Her head whips around and she stares at me with her eyes bugging out. "You did?"

"Of course," I reply. "I saw the whole thing."

She gulps again. Tears streak down her cheeks.

"So what did the assailant say to you in the car?" Detective Beckett asks again.

"He said...." She starts sobbing hard. "He said he would kill me if I didn't do what he said. He......he grabbed me by the hair. He kept yanking my hair every few seconds.....and telling me not to try anything."

"Anything else?" he asks.

She shakes her head down at the floor again. Her tears splash on the bedspread. "He told me where to turn off and park.....and then....he told me to get out of the car...."

"Can you remember when he struck you the first time?" Detective Beckett asks.

She barely whispers, "Not really. I think it might have been when I got stuck in the seatbelt."

He frowns at her. "What do you mean?"

"He kept yanking my hair....and trying to drag me out of the car......it took me a while to get the seatbelt off.....and then my arm got stuck in it.....that made him mad....and he hit me....."

"Anything else?"

"He kicked me....once I got out into the garage......I fell over.....and he kicked me.....I can't really remember where."

"Did he kick you in the head?" he asks.

She shakes her head. "He kept hitting me in the face with his gun. I think he kicked me in the ribs."

He nods. "Can you tell me what happened when you got upstairs to his apartment?"

She swallows hard. She won't look at him. I keep my hand on her knee. This is going to be the worst part.

Her voice cracks with strain. I have to listen hard to hear her. "When we got upstairs....he threw me on the floor.....and then he landed on top of me from behind....and started pulling my skirt up....and that's when Lane came in....."

"What did you see Mr. Prince do?" Detective Beckett asked. "We have his statement. We just need you to corroborate his account of exactly what he did to the assailant."

"When he first came in....I didn't really see.....because I was facing the other way.....The guy.....something hit him in the head....and he flew off me.....and he was holding onto me so he pulled me over onto my back....and Lane had his leg up in the air like he just kicked the guy. That's all I know."

"Then what?" Detective Beckett asks.

"He kicked the guy in the head again....and the guy pulled his gun on Lane....and Lane slapped the gun out of his hand.....and then the Police came in. That's all that happened."

He nods. "Thank you for confirming that. We don't have any other questions for you at this time, but we may ask you to come in to clarify anything....Oh, wait! I forgot. Could you give a description of the assailant?"

"Um....not really. I didn't really see him."

"Try," Detective Beckett urges. "Anything you remember."

"He was white.....and he had mousy brown hair.....that's all I can tell you.....and he was wearing jeans. That's all I saw."

"Thank you again. I'll be in touch if we need any additional information. Don't hesitate to call me if you need anything." He leaves his card on the table, says, "You have a good day, Mr. Prince," and leaves.

The door shuts behind him with an ominous click. Samantha buries her face in her bedspread, but at least she doesn't sound like she's crying anymore.

I rub her back through the thick bedspread. "You did great. I'm proud of you. I didn't think you would be able to get through that, but you did it. Now you don't have to think about it anymore."

She looks up at me and immediately looks away. She looks beyond miserable. "Thank you....for coming for me.....I couldn't.....I don't know what I'd do...."

"Stop it," I murmur. "Of course I came. I wouldn't let that happen to you."

She gulps again. "I just...." She glances around the apartment. "What's going to happen now?"

"I don't know. I guess we eat our breakfast."

"I mean....with the takeover and....and everything....."

Now it's my turn to look away. I don't dare to check the time, but the takeover must be happening right now.

How ironic that she already knows. She knows Derek's position is hopeless. Of course Samantha knows I'm going ahead with the takeover even while I'm sitting here supporting her.

"I really appreciate you staying over....and everything...."

"Don't mention it," I tell her. "Whatever you need."

"But.....it isn't a good idea....when we're on opposite sides....of the takeover, I mean.....and then.....after you do take over.....you'll be my boss.....remember?"

"I remember, but this is more important. Besides, I'm not your boss yet. I'm just a concerned citizen. If you need me to stay over again tonight, I will."

Her eyes float up to meet mine. My heart stops at that look. "I do need you to. I just don't think it's a good idea."

"I understand," I tell her and take a gulp of my coffee.

I eat my breakfast as casually as possible, but I don't want to leave her alone. She doesn't feel safe to stay alone. I don't like abandoning her when she admits she needs me.

She's right, though. We're supposed to be rivals. If we aren't rivals, then I am her boss. I might already be her boss if the takeover is already finished.

I need to check in with my team and I can't do that here.

"How about I give you my number?" I tell her. "You can call me if you need me. I mean....." I scramble to figure out what I mean. "You know what I mean."

She looks up at me again, but she doesn't quite manage to smile. "Thank you....for everything.....I wish.....there was some way to thank you....."

"Just feel better. You'll get back on the horse pretty soon. You can take all the time you need before you come back to work. I don't want you to feel any pressure. Understand?"

She nods. She looks like she's about to start crying again, but her eyes glow with so much warmth and gratitude that I can't stand it.

I finish eating and rub her back some more. "I'll take off, okay? You call me if you need me."

I scribble my phone number on the back of Detective Beckett's card. I really want to kiss her on the side of the head, but that would be taking this too far.

I rub her back and squeeze her knee through her bedspread before I say, "Bye."

She barely whispers, "Bye," and I walk out.

# Chapter 8: Samantha

I take a deep breath to steady myself. I know exactly what's going to happen when I walk into the office, but Lane is right. I need to get back on the horse. I can't keep hiding under the blankets.

I summon all my courage, get out of my new car in the Titanium Finance building underground parking garage, grab my leather laptop case, and set off for the elevator.

I'll never look at a parking garage the same way again, but that doesn't bother me nearly as much as the bruises on my face. I still look like I got hit by a truck.

I look like the elephant man, but I just have to bite the bullet and take my colleagues' reaction. I already know it will be bad.

I ride the elevator to the lobby and walk in. A bunch of people turn around to wish me good morning the way they usually do.

They all freeze with their jaws on the floor when they see my face. I say, "Good morning," to everyone I pass, but no one responds. They just stare.

I knew it would be like this, so I just go straight to the elevator. I usually ride up to the executive suite with a bunch of other people who are all on their way to work each morning.

They're all so frozen in shocked horror at my appearance that they don't get in with me. I have the elevator to myself.

I shudder when I imagine facing the executive team, especially Derek. I can't tell any of them about Lane helping me—especially not Derek. He's already touchy enough as it is when it comes to Lane.

The elevator dings again and the doors open. I get an identical reaction from everyone on the executive floor. I walk straight past them wishing everyone a good morning and head for my office. Please Dear God don't let any of the execs be waiting for me.

Of course they are. I make it within ten feet of my office door before Spencer Holt, Cesar Pound, and Reese McCall come out of Spencer's office.

All three of them head for my office. They must have been planning to talk to me.

They stop in their tracks when they see me. "Samantha!" Cesar gasps. "What on Earth happened to you?!!"

"I had an accident last night," I reply as calmly as I can. "It's nothing to worry about. The bruising will go away in time."

"An accident!" Spencer exclaims. "Do you mean like a car accident?"

I make a calculated decision to tell the truth. "Something like that. Anyway, what's going on with the Apico buyout?"

"There is no buyout," Reese tells me. "Derek refused to sell and now Apico is moving on our shareholders."

I only nod. I expected nothing less. I'm only surprised the takeover isn't finished by now.

"We've been calling in every favor we can from all our major investors, but we can't stop the automatic trigger," Cesar goes on. "All those shares are landing on the open market. Apico is buying them too fast for us to stop it."

"There must be something we can do," Spencer insists.

"Which investors have you called?" I ask.

Cesar opens his mouth to answer, but just then, Bradley Lenz comes out of his own office. He's heading for Derek's office, but Bradley changes his mind when he sees us.

He comes toward us. I have to remark how relaxed and upbeat he seems compared to the other three.

"The share price just hit a hundred and seventy-five," he informs us. "It looks like the Apico purchases are finally catching up with the auto selloff. Now we just have to wait for the....." He breaks off and frowns at me. "Jesus, Samantha! What the hell happened to you?"

"She got in a car accident last night," Cesar answers for me.

Bradley frowns even more. "Should you be working? You look like you need to go to the hospital."

"I've already been to the hospital and I'm fine. How close is Apico to gaining a controlling stake in Titanium?"

"They have forty-five percent," Bradley replies. "They need another two thousand units."

"Is there any chance they might not be able to secure the funding?" Cesar asks.

Bradley snorts. "Are you joking? This is Apico Acquisitions we're talking about. Funding is never a problem for them, especially when it comes to anything acquisitions-related."

"I hear Lane Prince hasn't even shown up to the office since yesterday," Reese suggests. "He's running everything remotely."

I can't listen to this. I turn toward my office, but just then, Derek comes out of somewhere.

He rushes over to us in a breathless panic. I can't tell at first which of us he's talking to or if he's just talking to himself. "The Silverberg Trust just dumped another five hundred units. The price fell another forty cents. Apico is having a feeding frenzy and one of my guys just spotted Lane Prince finally showing up at the office. We have to act now!"

"So you have guys staking out Apico and Lane Prince now?" I shake my head. "You really should have taken his offer, Derek."

He turns on me. He's too out of his mind with panic to notice my face. "You never said that! You never recommended that I take his offer."

I don't waste my breath pointing out that all his other execs did it for me. He wouldn't take that recommendation from them and he wouldn't have taken it from me.

"It doesn't matter now," I tell him. "As soon as the Silverberg shares hit the market, they triggered another dump from Global Intelligence Systems. They own a thousand units. That will trigger a dump from Labyrinth Enterprises and they own more than five hundred. We can't stop the takeover now. Our best bet would be to consolidate our remaining projects into....."

"We are NOT giving up!" Derek insists. "We still have the Global Intelligence shares and the Labyrinth shares. We can stop this."

"How?" Cesar asks. "I don't see a way."

Derek grabs my elbow and steers me into my office. He shuts the door behind us.

"Um....what are you doing?" I ask.

He hustles over to my desk, gets in my face, and lowers his voice to a husky whisper. "You can stop the takeover, Samantha."

"How? I can't stop the trigger dumps. That's all Apico needs to buy those shares on the open market."

"You can help me stop Global Intelligence and Labyrinth from dumping their shares."

"I can't stop that. The dumps are automatic. They're run by computer bots. I don't have any control over that."

"We can convince Global Intelligence and Labyrinth to intervene to stop the selloffs," he whispers. "I need you to do some research on Lane Prince. Find me anything we can use to discredit him with the Global Intelligence and Labyrinth boards. Once they realize what a lowlife he is, they'll stop the selloff and we'll be clear."

My eyes pop. "You want me to dig up dirt on Lane Prince.....to smear his reputation?"

"No! Of course not. Just find out about him. You know the guy is a cutthroat. He must have done something in his past that no one knows about. Once we find out what it is, we can convince everyone not to sell to him."

I open my mouth to tell him what a terrible idea this is. I can't tell Derek about what Lane did for me, but that doesn't matter. By the time I finish digging up this dirt, the selloff will be over.

Derek doesn't notice my hesitation. He only smiles. He really has cracked a cylinder this time.

He squeezes my elbow, murmurs, "I knew I could count on you," and slips out of my office.

I sink into my chair. Am I the only person around here sane enough to read the writing on the wall? Apico acquired Titanium a long, long time ago.

Lane Prince doesn't leave his acquisitions to chance. He lays the groundwork too carefully. He positions himself to strike, but the real maneuvering happens long before that.

He secured every piece of the puzzle before he entered the Titanium Finance boardroom. He made sure he had Titanium Finance in the bag before he ever sent Derek that proposal to buy the company.

Lane check-mated us. That's the bottom line.

The only thing left for us to do is accept it and start playing by the new rule book—whatever that is. We just have to wait for Lane to tell us.

I don't want to be the idiot who tears the wool off Derek's eyes, though. Facing reality will be hard enough for him once Lane takes over the company.

I turn to my computer. I don't think I'll find anything on Lane that we don't already know. His business record speaks for itself.

I do a search on him and come up with the laundry list of companies he's either started or acquired. It's a long list.

I roll back through the timeline to his first days in business. He started a tech robotics company called Trinity Processing that he sold for forty million. He used the money to stake him in a five-billion-dollar trading conglomerate and the rest is history.

That doesn't tell me anything, so I dig a little deeper. Now I'm just curious about Lane himself. He obviously isn't who I thought he was. A cutthroat business shark couldn't have acted as caring as he did toward me.

He was more than a Good Samaritan. He's practically a superhero if he followed me to that guy's apartment and attacked just in time to save me. Does Lane have anything in his past to show that he's been like this before?

He could have a list of hidden heroics—like Batman or something. He could have been out there on a regular basis stopping crime and helping the defenseless.

I do a broader search for anyone by the name of Lane Prince. I find a bunch of social media accounts, none of which belong to him.

I'm just about to give up when, on the fifth page of the search results, I spot something. *Court Docket #3250, City of New York Criminal Court.* The date is twenty years ago.

My heart stops. Could this be the smoking gun? Do I really want to find out something that could ruin Lane Prince forever? How can I do that after what he did for me?

I don't seem to be able to stop my hand from moving the mouse to the entry and clicking on it.

There's no question that this is the same Lane Prince, but he looks so different. He was only fifteen at the time.

He stares out of his mugshot with messy, unwashed blonde hair and a dull, miserable expression.

My stomach drops when my eyes skim over the charges. *Assault with a deadly weapon. Grievous bodily injury. Reckless endangerment. Attempted murder.*

The attempted murder charge got dismissed, but he got convicted of assault with a deadly weapon and reckless endangerment. He got an extra harsh sentence due to the severity of the victim's injuries. Lane served two years in a youth prison for his crimes.

I stare at the screen feeling sick. This is definitely the information Derek wants—if it isn't too late already.

What am I supposed to do about this? How am I supposed to cope with this?

I get a flashback of the carjacking with that guy sticking his gun in my face, threatening to kill me, and then smashing my face in with his weapon.

Did Lane do that to someone else? He must not be a dark knight if he could do something like that. What am I supposed to think?

The guy slept in my apartment last night. I slept in my apartment last night with my head in his lap. He's been touching me nonstop since he came to see me in the hospital.

I shut my eyes and try to shake those thoughts out of my head, but they won't go away. Lane's touch, his kind expression, his soft encouragement—it all gets mixed up in my mind with memories from the carjacking......that guy lying on top of me.....the gun in my face...

I shoot out of the chair. I barely take the time to close the web page so no one else sees it.

I can't deal with this information right now. I might not ever be able to deal with it, but when I leave my office, I only wind up taking the information with me. I'll never be able to get rid of it.

I can't stay here. I have to leave. I have to get away from Derek before he finds out about this—at least until I decide what to do about it.

In a few hours, Lane Prince will be my boss. How am I supposed to act around him when I'm carrying this secret? How can I work for someone that unethical?

I don't even know if he is unethical. There could be a perfectly logical explanation for this.

How can there be a perfectly logical explanation for Lane doing to someone else what that guy did to me? How can I ever let myself be in the same room with Lane again?

I'll have to be—or I'll have to quit Titanium Finance. That's all there is to it. I might even have to move out of New York. I wouldn't want to live in the same town with him.

I turn toward the exit. I have to walk past everyone again to get to the elevator.

Just then, Bradley comes out of his office and sees me. "Global Intelligence just dumped their shares. It's all over but the crying."

# Chapter 9: Lane

The champagne cork pops, whistles through the air, and hits the ceiling. Everybody cheers.

Excited talk breaks out in the Apico Acquisitions executive suite. Everyone laughs, claps each other on the back, and I bend over the table to pour champagne into dozens of glasses.

It's a little hard to pour without spilling when so many people are trying to hug me, squeeze my shoulders, and talk to me at once.

I finally clear the mob by handing out champagne to everyone. I take a glass for myself and raise my voice over the noise.

"Here's to the greatest team in corporate history!" I tell them. "We knocked this out of the park and now we're going to ride off into the sunset on a river of money."

More cheers break out and then the group dissolves in endless talk. All the executives, their assistants and deputies, and most of the company department heads crowd around the floor congratulating each other and themselves on executing a textbook hostile takeover of Titanium Finance.

I wander over to Marco Van Sant, Ethan Rosch, and Ricardo Thorn in a cluster. "We have to get rid of Reese McCall first thing tomorrow morning," Ricardo is saying.

"You might want to check his contract first," Ethan replies. "He could have stipulations that he needs a certain amount of severance notice. It could be a while before we get rid of him entirely."

"I don't care when we get rid of him as long as we get rid of him," Ricardo returns. "I don't care if we have to keep him on a full salary for a year. We can send him home and he can finish the year in his underwear while one of our own people handles Titanium's marketing. The guy is a walking timebomb and we all know it."

"What about Cesar Pound?" Marco asks. "We definitely need to keep him."

"He might be good, but he isn't as critical as Samantha Mulholland," Ethan replies. "We have to keep her. She's the best there is. She's better than anyone we have at Apico or in any of our companies."

"We won't be able to keep her," Marco points out. "She's loyal to Derek Salazar. As soon as we take over Titanium, she'll resign on us."

"You might be surprised," Ethan replies. "She's too smart not to have seen this coming. If Derek is that blind, she might be ready for a change. Give her a chance."

Ricardo turns to me. "What do you think?"

"About what?" I ask.

"About Samantha Mulholland quitting Titanium because of the takeover."

I try to shrug it off. I don't want to talk about Samantha Mulholland, in this context or any other.

The last two days have given me a history with her that could turn out to be incompatible with any future working relationship.

It might get real interesting to work with her—now that I know what I do about her. My life would probably be a whole lot easier if she did resign, but I don't say that out loud.

I realize in that moment that I'm no longer unbiased about Samantha—not the way I should be.

I don't know if I'm biased for her or against her, but I might not be able to think straight about her ever again.

"I agree she's too good to lose, but she's also the most loyal of the whole Titanium board," I reply. "I'd be surprised if she didn't resign. Besides, she can get another job anytime she wants anywhere she wants. She would probably get a hefty raise if she went somewhere else."

"Then we need to start looking for someone to replace her," Ricardo replies.

"We can't replace her," Ethan counters. "She knows Titanium better than anyone. She's the brains behind the operation."

Marco snorts. "Derek Salazar certainly isn't."

Just then, Russel Shauer and Marshall Weiss come over to join us. "We're all going downtown to Salvini's for dinner," Russel tells me. "You should come with us. We need to celebrate before we tackle Titanium tomorrow morning."

I smile at him and say, "Okay." It feels good to be back here. The last few days with Samantha cast a shadow over my life. I need to shake that off.

I don't regret anything I did. I don't regret being there for her and spending that night in her apartment. I just need to get my head back in the game.

I call Eddie and drive everyone down to Salvini's in my limo. Eduardo Salvini is working the front desk. He gives us a big table on the upper level away from the other diners. We order another bottle of champagne.

Talk flows to the Titanium acquisition and every detail of the sell-off. The other execs fill me in on everything that happened while I was out, but it all went by the numbers.

"It was a textbook Lane Prince takeover," Marshall gushes. "You're the man, Lane. No one stands a chance against you."

"So who are we acquiring next?" Ethan asks.

I laugh. "Titanium isn't even cold in its grave and you're already planning our next takeover."

"I like to win," he points out. "Mud-wrestling all these uncooperative employees into line is someone else's job. Just ask Lane. He'll agree with me. Who do you have your eye on next, big guy?"

"Takeovers aren't as interesting as the money we'll make from them," I tell him. "We have to make sure Titanium is on the straight and narrow and earning as much profit or more before we move on."

Ethan slumps. "Do you have to rob me of my only hope in life? Why can't we start researching our next conquest now?"

We all laugh until Marshall murmurs under his breath. "Don't look now, but a certain someone is sitting at the table in the corner."

We all turn around to look. My heart stops when I spot Samantha at a table by the windows. She's alone and gazing out the windows at the East River flowing by.

"My God! What happened to her face?!" Ricardo whispers. "She looks awful!"

"She looks upset," Marco adds. "She's probably planning how to resign from Titanium to support Derek."

"I'll go talk to her." I put down my napkin. "I'll see if I can convince her to stay on."

"You'd be the last person she'd listen to," Ricardo points out, but I don't answer.

All my colleagues' eyes follow me across the restaurant to Samantha's table, but the other execs won't be able to hear our conversation from over there.

I walk up behind her, around the table, and approach the chair opposite her. "Good evening," I greet her. "You must be feeling better if you're out here having dinner."

She jumps out of her skin when I come near her. She whips around and stares up at me in shocked horror before she realizes who it is.

She slumps back in her chair and looks away. "You scared me."

"Sorry." I wave to the seat opposite her. "Do you mind if I join you?"

She only shrugs. She won't look at me.

I sit down. She's still jumpy from the carjacking—or maybe from the takeover. I can't imagine why she would be nervous about that. She acted so nonchalant at the board meeting.

"I'm sure you heard by now that Apico acquired a controlling share of Titanium earlier today," I begin.

She doesn't stop looking out the window when she nods.

"My associates and I really hope you stay on. We know how valuable you are to the company. Losing you would be a terrible loss. If there's anything I can do to convince you...."

She spins around to confront me, opens her mouth to say something, and falters. "I...I have to tell you something, Lane."

I frown and then shrug it off. "Okay. What is it?"

"I'm.....I'm really sorry.....I feel terrible.....after everything you did for me....."

"I understand if you feel you need to resign," I tell her. "I know you and Derek....."

"It isn't that," she blurts out. "He asked me......he asked me to do some research on you.....to use it against you in the takeover......I know

I shouldn't have.....I didn't think I'd find anything....and then.....I found out about your criminal record.....and I didn't know what to think.....I......I don't think I can work with you while I'm carrying around this secret. I'm really sorry. I didn't know. I swear it. I feel awful. I don't know what to do about this. I understand if you don't want to work with me because of it...."

I relax back in my chair. I'm over the top relieved all of a sudden that she doesn't plan to quit. "Oh, is that all? I thought it was something bad."

She gapes at me with her mouth open. "You.....you don't care?"

"Not at all. I thought everyone already knew. I'm only surprised someone didn't bring it up before. It's right there on the internet for all the world to see. It isn't like I'm keeping it a secret or anything."

Her eyes fall even farther out of their sockets. "You aren't?"

I burst out in relieved laughter. "No, sweetheart. I'm not keeping it a secret—and I don't care who finds out. You can tell Derek or anyone else. I really don't care who knows. In fact, I'm glad you know. I'm glad you're the one who found out."

"You are?" She frowns. "Why?"

"Because I know you wouldn't do anything with it to try to ruin my reputation. I know you wouldn't use it to destroy me the way someone else would. The fact that you're telling me to my face proves your heart is in the right place."

"But Derek wants to use it to ruin your reputation. Wait a minute. How can you act so dismissive of this? It *could* ruin your reputation."

I can't help beaming at her. She has such a pure, kind, caring heart. She really cares about protecting me. "He can't, sweetheart. He can't do anything to me."

"So...." She furrows her brow again. "You really don't care? But.....I don't understand."

"The takeover is finished. Apico owns Titanium now. Derek can't stop that. If he tried to use this against me, it wouldn't change anything. I'll make sure you get a very healthy severance package if you need to resign, but...."

"I'm not going to resign!" she exclaims. "Are you insane?"

"You aren't?"

"NO!!" she practically shrieks before she fights her voice under control. "I'm not going to resign."

I get another wave of relief. I really didn't want to lose her.

"I'll handle Derek," I tell her. "Thank you for warning me about him. At least I'll see him coming when he starts broadcasting this all over town."

"He doesn't know yet. I didn't tell him."

My head snaps up. "You didn't?"

"I didn't get a chance to. I found out....and I got so confused about it that I left the office...." She breaks off again. She stares at me with a very different expression. "You threatened someone with a weapon. You hurt someone. You did the same thing to someone that that guy did to me."

I make a face. "I didn't do anything to anyone that that guy did to you. What I did was nothing like that—not at all."

She tries to speak and fails before she manages to get the words out. "What did you do?"

I hesitate. She never had a problem with me touching her or staying in her apartment before. Now I see a million questions wrestling in her head.

I can't have her thinking I did to someone else what that guy did to her. I have to tell her the truth.

I tell myself I don't care. Now I realize how hard this is.

I want her to know. That's the truth. I really don't care what anyone else thinks, but I want her to know. I want her to feel safe with me the way she did in her apartment. She can only do that if she understands.

"I would have to show you something to explain it to you," I tell her. "If you come with me, I'll show you something that will make everything clear to you. I swear no one will hurt you or threaten you. If you really want to understand, you have to come with me."

Now it's her turn to hesitate. She glances toward the window and the river again.

Maybe she thinks she would be taking a big risk by going somewhere with someone with my criminal record. I wouldn't blame her if she thought that.

She finally throws back her shoulders, shakes her hair out of her face, and says, "All right. I'll go."

# Chapter 10: Samantha

My heart skips a beat when I slip into Lane's limo again. He stands behind me holding the door open the way he did that night when he took me home from the hospital.

I might be making the biggest mistake of my life going anywhere with him, but I can't think of him that way.

He's still the kind, caring, protective man who saved me from the attack. He's the man who's been taking care of me ever since.

If he is a violent, dangerous criminal underneath all that, I need to know right now. I need to know who he really is. I can't go any further until I know the truth—the whole truth.

He restored my faith in humanity when he rescued me from the carjacker. Lane is the only reason I still believe I can be safe anywhere. I need to know right now if that was all a giant mistake and he's really a monster after all.

He gets into the limo behind me and I jump again when he slams the door. He notices, slides his hand across mine, and squeezes. "It's all right," he murmurs. "You're safe. No one is going to hurt you."

Heat rushes up my arm from his hands. I shouldn't let him touch me like this—the way he touched me in the hospital and in the apartment. I should protect myself from him, but I find it impossible to believe that he would ever hurt me.

I want to believe more than anything that he's telling the truth about me being safe with him. I can't lose that—not now.

He doesn't let go of my hand. I should read something into this and probably take my hand out of his, but I can't do that, either.

The last three days somehow established this routine of him touching me, comforting me, and taking care of me. I don't seem to be able to stop it. I don't want to stop it. It's the only thing keeping me going right now.

I didn't hear him give instructions to his driver, but the limo glides away into the darkness by itself. We drive for a long way uptown, past Central Park, and into the worst neighborhoods in New York.

I really start to freak out when some grungy street people come up to the limo at a red light. They bang on the windows and the hood. I hear them yelling, but I can't make out the words.

Those people look like monsters with ragged clothes, missing teeth, and bleary eyes. I cringe and Lane slides a little closer to me on the seat. "It's okay," he murmurs. "Nothing to worry about."

The light turns green and the limo eases forward. "Nice and easy, Eddie," Lane calls through the window. "Don't hurt anybody."

The driver replies, "Yes, Sir," and enters the intersection slowly and carefully.

The limo attracts people like moths to a flame. Young gangbangers with their pants sagging down to their thighs surround the car. The driver has to inch up the curb before he stops outside the most run-down apartment building I've ever seen.

Lane squeezes my hand. "Stay here," he tells me. "I'll handle this."

I don't see how he can survive out there with all these thugs packed around the car, but he gets out anyway.

He forces the door open, stands up, and the crowd surges back to make room for him.

"All right! Calm down!" he calls over the mob. "There's nothing to see here. Go back to what you were doing. Go on. The show's over."

Someone replies from the sea of bodies. "We didn't know it was you, Mr. Prince."

"No problem, Rico. Just go back to your business. The show's over."

Like some kind of miracle, the crowd disperses and leaves the limo sitting there alone. No one bothers Lane at all.

He waits until the coast is clear before he sticks his head inside the limo. "It's safe now. You can come out."

I don't want to go out there, but he takes my hand and pulls me out anyway. The sidewalk is deserted, but a few of the bystanders watch us from street corners down the block.

Lane keeps a grip on my hand. "Follow me." He leads me toward the apartment building.

I glance over my shoulder, but no one comes near us. "Where are we going?"

"I grew up in this neighborhood—in this very building, in fact. My mother still lives here."

I stop dead in my tracks and gape at him. "Are you serious?"

He only smiles at me. "Why are you so surprised? It wasn't easy growing up here. One of the local gang lords tried to get my sister to become a prostitute for him. The guy wouldn't stop harassing her, so I threatened him and beat him up. That's why I went to jail."

I can't stop staring at him, but he doesn't react to my shock at all. He just smiles.

He must have realized this would convince me that he's as good as I thought he was. That's why he's telling me.

He leads me into the building, but it looks much nicer on the inside than it does on the outside. The stairs and wallpaper have been restored and the elevator looks almost new.

He pushes the button and we get inside to ride upstairs. "I decided while I was in jail that I would make enough money to get my mother and sister out of the ghetto. I studied in prison and came out and started my own company while I worked for another firm. I sent my sister to college and then to law school. She works for a law firm downtown. I tried to buy my mother a nice house in a better neighborhood, but she refused to move. She feels comfortable here, so I bought the building. I can maintain it and make sure it's at least safe enough to live in."

I can't answer. I don't know what to say. It's such an incredible story....and it explains everything. Lane is nothing like the guy who attacked me.

My knees sag in relief. I wouldn't be able to handle it if he was some violent, dangerous criminal.

We exit the elevator on a floor halfway up the building. The wallpaper here has been replaced, too. The carpet isn't new, but it isn't threadbare, either. Every door looks solid with at least two locks on each one.

He knocks on a random door and we wait until a little lady comes to answer it. She isn't that old, but she acts like it—or maybe her height gives the appearance of age.

She has a round figure and wears a Hawaiian-style momo to hide her size. She hobbles when she walks.

Stray wisps of greying hair fly loose from a badly tied bun on the back of her head. Her face is more deeply etched with lines than it should be for a woman her age.

She immediately brightens up and bursts into a glowing smile when she sees Lane. His tailored business suit makes him look like he comes from a different planet—and I guess he does.

"Sweetheart!" She grabs him in a hug. He has to bend all the way over from the waist to reach her. "It's so good to see you!"

"Hi, Mom," he replies and stands up.

I wouldn't have believed this was the same guy when I see him smiling down at her. He doesn't look like a billionaire business tycoon at all. He actually looks like the boy in his mugshot.

"This is Samantha Mulholland," he tells her. "She's working for one of my companies now. Samantha, this is my mom, Anne Prince."

"It's so good to meet you, sweetheart!" His mother comes toward me and gives me the same warm hug.

"It's my pleasure, Mrs. Prince," I reply.

She bursts out in musical laughter. "You don't have to call me that! Call me Anne. Come in, come in. No need to stand on the doorstep." She laughs at her own joke.

We follow her into an apartment that has seen better days. Mrs. Prince is a packrat with piles of magazines, plastic totes full of craft supplies, ancient newspapers, thousands of knickknacks, and a bunch of other stuff so cluttered with dust and hidden behind other stuff that I can't see all of it.

Homemade crotched blankets cover the tattered couch and a slumped corduroy armchair. A lamp stands over the armchair with a side table loaded to the breaking point with more stuff, including books, magazines, unfinished craft projects, and God only knows what else.

The kitchen on one side of the living room looks unnaturally clean compared to the rest of the apartment. She hasn't left out any dishes or uneaten food. The kitchen doesn't look like part of the same apartment.

She hobbles to her armchair and collapses into it. Lane takes me to the couch and we both sit down.

He immediately leans back on the cushion like he's completely at home here. I find it hard to imagine the great, astoundingly wealthy corporate shark Lane Prince living like this.

I can imagine the boy in his mugshot living like this. I can definitely see how this lifestyle would inspire him to something greater.

"I've been meaning to call you," Anne tells Lane. "That tap in the bathroom keeps leaking. It keeps me awake at night....and the fridge keeps leaking, too. I wake up every morning to a puddle on the floor."

"I told you the fridge was leaking because the inner drain hole was blocked." Lane stands up and heads for the kitchen. "All you have to do is clear it out."

"I know, sweetheart," she calls over her shoulder without getting up. "The only problem is it's so far down in the bottom of the fridge. I can't get to it. My knees hurt too much for me to kneel on the floor...."

He opens the fridge and his voice drifts from inside. "Try moving some of these old condiment bottles out of the way. You'd be able to see it better."

She changes the subject. I dread seeing what her fridge looks like. She might have condiment bottles in there from the early fifties.

"What about the bathroom tap?" she asks. "That plumber you called was useless."

"What did he do?" Lane asks from inside the fridge.

"Oh, I don't know. I didn't watch him to see."

"I'll take a look." Lane rummages around in the fridge for a minute and goes silent. Then he mutters under his breath. "Is this fridge even still working? You have it set on the coldest setting, but the butter is soft."

"I know, sweetheart. I keep turning it up, but it doesn't help."

"I'll get you a new one." He leaves the kitchen and gives me a look when he passes through the living room. "You two talk amongst yourselves."

I find myself grinning at him. "You two are doing just fine without me."

Anne bursts out laughing again. She has a childish, infectious laugh that immediately makes me like her.

Lane crosses the living room to one of the many cabinets against one wall. He has to pull a bunch of the plastic craft totes out of the way. "You really need to become a minimalist, Mom."

She laughs again and her eyes twinkle at me. "He says that every time he comes to visit. He always gets on my case about organizing my things, but I just don't see how I can get rid of anything. It's all important stuff, you know."

He snorts. "Most of it is so old it's useless."

He pulls a heavy, drab-green canvas army bag out of the cabinet. This definitely isn't old or useless. It doesn't even look dusty.

He unzips it on the floor, takes out two plumber's pipe wrenches, and goes into the bathroom. It opens right off the living room.

"When did the plumber come?" he calls through the open door.

"Oh, I don't know," Anne replies. "It was only a few days after your last visit."

"That was over a month ago. Has the tap been leaking all this time? Why didn't you tell me? I could have come to check it."

"You know....I know you're busy. I didn't want to bother you." She leans closer to me. "He always comes over to fix anything I need."

# Chapter 11: Samantha

I can only sit here and marvel at the interaction between Lane and his mother. This is a side of Lane I never knew existed. I never would have believed it could exist, but I suppose everyone has a past.

Banging noises drift out of the bathroom. "The washer is blown out," he announces. It sounds like he has his head under the sink. "Did the plumber check that?"

"I don't know what he did, sweetheart," she replies. "He fiddled with it and said it was fine."

"I'll never use him again," Lane mutters.

"Do you need to buy a replacement washer?" I ask. God knows why I'm getting involved in this conversation.

"I have an extra one here. I'll use that." He keeps banging away in there. "It looks like water is leaking into the wall here. I'll need to fix that, too."

Anne leans forward in her chair and frowns at me. "Are you all right, sweetheart? You look like you got hurt."

"I'm all right." I seize on the most convenient excuse. "I got into an accident a few days ago."

"Do you mean like a car accident?"

"Something like that."

Lane comes in while we're talking and overhears us. He gives me a sharp look over his shoulder on his way back to his tool bag.

He's taken off his jacket and business shirt. He wears a white T-shirt underneath. It makes him look like a working man who might actually live in this neighborhood.

He digs through his tool bag and brings out a rubber plumbing washer still wrapped in its plastic package. He rips it open, throws the wrapper in the kitchen garbage can, and takes the washer back to the bathroom.

He is NOT in there doing plumbing on his mother's apartment. He's rich enough to hire any plumber in the city.

He must fix things for his mother all the time. That must be why he keeps this tool bag here—so he'll be ready to fix whatever she needs.

"So when did you start working for Lane's company?" Anne asks.

"Well...technically I haven't actually started working for him. He just bought the company I work for.....so I guess you could say I'll start working for him once he starts running it. We haven't exactly ironed out the details. We don't even know how he wants to run it or what he wants us to do."

She beams at me. "That's so nice! I always thought Katrina would go to work for one of Lane's companies, but she always did want to be independent."

"Who's Katrina?" I ask. For a second, I experience a moment of sheer terror that Katrina will be some psycho ex of Lane's who will open up a whole new can of worms from his past.

"Katrina is my daughter—Lane's sister," Anne tells me. "She's a lawyer in a firm downtown."

"Oh, right." I nod. "Lane told me."

"They were so close growing up. I always thought they would do something together, but then Lane went off to work and Katrina went to college. I thought that was the end of it and they would drift apart, but they've stayed close." She frowns. "I think they have lunch at least once a week even now."

"That's sweet that your family stays so close."

"Where is your family, sweetheart?" she asks.

"My parents live in Maine where I grew up. My brother and sister both live here in New York. My brother is a lawyer and my sister works in an investment firm. We see each other all the time, too."

She beams at me again. "That's nice. It's always nice to stay in touch with family."

Lane comes back just then. He pulls on his shirt, buttons it up, and then puts on his jacket. "I replaced the washer, Mom. The faucet shouldn't leak anymore, but I need to come back and find out what's wrong with that wall. I might have to tear it out and find a leak in the pipes if that's what's causing the problem."

Her face falls. "Do you have to?"

"I said I might have to. I need to check it more thoroughly and I can't do that tonight. Samantha and I will get out of your way now. It was nice to see you."

He bends over and kisses her on the cheek. She tries to hug him without standing up.

I stand up and hug her, too. I wish I could stay and get to know her better.

Everything about this apartment and Anne gives a feeling of comfort, relaxation, and total acceptance. None of the pressures of the outside world can bother anybody here. This apartment really is a home.

"It was wonderful to meet you, Mrs. Prince," I tell her. "I hope we meet again sometime."

"I hope so, too, sweetheart. You two have a good evening."

"I'll come by in a few days to check on that wall, Mom."

"Okay, sweetheart. I'll see you then."

Lane leads me out of the apartment and back down the hall to the elevator. "She's so sweet," I remark on our way there.

"She has a heart of gold," he replies. "She worked hard to raise us alone."

I don't answer that. Lane isn't the rich snob I thought he was. He isn't a dangerous criminal, either.

"Thank you for confiding in me," I murmur as we step into the elevator.

"I meant what I said. I really don't care who you tell. I'm not ashamed of my past. I'm proud of it."

I nod. "I can see that. You have every right to be."

The elevator starts going down and Lane's driver meets us outside with the limo. None of the neighborhood people come around to bother us when we get in.

Lane waits until we're already driving away before he breaks the silence. "Do you think the rest of the Titanium employees will quit to support Derek?"

"I doubt any of them will."

His head shoots up. "Really? Derek made it sound like...."

I roll my eyes to Heaven. I never let myself express this to anyone else.

I can express it here because Lane and I are alone in the back of his limo. No one will hear me saying anything negative about Derek.

He's the reason we're in this situation. He had his head so deeply buried in the sand that he didn't see Lane out-maneuver him with that sales offer.

"Derek is right that Titanium couldn't function without our company culture," I tell him. "It definitely won't be as profitable without that—if it could stay in business at all. Our clients and customers do business with us because they believe in what the company stands for."

"Then why wouldn't that suffer when Derek leaves—if he leaves?"

"He'll leave. He's too headstrong to stay on as an employee in someone else's company. You just have to convince the employees that they'll still be working for the company values by staying on. We all joined to support those principles, not because of one man. The employees won't quit. I'm certain of it."

"Could you convince them to stay?" he asks. "Could you talk them into continuing the work they did under Derek?"

"Absolutely. That would be easy."

He studies me for a while....and he doesn't look away. The car keeps gliding down the street. The streetlights pivot through the windows.

The eerie light gives Lane a haunted look. There's so much more to him than I thought. I don't know half of what he is, but I've already seen enough to know he's better than I ever imagined.

Without warning, he slides his hand across the seat, covers mine with his warm palm, and squeezes.

This is nothing like all the touches he's been giving me these last few days. He did that to comfort me and support me.

He has no reason to do that now. I'm not scared and I don't need support. He does it for some other reason.

His eyes gleam so close to mine. I get enthralled by the depth of him. I can't look away....and then those eyes dart down to my mouth. Is he going to kiss me right now?

He might never have intended to, but that one look tells me he wants to. That moment changes everything between us—and yet it doesn't change anything.

He showed me something tonight—something no one else knows. Even if he doesn't care who finds out, he still shared something intimate and personal. He gave me something that would allow me to understand him in ways no one else does.

Does that mean anything? It means everything—almost as much as him knowing about my carjacking.

I wouldn't want anyone to find out about that. I have nothing to be ashamed of, but I would still hate for anyone to find out.

Knowing that he knows is the greatest relief of my life. My secret is safe with him. One person knows—the most important person.

Am I really thinking of Lane like that—as the most important person? I don't want to go there with him, especially not when he's about to take over Titanium Finance.

Neither of us moves or looks away until the limo pulls up in front of my apartment building.

Lane gets out and offers me his hand to help me get out. He walks me inside, but he stops in front of the elevator. "Good night," he tells me
.

I want to say something to keep him here. I don't want him to leave. "Thank you again for tonight. I was really worried."

He bursts into a grin. "Don't worry about it. It's nothing."

"I guess...I guess I'll see you tomorrow at work."

"You bet. I can't wait."

Now it's my turn to grin and I find myself blushing. "Good night."

He stands there in the hall and waits for me to unlock my apartment door. He's still standing there when I slip inside. I shut the door.

He isn't here anymore. He'll go home now, but he's still here. He'll always be here. I know that now.

# Chapter 12: Lane

D ante Helme raises his glass of whiskey and clinks it against mine in The Billionaires' Club bar. "Congratulations, man—as if any of us doubted you would get Titanium Finance."

"Thanks," I mumble. "I'm proud of it."

"You should be," Judah Hayes tells me. "You set 'em up and knocked 'em down like a pro."

"That's because he is a pro," Jackson Metcalf interjects. "He's done this before, remember?"

"It's ancient history now," I cut in. "Now we just have to run the operation and get everything back on track through the transition."

"What are you going to do about the employees?" Kevin Drake asks. "I hear there's already talk about a mass walkout."

"That's not good," Jackson remarks.

"I'm not worried about it," I tell them. "It's all under control."

"How?" Dante asks. "What are you going to do to win them over?"

I can't help grinning. "I can be very persuasive when I need to be."

Judah laughs, but right then, a scuffle breaks out near the club entrance. Someone yells, "I don't care! Get out of my way!"

The tension in the room spikes when Derek Salazar storms in. He casts a flinty glance around the club, spots me talking to the other guys, and barges over to us.

"You stole my company, you piece of shit!" he blares. "You took my life's work and destroyed it! You have no honor and no integrity. You're a monster."

I try to shrug it away. Everyone in the club turns around to stare at us. "I offered to buy your company first," I tell him. "I made you a very generous offer—much more generous than Titanium Finance was worth."

"You son of a bitch!" he rages. "You made that offer knowing I would turn it down! You did this so you could screw me over."

I snort in his face. "Believe it or not, pal, I don't lie awake at night thinking about you. You're so arrogant that you short-changed your own employees that you care so much about so you could save your own face. You don't deserve Titanium Finance."

"Don't you dare say anything about my employees!" he fires back. "I care about them a lot more than you do. We have a community. We understand each other in ways you never will."

"You think so? Your employees joined to support their common principles, not for one man."

He narrows his eyes at me. "You bastard! Who told you that?"

"Actually, Samantha Mulholland told me and she should know. You should treat your people better. You should think less about yourself and take care of them. Then maybe you'd be walking away with a nice fat payout instead of the shirt off your back."

"You turned Samantha against me?!" he roars. "You went behind my back and corrupted her against me? You cocksucker!"

"You did that all by yourself, pal. You could have avoided this whole thing if you'd only listened to your executive board. I know they advised you to take my offer and avoid a hostile takeover. You were too stubborn and self-centered to do that. Now you're out in the cold. That's your problem, not mine."

He glares at me so ferociously that I really think he might attack me. Fortunately, Judah, Jackson, and Dante are still standing here. The three of them will be able to restrain Derek if he tries anything.

He stands there with smoke coming out of his nostrils. Then his hard eyes flick to the men on either side of me.

"Did you know this piece of shit has a criminal record?" Derek snarls. "He did time for assault with a deadly weapon and reckless endangerment. Didn't you know? You guys might want to think about who you associate with. His bad reputation might rub off on you."

Dead silence falls over the club. I hold Derek's gaze no matter what. I don't dare to look away. Looking away might make him think I'm concerned about this.

"Is that all you got?" I ask. "Did Samantha tell you that?"

Derek's jaw drops. "Samantha.....she knew?"

My stomach clenches. She knew, but she didn't tell him. She kept the secret to protect me.

I see the wheels turning in his head. He was the one who told her to dig up some dirt to use against me, but she didn't tell him. She kept it from him.

She's better than I ever dared to hope. She's priceless beyond words. She felt terrible for looking me up....and then she told me the whole sordid tale. She couldn't live with the guilt.

What a prize she is, but I can't even tell her. She's my employee now. We have to keep it professional. I'll never be able to express how grateful I am to her for this.

I watch Derek make all those connections. He really blew it when he lost her. Losing Titanium was bad enough. He crossed a line with her.

"Well?" I demand. "Come on. Hit me with your next shot. You can do better than this."

"You piece of shit," he snarls. "You'll pay for this."

"I can't wait," I tell him.

He turns on his heel and storms out of the club. I take a sip of my whiskey, but I can't help feeling the tension all around me. No one says a word until Dante walks away.

Jackson, Kevin, and Judah remain silent. I don't let myself look to see their reactions. Now they all know about me.

I tell myself I don't care and that I'm proud of my history. Life is going to take on a whole new dimension of complicated now that this is out of the bag.

Some people might turn away from me. Some of the men in this room right now might not want to do business with me.

That's okay. I can live with that. I just wish it didn't have to be that way.

It is that way because that's who I am. I can't change my past and I don't want to. I just wish I could change how everyone else sees it.

# Chapter 13: Samantha

The elevator dings in the Titanium Finance lobby. A dozen people rush me as soon as I step through the doors.

"Is Apico going to fire all of us?" a woman from marketing asks.

"How do we know any of us will have jobs on Monday morning?" a man asks. "Should we start looking now?"

"Come on, Samantha. Don't leave us in the dark."

More people crowd around me when I get to the elevators.

"You know what's going on with the executive team," a different guy cuts in. "Tell us what's going on upstairs."

"Did Lane Prince ask you to resign?" another woman asks.

I stop by the elevators and turn around to face the crowd. No one seems to notice my bruises anymore.

I raise my hands for silence. "Listen up, all of you! Apico hasn't given anyone notice of termination and no one is asking anyone to resign. None of you has anything to worry about if you're working hard and giving the company your best. I talked to Lane Prince yesterday. He plans to keep as many of you in your current roles as possible. We'll be holding a company-wide meeting later today where the Apico executive board will announce our next steps forward."

"How do we know what projects we're supposed to work on?" the first man asks. "We don't know what to do until they tell us."

"Just keep doing exactly the same things you were doing before," I reply. "Keep working exactly as if Derek was still in charge. Don't change anything unless someone tells you otherwise."

"How will we know if the person telling us to change has the authority to make those decisions?" the second woman asks.

"Keep the same hierarchy you had before. Follow your department heads' instructions, keep your projects going, and keep giving Titanium your best. That's what I'm doing, so I'm in exactly the same situation you are."

The employees exchange glances. None of them goes back to work.

"I'm going up to the executive suite right now," I tell them. "I'm going to keep working and I suggest you do the same thing. You'll hear everything you need to know at the company-wide meeting soon. I promise. We're all going to keep Titanium going and make it as good as it's always been."

I step into the elevator. No one enters with me or accosts me for answers I don't have.

I ride up to the executive suite and walk into a wall of tension just as stiff and dangerous as the one downstairs.

No one does any work. The employees stand around whispering and shaking their heads.

I know they didn't get bad news—not yet. I would have heard by now if Apico Acquisitions wanted to come through with a chainsaw and a blowtorch and cut Titanium to pieces.

I go to my office and sit down at my desk. I don't know what to do about all my own projects, either, but I have to keep the wheels turning.

I go over the quarterly earnings report first. I would have to do that no matter who owns the company.

I'm just getting back into the swing of my morning schedule when Derek storms in. I didn't even know he was still in the building.

He slams the door behind him and leans over to my desk. "Why the hell didn't you tell me about Lane Prince's criminal record? I specifically asked you to find some incriminating evidence against him that we could use to stop the takeover—and you kept it from me! You found it and you kept it from me! I had to find out from someone else."

I sneer at him and lean back in my seat. Now I know what this is all about. "You had no right to tell me to dig up dirt on Lane. That was unethical—but you don't care about that. You only care about yourself. You screwed all of us over by trying to stop the takeover. Now you can read 'em and weep."

His mouth falls open and his eyes drop out of their sockets. "I can't believe you actually have the nerve to justify this behavior."

"Lane did his time for what he did. He has every right to put it behind him and prove himself. He's never done anything illegal since...."

"Except steal people's companies."

"He didn't steal Titanium or any other company, Derek," I snap. "He took advantage of your stupidity—which is your fault. The rest of us could have wound up on the street thanks to you."

He stands back and props his hands on his hips. "I really thought you were loyal. I thought you stood for something."

"I'm loyal to the company, Derek—which is more than I can say for you. I'm loyal to what this company believes in, which is doing the right thing for our customers and co-workers. We can do that a whole lot better without you."

"How dare you?!" he gasps. "You're sitting in this office because of me! You're where you are because of me."

Now it's my turn to glare at him in fuming hatred. I lower my voice to a deadly snarl. "Don't you dare! Don't you even dare! I could go out there and get another job in ten seconds if I wanted to. You didn't do shit for me, Derek. I'm the one who's been carrying *you* all these years, not the other way around. If you care half as much about this company as you say you do, you'll go right back to your office and get back to work. You'll do everything in your power to make sure the transition to new leadership happens as smoothly as possible. If you don't do that, then you're every bit as selfish as everyone already thinks you are."

I sit down and deliberately turn to my laptop. I pretend to erase him from existence. I don't have time for this idiot.

"You know," he murmurs under his breath. "I really thought our relationship meant something. It obviously doesn't mean as much to you as it does to me."

"You better not mean what I think you mean by that," I fire back. "That would be massively out of line."

"I didn't mean that...."

"Then don't say it. Get out of my office. You can either prove everyone wrong about you by actually doing the right thing for once or you can prove everyone right by sticking your head up your ass again and making this all about you. I really don't care. You're finished as far as I'm concerned."

I don't look at him again before he lets himself out of my office. The bastard! How dare he accuse me of being disloyal!

He better not have been implying that there was ever anything between us—and that bullshit about making me what I am. How dare he even suggest that?!

I'd like to slap him into next week, but watching him disappear into the woodwork of corporate obscurity will be just as good.

I throw myself into my work with a vengeance, but in a few hours, I have to hustle downstairs to meet the Apico board.

The Titanium board meets me near the elevator. "Are we ready for this?" Cesar asks.

"At least we won't have to wonder what they want from us," Spencer murmurs. "I can't live with the anxiety anymore."

"Everything is going to be fine," I tell them. "You'll see."

"You talk to them, Samantha," Cesar tells me. "Everybody loves you."

I laugh nervously. I'm about to protest when I catch a glimpse of Derek in his office. He's still working here. I guess he made his decision.

# Chapter 14: Lane

I get out of the limo with my executive team and enter the Titanium Finance building lobby. Word must have spread about our visit because everyone present stops what they're doing to stare at us.

The rest of the team follows me to the reception desk. A young Asian woman with glasses and a very Japanese-style, shoulder-length hairdo stands behind the desk in her business suit.

"Good morning...." I read her nametag. "Good morning, Jennifer. We're here for the company meeting in....." I check my watch. "In twenty minutes."

She opens her mouth like a stunned mullet, but just then, the Titanium board comes out of the elevator—without Derek. I hope he doesn't plan to make trouble for us.

The other execs hang back, but Samantha comes toward me grinning. "Welcome. It's wonderful that you could make it. We've been looking forward to this."

I glance around at the employees. They all stand petrified like statues. "You could have fooled me."

She laughs. "Don't worry about them. They're just anxious because they don't know what to expect from the takeover. I tried to reassure them, but they won't believe anything until they hear it from you."

She glances around the group. She knows everyone here from our negotiation on my purchase offer.

She goes through the group shaking hands with everyone. "Welcome, Mr. Thorn—Mr. Van Sant. It's a pleasure to make your acquaintance at last."

"Thank you for having us, Ms. Mulholland," Marco replies.

She turns to Marshall, Russel, and Ethan. She greets them all by name and shakes all their hands. "I really hope we can work together and make this transition as seamless as possible. All the employees want that, I can assure you."

"I'm glad you think so," Marco mutters from the back.

"I'm certain of it. I told them this morning that the company's continued success depends on all of them staying in their roles and continuing to give the company the same effort and dedication they always have."

"You mean....they actually want to continue with it?" Ricardo gasps. "Are you sure? We heard the opposite."

She holds up both hands. "We all want to continue dedicating ourselves to the principles that made Titanium great in the first place. If we can convince everyone that they can continue doing that, I don't see the transition causing any hiccups. Everything can go on as before."

"We?" Russel repeats. "Do you plan to help us make this transition as seamless as possible? How do you plan to do that?"

Her eyes dart to me, but she doesn't tell them about our conversation in the limo last night. She doesn't reveal anything about what's passed between us.

"I'm going to give a statement at this meeting," she tells them. "I'm certain I can convince all the employees to stay on board."

"Thank you, Ms. Mulholland," Ricardo exclaims.

She smiles at them all. "Please—call me Samantha." She waves at the people behind her. "I think you know Reese McCall, Bradley Lenz, Spencer Holt, and Cesar Pound."

She introduces both boards to each other and everyone shakes hands. Then she waves us toward the elevator. "If you follow me, I'll show you to the auditorium where we'll hold the meeting."

She takes us back to the elevator. We have to jam in tightly so we can all fit.

I wind up standing right next to her. Her eyes keep darting up to meet mine before she immediately looks away.

I get a sizzling sensation of her body pressed right against mine. I shouldn't think of her that way.

Everything I've ever done with her has been totally innocent. Don't ask me what changed to make me think of her differently.

I probably would have thought of her differently if I hadn't gotten involved in that carjacking. That somehow turned our interaction into something purely innocent and selfless on my part. I never thought of her as anything else—until last night.

She's the first woman I've ever taken to meet my mother. I never would have dreamed of showing any other woman where I grew up—but it seems so natural with Samantha. I don't know why.

Sure, she's a knockout—not to mention successful, intelligent, and caring. Maybe finding out that she kept my secret from Derek tipped the scales—except that I found out about that after I took her to meet my mother.

I don't understand all this except that I feel differently about her. I want to feel that body pressed up against me in a different way. Does she feel it, too?

I know she does. I saw it in her eyes last night on our way home in the limo, but neither of us would ever act on it.

Now we're both here in the Titanium Finance elevator in a professional capacity. That just proves how impossible it is. Every minute of every day carries her farther out of my reach even as it brings us closer together.

It would have been nice, but it will never happen. At least I found out what she was worth.

I found out she's honest, loyal, caring, and protective. That will make her even more valuable as an employee. I don't want to risk that.

# Chapter 15: Lane

Samantha takes me and the rest of the Apico executives on a tour of the Titanium Finance building through a few different departments.

The Titanium board hangs back and follows us in silence. They let her do all the talking unless someone asks them a specific question.

We're just leaving the executive floor to get in the elevator to go back downstairs to the auditorium. We're waiting for the elevator to come when Derek steps up to his office door.

He eyes us out in the hall, but he doesn't speak or come out to greet us. He just stands there brooding in silence.

I don't know what to think of his reaction. Does he plan to cooperate? Is this going to turn into some kind of vendetta against me? It better not or I'll have to shut him down.

The elevator comes just then and we wind up sandwiched into it a second time. I get squashed against Samantha in one corner. She wedges herself against the wall by the elevator buttons with me standing right in front of her.

I get another wave of sensation. I can just imagine my body jammed against hers, but in a very different way. I feel what it would feel like to pin her against the wall.....with her back to me.....that ripe, round ass sticking out for me......and her panting and gasping in desire for me.....

I can't think like that. I have to pay attention. I look at the elevator doors instead, but her deep soft eyes draw me back. I find it impossible to look away.

Her eyes glow with questions and buried passion. Is she thinking about me groping her all over? My hands itch to take hold of her....and her clothes....

I feel myself starting to get hard, but right then, the elevator doors open and we exit into a wide corridor crowded with employees.

They're all talking when the elevator opens, but they fall silent when they see us.

Samantha walks straight through them, smiles at everyone, and stops a few times to greet everyone and thank them for coming.

She leads the way to the entrance at the top of the auditorium. Curved rows of seats surround a stage at the bottom.

She murmurs, "Follow me," and enters the giant room.

We climb down between the seats and up another set of steps to get onto the stage. Our arrival signals the employees. They follow us inside and start taking their seats.

Someone has set up a bunch of chairs for us on one side of the stage. Some bright spark put all the executive seats together. The Apico board and the Titanium board sit together—all except Samantha.

She busies herself setting up a microphone and hooking it up to the auditorium's sound system. Then she tests it.

The employees fill the hall. Their conversation washes down the tiers to the stage, but none of this seems to bother Samantha.

She doesn't show any sign of nerves, not even when she catches me watching her. She smiles at me.

I don't know what she'll say to the employees except that I do know. She already told me.

This moment will make or break her and us. If she doesn't pull this off, we're going to have a hard time transitioning Titanium under Apico's control.

She acts like this is no big deal, though. She's so relaxed and confident. She finishes messing with the microphone and comes over to sit with us.

"Don't look now, but Derek is here," Bradley Lenz murmurs.

We follow his gaze to the very top tiers of seats. Derek comes to the doors, but he doesn't enter. He stays standing there looking down over this meeting.

"Don't worry about him," Samantha tells us. "He won't bother us."

"I wish I could share your confidence," Russel replies. "He has more pull with the employees than you do. If he speaks against us....."

"He won't," she insists. "I'm certain of it."

Don't ask me how she's so certain, but Derek doesn't intrude on the meeting at all.

He stays standing there when Samantha stands up, retrieves her microphone, and starts speaking to the assembled employees.

"As you all know by now, Apico Acquisitions carried out a hostile takeover of Titanium Finance last week. Whatever your personal feelings might be about how this happened or who might have done what to whom, Apico Acquisitions now owns Titanium Finance. There's nothing we can do about that, so talking about the past and dwelling on how it happened won't make any difference. Starting right now—today—we only care about the future and making this company as good as it can be. I know each and every one of you dedicated yourselves to that mission and I did the same thing. We've pulled together, struggled together, and worked our tails off all these years to make Titanium Finance the powerhouse that it is today."

I find myself barely listening to her words. I get another surreal flash of imagery of her body in my hands.

Her tight-fitting suit blazer hugs her sides and flares around her hips at the bottom. The cut shows off her full breasts and the luscious sweeping curve of her glorious ass. Her muscular thighs move back and forth under her skirt when she paces back and forth across the stage.

Her hair sways against her shoulders and I catch a glimpse of her neck underneath—right beneath her ears. Her gold earrings flash in the shadow under her hair.

That neck.....that waist.....those thighs.....What I wouldn't give to crawl inside them and taste all her delights.

I don't want to hurt her, though. I don't want to scare her or put her in a compromising position.

She feels safe with me now. I want it to stay that way. In a way, dreaming about her is sweeter than actually going there—especially when I know what going there would cost both of us.

She's so perfect, though. I can admire her like this—all done up in her business suit and high heels—but it was somehow nicer to see her in her pajamas and bathrobe with her wet hair combed and her curled up on the couch in a big fluffy bedspread.

I loved drinking coffee and eating breakfast with her like that. Holding those two images side by side in my mind—it gives me a complete picture of just how outstanding she is in every possible way.

She can hold both those images about me now, too. She knows me from the corporate boardroom, but she also knows my past. She knows where I come from and how I grew up.

Applause snaps me out of my trance in time to hear the end of her speech. "We're still on top! We're still the best in the industry—be-cause of you—because of all your hard work and dedication. We're going to keep kicking ass. We're going to keep dominating the industry. We're going to keep taking care of our customers the way they expect us to. We're going to keep providing value and holding each other to a high standard. None of the principles that brought us all to work here will ever change—because we won't let them. Those standards will always rule this company because we'll make sure they do. They'll rule all our actions, every hour, every day, every project, every client, and every sale."

People out in the seats whistle and pump their fists. Some cup their mouths to yell back at her.

She waits for silence and then points to the chairs near her. "Most of you will never see the people in the executive suite except on this stage at these meetings. Most of you couldn't identify which of these people comes from Apico Acquisitions and which of them are Titanium executives. None of that matters. Most of you will never see or know anything that happens in the executive suite—because it doesn't matter. Your lives won't change. Your jobs won't change. The standards we all hold for ourselves won't change. We'll keep doing things the way we always have and Titanium will still rise to the top. No one will ever b eat us."

More cheers answer her and a bunch of people get to their feet. I spot Derek still standing in the doorway, but after a few more minutes, he leaves. He doesn't come back.

I feel sorry for the guy. It must be terrible to watch everything you've ever worked for slip through your fingers.

He banked everything on his employees sticking by him. He just didn't realize what that meant until it was too late. Now it's gone.

Samantha keeps striding back and forth yelling into the microphone to make herself heard over the noise. I don't listen to the rest of her speech. It's nothing she hasn't already told me she would say.

I just never thought she'd deliver it this way. I never dreamed she would rally the employees like this.

The meeting breaks up and she puts her microphone away. All the employees go back to work talking much more excitedly. The relief in the room becomes palpable, now that they know they can keep doing their jobs the way they want to.

Samantha comes over to us smiling. The other execs stand up.

"That was spectacular, Samantha," Marshall tells her. "That was beyond anything I ever thought possible."

"Yeah," Russel murmurs. "I never thought I'd see them standing up and cheering the takeover like that."

She beams at all of us, including me, but she isn't thinking that way about me.

"I knew they'd come around. These people have dedicated everything to Titanium. They don't want to give it all up just because different people are in the executive suite."

"*You'll* still be in the executive suite," Bradley points out. "You aren't going anywhere...but what about the rest of us?"

His question throws a bucket of cold water on us. My team and I turn around to face the Titanium board.

"We'd like to meet with each of you individually," I tell them. "We'll hold these meetings later today and discuss each of your positions and how we want to move forward. Then each of you will translate our decisions down to the rest of your departments."

Samantha nods. "No problem. Let's go back upstairs. We can meet in the boardroom and you can discuss whatever you need to discuss before you meet with each of us there."

# Chapter 16:
# Samantha

I step into the Titanium Finance boardroom, but this is nothing like the other times I've been in here.

None of my fellow Titanium execs are here. I'm all alone.

The Apico board sits across the table in a line. Lane sits at the far end and leans extra far back in his chair like he isn't part of this even though he is.

I'm the first Titanium exec to meet the Apico board in here. I'm about to find out if I still have a job.

I know I do. I'm not worried. Bradley wasn't lying about that. I'm safe. They won't get rid of me—especially not after the way I rallied the employees at the company meeting earlier.

"Take a seat, Samantha," Russel Shauer tells me.

I pull out a chair and sit down alone on this side of the table. They all sit on the other side of it facing me.

"We just want to say we're ecstatic about your speech just now," Marco tells me. "We couldn't be happier and we definitely want to keep you on as CFO of Titanium."

I only nod. This is nothing less than I expected. "Thank you. I'm grateful."

"We plan to keep Spencer Holt, Bradley Lenz, and Cesar Pound, but we have to let Reese McCall go," Marco goes on. "I'm sorry if this hurts you, but his work has been substandard and he's a weight on the entire marketing division. We can do better. Almost anyone would be better."

I nod at that, too. "I guess I can't fault you for that."

I become aware of Lane's eyes drilling into me from the other end of the table. He stays reclined back in his chair and doesn't join the conversation, but he takes in every word.

"I'm glad you feel that way," Marco goes on. "We value your contribution to this company and we don't want to do anything to alienate you."

"You won't be alienating me by getting rid of Reese."

"Because you made it clear in your speech that everyone would continue in their roles. You gave everyone to believe nothing would change and that everyone would keep their jobs."

"I made it clear that everyone would continue in their roles and nothing would change as long as they maintained the high standard of conduct and customer care we've always prided ourselves on providing. Reese hasn't done that. We all know that. I thought I made it clear in my speech that our mission going forward was to make Titanium as great as it could be and that everyone working here was a part of that. If someone isn't a part of that, then they don't have a place here. I thought I made that clear."

"You did," Ricardo chimes in.

"Do you think Reese understood all that?" Marco asks. "Do you think the rest of the employees see that Reese is a weight on the company and not an asset? Do you think everyone else sees that he's failing to live up to that standard?"

"I think Derek let Reese slide because Derek didn't want to confront Reese about it. I think Derek talked a good line when it came to motivating the employees. Then, when it came to enforcing that standard within his own executive team, Derek lacked the balls to actually enforce those standards." I wince. "I shouldn't be talking about Derek behind his back like this."

"We need to know where we stand with everyone in this company," Marshall interjects. "You're the only person here we can ask about the company's internal workings."

"Well, that about sums it up. Derek liked everyone who worked here. He valued everyone, which made it impossible for him to fire anyone—especially those closest to him. He inspired enough of the employees and the culture spread from there, but he didn't do anything to make sure the executives held the same standard. Some of us did....."

I trail off when I realize I might be spewing too much information.

The Apico board sits there in silence listening until Marco clears his throat again. "How cooperative do you think Derek will be with the transition?"

I can only shrug. "Your guess is as good as mine. To be honest, I'm surprised he's still here at all. I thought he would have left by now."

"We thought the same thing," Ricardo replies. "That's why we were worried when he came to the meeting. We thought he would try to rally the employees away from us."

"But we see now that he no longer has that power within the company," Russel goes on. "We won't have to worry about him again thanks to you."

I turn bright red. "You're too kind. I'm only trying to do what's best for the company and that's obviously Apico."

"I'm glad you see it that way," Marco tells me. "We'd like to assign Ethan here to stand in for Reese until the Board of Directors hires another more permanent CMO. We'd like you to orient Ethan and help him merge with the company so he can start ironing out the marketing department as soon as possible."

I nod across the table. "No problem. I can do that."

"Thank you for your excellent work, Samantha. We're all grateful for your dedication and enthusiasm. We couldn't do this without your ongoing help."

I want to say again that I'm only doing this to help the company, but I already said that.

I become aware again of Lane scrutinizing me. I can't even lie to myself anymore that he's scrutinizing me. He sits there simmering with barely concealed power.

He undresses me with his eyes. He probably doesn't realize how obvious it is what he's thinking about.

I saw it and felt it in the elevator, too. His body throbbed with buried passion just waiting to explode.

The depth and volatility of it scares me, but it also turns me on beyond anything I've ever experienced.

He's by far the hottest guy who has ever shown an interest in me, but he's also the kindest, the most caring, and the most protective.

He's been touching me all this time—ever since the carjacking. He's been holding my hand and stroking my hair and rubbing my back. He's been sitting right next to me and putting his hand on my knee.

None of those touches meant anything at the time. They mean everything now and he isn't even touching me anymore.

He knows better than anyone that we have to keep our distance. He's my boss now. We'll never do anything.

My knees tremble with desire just from being in the same room with him. I feel his eyes tracing all my curves and seeing my body exposed underneath.

I want to crawl inside him for protection, but I also want him to unleash all that ravenous animal hunger on me. I want to feel the full power of his appetite satisfying himself with me.

I have to shake that off before I start getting wet from thinking about it. Who am I kidding? I'm already wet from thinking about it.

His body felt tight and strong in the elevator. His eyes bored into me with such intensity. Is that how he would look at me when he took me against the wall? Is that how he would look when he ripped my clothes off and claimed me for himself?

I shouldn't be thinking that after what happened during the car-jacking, but I am thinking it. I can't imagine thinking it about any other man.

He's the only man I would feel safe enough going there with. He's the only man I could really let myself go with. I wouldn't want anyone else to see me like that. They might get the wrong idea.

I don't know what wrong idea they might get, but he would never get the wrong idea. He knows me better than anyone, including my own family. He knows the worst thing about me and he still wants me.

I see that in his eyes. He wants me. He wants me real bad. He just can't have me—and I can't have him no matter how wet I get for him.

My nipples tingle just thinking about him sitting there watching me. I want him to touch me. I want him to tease me and excite me. I want him to own every part of my body and make me succumb to his desires and my own.

I barely notice when Marco ends our meeting. I meet Ethan outside. He's a young guy of thirty-five with black hair, black eyes, and fiery blue eyes. He grins at me. "I guess I'll see you tomorrow morning."

I smile back as genuinely as I can and bolt back to my office. I shut the door and collapse panting in my chair.

I can't start thinking about Lane like this, but it's already too late. I can't get him out of my mind. Everything he does turns me on.

I shut my eyes, but that only floods my mind with a million images from our time together. The back of his limo, the couch in my apartment—did all those mean something? Did they mean the same thing to him that they mean to me?

Thinking about doing it with him in all those places gives me a rush of slippery heat between my legs. I squirm in my chair, but that only excites me even more.

Every movement of my thighs under my skirt reminds me of him slipping his hand between my legs....and higher....

I gasp, but just then, my phone rings. I don't recognize the number. I answer it. "Hello?"

"Ms. Mulholland? This is Detective Beckett from the NYPD. I took your statement on the carjacking incident...."

"Yes!" I practically shriek. "How are you? Sorry. I wasn't expecting to hear from you."

"I get it. Most people hope they never hear from me ever again."

I pretend to laugh. "Yeah, actually, I kinda hoped that, too."

"Sorry to disappoint you, but would you mind coming down to the station to clarify a few things about your statement? Don't worry. Your assailant isn't here. He's been transferred to a holding facility upstate. There's no chance you'll see or bump into him here."

I sigh with relief. "Thank you, Detective. That was going to be my next question."

"I understand. So...what about it? Would you mind coming in?"

"Not at all. When would you like me to come?"

"Anytime that's convenient for you. I'm here all the time."

I check the time. It's four o'clock in the afternoon. I wouldn't normally leave the office now, but I need to put some distance between myself and all these feelings raging inside me.

What better way to do that than to give a statement on the carjacking? That will dampen any thought of doing it with anyone.

"How about now?" I ask. "Is that too soon?"

"Not at all. That would be great."

# Chapter 17: Lane

"You can take the car home, Eddie," I tell him. "I don't know how long I'll be, so I'll just text you when I'm ready to leave."

"Yes, Sir. No problem, Mr. Prince."

"Thanks, man." I get out of the limo and shut the door. He drives off and I turn to face the New York Police Department.

I'm going to have a chip on my shoulder about this place for a while after getting arrested during Samantha's assault, but I can put that aside. The cops were just doing their job. I can't hold that against them.

I don't mind coming back here to answer questions. I don't care how long it takes for the Police to get it through their heads that I was just trying to help her.

Detective Beckett has been super supportive and understanding about the whole thing. He keeps insisting that they know I saved her and all of this is just procedure.

Still, it's kinda hard not to get defensive when I walk into the place. I approach the sergeant at the reception desk. "I'm here to see Detective Beckett. He asked me to come in. My name is Lane Prince."

"He's expecting you, but he's in another meeting right now. Just take a seat, Mr. Prince. He'll be with you shortly."

I turn to the waiting area. It's clogged with the dregs of humanity, including a few people who look like they're about to fall over dead right in their seats.

I make a strategic survey of the area to decide where I'm going to sit. I'm just trying to make up my mind when the doors next to the sergeant's desk opens.

I gasp when Samantha comes out. "Samantha? What are you doing here?" I ask.

She rubs her hands up and down her arms and her eyes dart around the waiting area taking in the gruesome scene. Then she jumps out of her skin when the door slams behind her.

All her calm confidence from the meeting evaporates. She's back to being jumpy and jittery. Nothing better have happened to her—again.

I ease closer to her, lower my voice, and just because it feels right, I put my arm behind her back. "You okay? What are you doing here? Did something happen?"

"No, I just...." She shuts her eyes and tries to shake it off. "I just had to answer some questions about my statement. I just...I just finished talking to that detective."

"Oh. Me, too. I mean, that's why I'm here. I'm supposed to see him right now."

She doesn't hear me. Her eyes travel back to the waiting area and she shrinks a little closer to me. She would have to walk through all those people to get outside—and then it hits me.

She owns her own car. She may have driven here from the office. If she did, she probably dreads driving home—or anywhere else for that matter.

"Would you like me to drive you home?" I offer. "You don't have to drive alone."

Her eyes shoot over to me. "Really? I feel like an idiot for not being able to handle this better."

"Forget it. You can handle it any way you want. Stick around. I'll talk to the detective and then I'll call Eddie to come and get us."

She looks out at the waiting area again. I barely hear her when she half-whispers, "Okay."

"Come over here and sit down."

I lead her to the seat I was planning to take for myself. It's at the end of the row. An overweight black lady in her sixties hunches sound asleep in the seat next to this one. There is no other seat. The sleeping lady will be Samantha's only neighbor.

"Stay here. I'll be back as soon as I can. Okay?" I squat down and position my face right in front of her eyes so she has no choice but to look at me. "Okay?"

She nods and closes her eyes again. "Thank you. I don't know what's wrong with me."

"I do." For no reason I can think of, I kiss her on the forehead, but right then, Detective Beckett comes to the door.

He sees me and Samantha together, but I really don't give a shit.

I squeeze her shoulder once and go over to him before he can call me. He glances past me at Samantha in the waiting area. "Is she okay?" he asks.

"Not really. She's still jumpy after the attack and she's scared to drive by herself. I offered to take her home after this."

He nods and opens the door for me. I go into the back and he leads me to his office, which is the same place he questioned me after my arrest.

He sits down behind his desk. "Take a seat. We've just been going over the evidence we have and comparing everyone's statements. The assailant is claiming you held him at gunpoint...."

"That's bullshit. I never touched his gun except when I slapped it out of his hand."

"I know that, Mr. Prince," the detective murmurs with exaggerated patience. "We fingerprinted the gun. He was the only person who handled the weapon on the night in question. We also have Ms. Mulholland's statement to the same effect. This is just a routine cross-check."

I stiffen in my chair. I need to keep my cool here, but cops always did have this effect on me.

I try not to squirm. "What else do you want to know?"

"A few of the arresting officers said you started speaking to Ms. Mulholland as soon as they entered the premises. They heard you reassuring her and calling her by her first name in a way that seemed to indicate that you knew each other beforehand."

Now he's the one who squirms in his seat. Is he as nervous about this interview as I am?

"Anyway, when I saw you at her apartment, it appeared as though you weren't just helping a random stranger."

"Of course I knew her beforehand." I have to check myself when I remember that he doesn't know about any of this. "She works for a company—a finance company. My company took over her company last week. I made an offer to buy her firm before the takeover and we met at a negotiation between my board and her board—so yes, I knew her beforehand."

"Is that the only time you ever met her—at this board meeting?"

I try to think and then remember seeing her at the bar. "Actually, I met her one other time at the Revelation Steakhouse."

"What happened there?"

"I tried to talk to her. This was between the purchase negotiation and the takeover itself, so she was hostile and told me to take a hike.

I didn't do it fast enough and her brother stepped in and told me to buzz off. That's it." I shrug. "I guess that's the only reason I saw the carjacking in the first place—because I recognized her through my window and I was watching her drop off her sister. I wouldn't have noticed otherwise. I wouldn't have been paying any attention to her so I wouldn't have seen it."

"The assailant also claims you were on that side of the street prior to him getting into her car."

"He's lying. I never got out of my car until after he took Samantha to the underground garage. Besides, how does he explain winding up in her car with her if I was on that side of the street? How does he explain hitting her in the face and ripping out half her hair?"

"I know that, Mr. Prince," he groans. "We have the doorman's testimony that he never saw you before—on that night or any other."

I pull my head in. This isn't about me. I'm not being accused of anything—not by anyone that matters. Of course the dirtbag that did this is going to make up any lunatic shit off the top of his head to deflect blame away from himself.

Detective Prince checks his notes on his laptop. "I'm sorry to put this so indelicately, but I have to ask. You and Ms. Mulholland are the only witnesses apart from the assailant himself. He denies that he was trying to rape her when you entered his apartment."

I have to fight down rage threatening to blow me apart. "Well, he was trying to rape her—and he had his gun to her head, too—just in case he gets any stupid ideas about claiming it was consensual. I mean, just look at her damn face, man. Are you telling me that was consensual?"

"He doesn't deny hitting her in the face. He denies that he was lying on top of her trying to pull up her skirt the way she claims."

I glare at him in pure boiling fury. I have to remind myself that this detective isn't the one saying these things. "Well, he was trying to pull up her skirt."

"You're the only other person who was in the room, so I'm afraid I have to ask this. How far did he actually get? How close did he come to actually raping her?" He spreads his hands. "I only ask because she might be inclined to gloss it over by saying he only tried to instead of saying he actually did it."

I have to look away. I want to hurt somebody right now. It's a damn good thing the bastard isn't in the building right now or I don't know what I'd do.

"He didn't get her skirt up," I snarl. "He got it a few inches above her knees before I got there. He didn't actually do anything."

"Did you hear him threaten her—verbally, I mean—apart from just seeing him holding his gun to her head? Did you hear what he actually said to her? She claims he threatened to kill her if she didn't cooperate. Did you hear that?"

"No," I mutter. "I didn't hear anything he said. I walked in. I saw him on top of her and I kicked him in the head. That's all. It happened in seconds."

"Did you hear him talking to her without hearing the actual words? Can you confirm that he was talking to her at the time?"

"I can't confirm that. I didn't hear anything. I mean, I didn't hear whether he was talking to her or not. I was too damn mad."

"Okay, Mr. Prince. That will be all for now. I appreciate you coming in. I'll let you know if we need anything further."

# Chapter 18: Lane

I get out of Detective Beckett's office as quickly as I can, but I have to calm myself down in the hall before I go see Samantha.

That son of a bitch! How dare he deny that he tried to rape her? He deserves a slow, painful death for that at least.

Now I know why she was so jumpy after talking to the detective. He must have asked her the same questions. That must have been awful.

I really wish I could have been there for her during the interview, but I guess that's kind of the point. We're the only two witnesses and she's the victim. Detective Becket has to interview us separately to make sure we don't influence each other's statements.

Thinking about her makes me hustle downstairs. I send Eddie a text and find her sitting in the same place.

Seeing her calms me down instantly. She needs me to be strong and steady right now—not ready to kill anyone who looks sideways at her.

I squat down in front of her again. "You okay? Are you ready to go home?"

She nods. Her eyes focus on me much better now.

I take her hand and lead her outside. We have to stand and wait for Eddie to show up before we climb into the limo.

She gazes out the window at the streetlights drifting past. I really don't care about all these fantasies floating through my head. Thinking about her scared or in danger cools my jets. I just want her to be okay.

"Don't worry about all this," I tell her. "It doesn't mean anything. The Police just have to dot all their Is and cross all their Ts. You know that, right?

She turns around....and those eyes lock on me. She looks at me the way she did in the elevator....and just as fast, I forget about her being scared and in danger. She's right here in my limo—close enough to touch, close enough to kiss.

Her eyes glisten with something other than fear. She wants it. She must have been thinking about me the same way—ever since I held her hand on the way home from my mother's apartment building.

That's when she knew I wanted it, so that must be when she started thinking about it, too.

Her eyes pulse with heat. Her whole body radiates it.

I don't think twice. I lean in and kiss her......and she responds. Her lips melt in a river of warmth and satin softness. Her tongue tastes mind-blowing in my mouth.

All my dreams come true when my hands appear on her slim waist.....and then glide down to her hips.....and up to her chest.

She exhales a sudden puff of hot air through her nostrils and then moans one high, tortured sob of desire. Holy shit, she's so damn hot! I have to have her.

I try to pull myself back. I have to be gentle with her. I don't want to be. I want to attack her and pin her to the limo seat right now.

Her hands fly up to my face and shoulders and chest. Before I can think, she burrows under my jacket and touches me all over through my shirt.

That touch shoots a lightning bolt of electricity to my crotch. My package swells to painful hardness, but I can't let her find out about that. I don't want to scare her when we're just kissing.

I can't stop my hands from touching every inch of her. I squeeze her breasts just to hear her whine like that again. The sound twists in my nuts. Christ, I want to make her moan like that all the time.

She grabs my jacket and starts tugging it off....and then, just when I think this can't get any crazier, she slips her hand between my legs and feels me.

I freeze at her touch, but she's definitely doing this. She squeezes and then starts rhythmically stroking me through my pants.

I stare at her in stupid shock. I can hardly kiss her with these crushing sensations shooting into me. They flood up my shaft, into my guts, and through the rest of my body.

I'm going to lose it completely if she doesn't stop, but I can't move. My head will explode with all the thoughts and emotions pulsing out of me and into me from her hand.

Her eyes float open in front of me. They shimmer in two glossing brown pools of deep passionate emotion. Does she have a clue what she's doing to me?

She stops touching me and goes to work on my jacket again. She tugs it off my shoulders.

That feeling snaps me out of my trance and I pounce on her. I tear her blazer open and don't give myself a second to hesitate.

If she second-guesses herself about this, if she changes her mind and pushes me away and says no, she can't, I have to take it to the limit before that happens. I have to experience all of her while I can before the door slams shut in my face.

I grab her around her back and plunge my face into the cleft of her blouse. God only knows I've dreamed about her cleavage enough times.

I nudge her shirt open and bury myself up to my eyes in her sweet, soft breasts. She whimpers and hugs my head close. Her fingers rake up my back, into my hair, and her delicious sobs float into my ears.

She makes me so damn hard I can't stand it. I lower both hands to her thighs and try to push her skirt up before I remember. He did that. I don't want to do anything that might remind her of that.

Before I can change tack, she slips her hands under my jacket again and starts tearing up my shirt. The sensation of her exposing my body drives me wild. She really wants this. She really wants me to do it with her right here in the limo.

Right then, right when I think I can't stand this a second longer, Eddie brakes to the curb. "We're here, Mr. Prince," he tells me through the window.

I don't worry about Eddie seeing me with her. He's seen me with enough women in the back of the limo.

This is different, though, because it's her. She means more. I don't want her to be a backseat conquest I never see again.

I pull off her lips. I'm ready to walk away and call it a hot make-out session. I don't need or necessarily want it to go any further.

She floats off my mouth and whispers in a deep, sultry undertone, "Come inside, Lane."

Her eyes consume me with that cosmic magical power. She did NOT just invite me inside.

Just to confirm it, she squeezes my leg again—on my thigh this time. She is definitely suggesting that.

I don't know what to expect and yet I do. I get out of the limo and tell Eddie to go home for the night. He doesn't make eye contact before he drives off.

# Chapter 19:
# Samantha

I fight down serious heart palpitations when I unlock my apartment door and lead Lane inside. He's been here before, but never like this.

We just kissed in his limo. I touched him—and he touched me.

"Can I get you something to drink?" I ask for no particular reason.

"Uh....sure. Thanks."

He wanders into the apartment, but he doesn't make himself comfortable the way he did last time. Of course not.

I don't know why I invited him in—and yet I do. I want him. I want to do everything with him, but I don't know how to start.

I suppose I'm the one who started in the limo by looking at him like that. He would have to be blind not to see my reaction.

I go into the kitchen and pull open the cabinet. "I have bourbon, vodka, tequila, schnaps, Kahlua, and whiskey.

He spins around. "Are you a heavy drinker? I never knew."

I find myself laughing. "This is all left over from a party my sister and brother and I gave two years ago. I haven't touched it since. I swear, Your Honor. I never touched the stuff."

He laughs, too. At least we can laugh. This isn't deadly serious even though it is.

What am I thinking? Lane is my boss now. I shouldn't be making out with him in his limo or inviting him in for a drink afterward, but that's what I'm doing.

"I'll take a bourbon. Thanks."

"Straight or on the rocks?" I ask.

"Straight, please."

He keeps strolling around my apartment looking at everything like he's never seen it before. I take ice out of the freezer, put the ice cubes in my own glass, and pour the liquor into both glasses.

I take his over to him and sit down on the couch to sip mine.

He stops in front of a painting on the wall and studies it. "This is interesting. I don't recognize the artist."

"That's because it's mine."

He spins around to glance at me. "Yours?!"

I blush and grimace at him. "I know what you're going to say. I studied art in college. Let's be generous and call it a phase."

He goes back to studying the picture. "I think it's good. It's....pro vocative."

I snort and take another sip of my drink. "I'm sure I thought so at the time, too."

He stands there looking at it for way too long. I hope he's not going to make a big deal about it. "Why do you keep it if you think it's no good?"

"The subject," I reply over my shoulder without turning around. "I keep it for the subject."

He cocks his head the other way and scrutinizes the picture a little closer. The subject is the outline of a man. He's young—about thirty.

A dozen squares cover his face, head, neck, and every part of his upper body inside the picture frame. Each square shows a tiny landscape, each one also dotted with squares showing even more varied and layered landscapes.

Each landscape is a surreal mishmash of recognizable shapes, twisted faces, machinery, monstrous creatures, and regular images from nature.

"I know it isn't the most original idea, but it meant a lot to me when I painted it," I go on over my shoulder. "I put a lot into it and I've never been able to get rid of it even though I painted it so long ago."

"So who's the subject?" he asks also without turning away from the picture. "Who's the guy?"

I hesitate and then blurt out, "My father."

Lane doesn't answer nor does he turn around. He's told me everything about his past. I guess I don't feel right about keeping mine from him.

"He died when we were young. He died when he was about the age he is in that picture. That's the way I remember him—not with all those imagines all over his face, obviously, but the outline picture. He was young and strong and healthy."

"How did he die?" Lane asks still without turning around.

"He died in an industrial accident. He worked in a sawmill and there was an accident. He got knocked into the sawblade and his body got cut to pieces. That's all I know. I was only a kid at the time. We all w ere."

Lane stands there staring at the picture in silence for a long time. I don't see his reaction because he doesn't have one.

I don't know why talking about my father brings up so many emotions for me. I've always felt close to him—probably closer to him than I could have felt if he'd lived.

I've always felt that he was with me, watching over me, and proud of my accomplishments. He's one of the most important people in my life even though he isn't in it.

The only people more important are my brother and sister—probably because they went through it with me.

After a long time, Lane says, "I thought you said your parents live in Maine. You told my mom that."

"He's my stepdad. He married my mom less than a year after my father died. My stepdad raised us as his own. He's the one who took that place in my life. I guess that's why I felt like I had to paint a picture of my father. I needed a way to remember him—something that didn't threaten my relationship with my stepdad."

"Is he threatened by it?" Lane asks. "Would he be threatened by you painting a picture of how you remember your father?"

"No, not at all. My stepdad is always the one encouraging us to do things to remember my father and celebrate him. It's just kinda hard because it brings up painful memories. My mom hates it when he does that. She just wants to forget. Remembering makes her sad—and I guess she feels like she's betraying her husband by getting sad over another man—a man she can't have. I guess all of us feel the same way. I wouldn't want my stepdad to think I didn't appreciate him."

"Does he know you have this?"

"Yeah, he knows. He's visited me here. I don't know if he recognizes who it is, but if he does, he doesn't mention it."

Lane takes a gulp of his drink and finally turns away from the picture. He comes over to the couch, but he doesn't sit on it next to me.

He sits on the coffee table in front of me, puts his drink down next to him, and leans forward.

I don't know what he's going to do until his arm, powerful hands land on my knees. He grips them and, very slowly, inches his hands up to my thighs.

He puts just a little pressure on my legs to push them apart—not enough that I can't resist him. My skirt holds my legs together, but that sensation shoots another rush of heat straight up my legs into my crotch.

I gasp at that sensation. Lane's blue eyes blaze at me from inches away. His face smolders with volcanic power.

"Do you want this, baby?" he whispers and crawls his hands just a little higher. He very gentle, very slowly, very deliberately pushes up my skirt before he squeezes my thighs....a little higher.

I pant under my breath at the intoxicating look in his eyes. I can't look away. My mind spins in a delirium of wanting everything he could possibly do to me.

I reel under his thrall. I can't resist him—not anything he does. Those hands—they'll pry my legs apart.....and then I'll be his for the taking. I can't stop it and I don't want to.

He creeps his hands another fraction of an inch higher.....and pushes my skirt up a little higher. Torturous throbbing heat drips between my legs. I want it. I need it. I need him.

"You want this?" he whispers again. "You want me to touch you like this?"

I can barely make myself heard when I gasp out, "Lane....."

"Come on, baby," he breathes. "Spread your legs for me. Show me how much you want it. That's right."

He scoots my skirt just a tiny bit higher, but not high enough to expose anything. His hands clamp on my thighs.

I sag there panting hard. I fight to breathe under the unbearable weight of all this desire. I need more. I need so much more. I need him inside every part of me. I need him to take over everything that I am. I can't hold back any longer.

He tightens his grip around both my thighs, leans the rest of the way forward, and kisses me.

All the passion from the limo erupts. I rock on the couch trying to reach him, but he's too far away. His mouth consumes me in a torrent of hot, wet, delicious kisses.

He rakes his fingers through my hair to push it out of my face. Those fingers follow down the back of my skull and tighten to pull me into his mouth.

I whimper at his power. He holds me in his grip steering my mouth where he wants it.

His tongue lights me on fire. That tongue traces through my mouth, but I feel him between my legs teasing me to the breaking point.

His hands range all over me, squeezing my breasts through my blouse, tugging my blazer off, scooping his hand down to my ass, and gripping my thighs again.

He never tries to push my skirt up any further, though. I want him to. I want him to touch me and strip me and take me in all his colossal power.

I yelp every time he crushes my breasts. His hands migrate back and forth from one side of my chest to the other.

He must have tugged my buttons open because, when he moves back to my right, my blouse falls open and his hand lands on my bra cup.

He squeezes once and then his fingers dart inside. He pinches my nipples without taking my shirt or my bra off. His masterful patience drives me crazy. I need him now.

I try to reach any part of him to touch him, but he's coming at me too strong. I can barely touch his shoulders, face, and neck. I can't get to any other part of him, especially not with his clothes in the way.

He tears off my mouth—just enough for me to see his eyes drilling into me. They blaze with ice-blue fire and make me catch my breath all over again.

The intensity of those eyes—and the sheer brutal intensity of his desire—they take my breath away. I don't know how to deal with this man—but it looks like I'm doing it either way.

He sits back just enough for me to see his face seething with all that pent-up desire, passion, and animal madness hidden just beneath the surface. It scares me to think he might release it on me.

It scares me a lot, but it also electrifies me. It ignites my deepest cravings. I need to feel that. I need to feel that he wants me to the bottommost core of his being.

His hot, strong hands fall on my thighs. "Is this what you want? Do you want me to take this?" He scoots his hand just a little higher to the hem of my skirt. "Like this?"

"Yes!" I whisper.

"Does this turn you on?" he breathes. "Does it turn you on to think of me touching you like this?"

My mouth says, *Yes!* but no sound comes out. I can hardly focus my eyes. His hands keep sending waves of blistering heat up my body. They wash over my face and make my eyes slip out of focus.

I teeter back to my senses and get another blast of scorching desire when I see him watching me. He's seeing me tremble for him. He sees me quiver all over and barely staying sane with all this overpowering heat pumping through me.

"You are so fucking hot, baby!" he whispers. "I can't keep my hands off you."

Just to confirm it, he dives in and bites me in the chest—right in my cleavage. He could have bitten my nipple through my bra. My shirt hangs open enough for him to reach it.

He chooses to bite on the fleshy bulge of my cleavage. I yelp and then moan as that sensation blasts to my crotch. I can't keep still.

That one jet of fire almost rockets me into a devastating orgasm, but just as soon as he lands his teeth on me, he pulls away and it's over.

Nothing will ever be over because he won't stop touching me. He crushes my thighs in both hands and pries them apart just a little more.

He leans back and I fall into the trance of his eyes glaring down at me. He eyes me with predatory intent.....and in that instant, he dives his hand between my legs.

He pinches me through my saturated panties, but he does it with his knuckles—just enough to skyrocket me out of my mind but not hard enough to hurt.

He kneads his knuckles into my flesh, but he leaves my panties in place so he doesn't touch my bare skin.

"Do you like that?" he half-whispers. "Is that what you want me to do?"

I can't answer. I'm moaning too hard as I reel off into another spiraling eruption of madness. I writhe back on the couch trying to take his fingers and everything they're doing to me.

I can't cope, but I don't try to stop it. He's taking me somewhere I've never been before. I don't ever want this to stop.

I see myself sprawled in front of him and clawing at the couch for some purchase. My blouse hangs open so he can see my cleavage heaving in front of him.

His other hand scrapes up my body and he grips my breast once before he dives his wicked fingers inside my bra to tease my nipples again.

I arch into his grip. I buck back and forth between trying to satisfy myself on his fingers and trying to shove my breasts into his groping hands.

I can't stop thrashing on the cushions as sweeping, destroying energy pulses through me. I can't hold it back.

I can't take it a second longer. I want to beg him to take me all the way, but I'm moaning too loudly and crying in ragged ecstasy. I can't form the words.

At that moment, he pushes off the couch, goes down on his knees between my legs, and leans in and kisses me.

He snatches at my lips, and before I realize what's happening, he yanks my panties aside and plunges his fingers all the way in to the hilt.

I scream into his mouth, but he's already shifting back onto the coffee table to sit where he was before.

He drills his fingers in again and again as my juices gush over his knuckles. I scream and convulse as epic spasms tear me apart. I spread my legs to take him deeper and grasp at the back of the couch above my head.

That makes my breasts stand up and he grabs them. He strips my bra down on both sides so he can maul and pinch and squeeze as much as he likes.

I barely notice except that his squeezes and pinches blast me even farther into outer space. I twist and corkscrew my hips on his hand as one explosion after another tears me apart.

I know Lane is still sitting there watching me, but I can't see him. When I manage to open my eyes, they won't focus on anything as one wave of rapture after another wipes out my mind.

His rhythm slows down. I become aware of it from a great distance. The pulses rushing through me slacken just enough for me to haul my hazy eyes into focus.

He stares down at me from the coffee table as his fingers keep thrusting into me again and again. He slows, but he doesn't stop. Will he ever stop?

I can't survive this tide of emotion and pleasure annihilating me. I want to cry and scream at the same time, this feels so damn good.

# Chapter 20: Samantha

L ane slides his other hand down my stomach to my waist. He follows the movement of my hips as I buck and grind on his hand.

He watches my body undulate in front of him as cosmic pulsations beat up to my face, blast out through my skin, and then rush down to his hand between my legs again.

I could go on like this forever. He doesn't move. Maybe he wants that, too.

The energy changes again. It softens, but it doesn't fade. It doesn't even ease. It just transforms into this steady, endless sea of bliss consuming both of us—or at least me.

Does he feel it? Does he even sense how much I want him? Does he know what he's doing to me right now?

He slows just a little more. I expect him to ease off completely or maybe decide to leave. Then what will I do? How can I ever come back from this?

The sensation of his hand between my legs and his fingers splitting me apart triggers another electric reaction all over my skin. Seeing him like this—seeing him take me like this—this is the hottest thing I've ever experienced. I never knew it could be like this.

Almost as soon as I think that, he pulls out, leans back to sit up straight, scoots my skirt the rest of the way off, and pulls down my panties.

He does it all so fast and so expertly that I don't have a chance to move before he pushes my thighs all the way apart, sinks onto his knees between my legs, and dives face first into my quivering, pulsating flesh.

I scream as his tongue lights me on fire and then a rocket goes off inside me. It propels me into the most shattering orgasm of my life.

I grab at his hair, but I have to hold onto the back of the couch to give me some purchase. My body takes over and I buck into his face trying to take as much of his tongue as I can.

His fingers find me again and I dissolve in heart-wrenching screams as ecstasy takes me over. I can't survive this.

I drive my hips down on his mouth as he devours me to the ends of the earth. He gnaws my clit and sucks the sweet juices from every inch of my body.

I can't feel any of that with these monstrous explosions going off in me. I want him all over me and inside me. I can't......

He pushes my thighs all the way apart. His fingers imprint on my skin and his hands flex with a powerful, possessive grip. He cups my hip to bring me closer into his face where he can maul me the way he wants to.

My mind will never come back from this, but he isn't finished yet. He straightens up in front of the couch and glares down at me thrashing and convulsing in front of him. I'm too wrung out to move.

He eases closer to the couch on his knees between my legs. They're wide enough now for him to shove between them.

He grabs me behind my back, lifts me upright, and pulls me into his kiss. He attacks my mouth, but that's nothing compared to him dragging my thighs on either side of his hips.

I freeze when he rips his fly open.....and then I feel him pushing into me. He holds my panties aside and my swollen, hungry flesh offers no resistance.

My deepest being caves to the burning hot scorch of his shaft breaking me apart. I try to scream, but that scream echoes only in my mind as his thickness blasts me to pieces.

I gasp for air. He's kissing me too fast.....and then his hand glides up my back to my neck. He cradles me there in a dream as his hips pump faster, deeper, harder, truer.

His other hand tightens on my thigh to bring me into him. I sit on the edge of the couch with my knees spread around him. This position feels so unimaginably hot that I can't stand it.

His fingers tighten in my hair. He steers me into his mouth and then snaps off to stare into my eyes.

Those eyes command me to look and never look away. They consume me in a tornado of destruction laying waste to all my fear and resistance.

He's taking me. He's owning me. He's claiming me and conquering me and leaving nothing but this quivering mass of aching desire for more.

"Come on, baby," he pants with each cruel thrust. "Come on."

I gasp to the same rhythm. Our tempo synchronizes. Those electric jets of heat pulsing through my channel become unbearable.

I wince and writhe in front of him so he can see exactly how I'm falling apart for him right now. I whine in a combined sea of insatiable desire and mind-blowing pleasure. I can't get enough of him, but at the same time, I don't know how to cope with all this.

I try again to touch him, but I can't get to him in this position. I want to put my arms around him and cling to him, but I can't even do that.

I just have to sit here and experience this—and let him see. He sees everything with those eyes. Does he see how much I want him—how much I need everything he does?

My rising cries echo in my ears. They escalate to screams again and I can't look at him as I fall apart in front of him.

He sees me pulsing with climaxes. He sees my eyes roll up in their sockets and my lips trembling with screams for all the rapture he's giving me.

He sees me grasp at him for my very life and my flesh quiver for his touch.

He watches my face wrench in excruciating, torturous pleasure as I dissolve in a torrent of unstoppable passion.

My channel throbs around his shaft and I feel him straining. His penetrating thrusts get stronger, more insistent. His fingers clench in my hair and he grits his teeth.

His nostrils flare faster and he narrows his eyes in deadly fury.

Seeing him like this disintegrates the last wall holding me back. I throw back my head screaming to the stars, and right then, he attacks my neck roaring out in completion as he ejects into me.

His voice stabs into my brain. That tormented sound of painful release drives me into another dizzy spiral and I lose all contact with reality.

I drift back to awareness sitting on the couch with Lane still kneeling in front of me. How much time has passed? I can't tell. I can't think much of anything right now.

He keeps kissing me in the depths of this deep longing. He keeps his eyes open and combs his fingers through my hair.

He trails his fingertips down my face. He doesn't show any sign that he sees my bruises.

I feel beautiful in that gaze. I feel like I look the way I did when we first met—like nothing in the world could ever make me less attractive to him.

I lose awareness of when he pulls off my mouth. That endless kiss just comes to its natural conclusion.

As soon as our lips break contact, he starts taking my clothes off. He pulls my blazer the rest of the way off, finishes unbuttoning my blouse, takes that off, too, and unclips my bra.

He unzips my skirt and pushes me very gently to lie back on the cushions so he can draw my skirt down over my knees.

I see him doing everything for me—everything in a caring, gentle way like he did that first night. His hands position me where he wants me to take the best care of me.

He undresses me on the couch, traces his hands down my naked body, and then lifts my legs to lie me lengthwise on the couch.

He keeps grazing down at me with that intense stare of deep emotion. I can't tell what he's thinking except that he really does think I'm beautiful. What is he really thinking right now?

Those eyes express so much warmth and approval—almost admiration.

He keeps stroking my body with those warm, comforting hands. His touch makes everything all right, but I can't help quivering with deeper desire. All those orgasms didn't satisfy me. If anything, they only made me crave him more.

He finally straightens up and attacks his own clothes. He rips off his jacket, unbuttons his shirt, and then strips off his T-shirt underneath.

I stare up at his chest and shoulders chiseled in muscle. I don't know why I expected his body to be any different. I knew he took care of himself—just not like this.

He pushes his pants and boxers down, sits on the coffee table to take off his shoes, and then leans over me.

He starts kissing me again as he lowers himself onto the couch with me, but he doesn't lie on top of me the way I expect.

He stretches out next to me still kissing me all the way to the bottom of my soul. His heat floods me and dissolves every trace of my reserve.

I erupt in another wave of passion as his warm, silky skin touches me all over from my lips all the way down my legs.

His muscles tense as my arms close around his neck. I want to rub my body all over him.

That wave translates down my face and neck to my chest. I shove my breasts against his chest and his arms snake around my back to pull me in tight.

My thighs glide against his legs. He's hard again. I thrust my hips toward him trying to reach him. I need him. I need him more now than I did before if that's even possible.

His hands stroke down my back to my hips and finally to my ass. He doesn't stop kissing me when he lifts one of my thighs and pumps into me on a slippery film of our combined essence.

I gasp as the first fireworks go off between my legs. He pulls away just enough for his eyes to take control of me again.

I pant to the rhythm of his slow, spiraling thrusts. He's taking me there again, and this time, we lie naked body to body with nothing hidden.

I swim in those eyes. His masterful power holds me spellbound. I can't even drift off into delirium anymore. Everything in those eyes looks beyond real.

He doesn't hide from my gaze, either. I see him so intoxicatingly magnetic, so self-possessed, and yet so caring, so attentive, so gentle in everything he does.

His hands claim my breasts, my hips, my ass. He claims my face and mind when he closes his hand around my jaw to steer my mouth to his. He claims my being when he laces his fingers into my hair and pulls my mouth into his devouring lips.

He watches me pant and grimace as another tidal wave of passion takes over. I don't have to hide from him how much I need this.

Without warning, he rotates onto his knees. One of my legs still lies outstretched down the couch. He doesn't try to lift it.

He straddles that leg and lifts the other onto his shoulder so he can drive into me without limit. He arches over me drilling me to kingdom come.

That soul-destroying sensation of his shaft invading me makes me scream again, but he swallows those screams with his ravenous mouth and tongue.

His muscles etch deeper with the strain of holding himself up. His stomach contracts all the way down to the tight V of his prick driving into me.

I feel myself losing all control and gushing hot juice on every inch of his rigid shaft. I can't stop this.

I want to turn away and look into his eyes at the same time. I want to fall apart, and at the same time, never leave the comforting certainty of those eyes.

# Chapter 21: Samantha

I wake up on the couch again, but this is nothing like last time. Sunshine streams through my big living room windows and I'm stark naked.

I only have to feel the slippery film between my thighs and all over my ass to remember last night.

Lane's warm arms around me and his naked body pressed up against me from behind complete the picture. We did it. Now we're lying naked under the down bedspread on the couch in my apartment.

I shut my eyes and groan silently to myself when I realize what I just did. I slept with the boss.

Everyone in five countries knows Lane Prince's reputation with the ladies. A guy as rich as he is can get any woman he wants—and he does. He doesn't dissuade them from throwing themselves at him.

Now I'm one of those floozies that threw myself at him. I'm the one who invited him in. I'm the one who made out with him in the limo.

He doesn't wake up when I do. He lies with his face buried in my hair. How long should I wait? I have to go to work this morning and so does he.

I don't dare to move to check the time, but just then, something vibrates against the glass coffee table. The buzz comes from his jacket. His phone is vibrating.

I wince when I pry myself out of his arms. I don't want to get up, but we have to face the reality of what we did.

"Lane...." I murmur. "Your phone is ringing."

He jerks a little bit. "Huh?"

"Your phone is ringing." I sit the rest of the way up on the edge of the couch. The bedspread covers most of me.

I fish his phone out of his pocket, but it stops ringing by the time I hand it to him. He coughs and then sniffs while he blinks the sleep out of his eyes.

He frowns at it and then sets it aside before he sinks back into the couch. He doesn't look like he's in any big hurry to get up and go to work.

He wraps his arms around me and pulls. "Lie down," he tells me. "Come here."

"I can't. I have to go to work today—and so do you."

"That can wait." He leans farther forward on the couch and burrows his head under my arm. He starts crawling his face and mouth around my stomach to my breasts.

His mouth feels unbelievably good. I get another wave of blissful desire. It would be so easy to fall back onto the couch and keep doing it with him all day.

"Lane...." I have to stop and gasp for air. "Lane.......we can't....."

"We already did," he mumbles with his mouth full.

I hold it together for a second before I try again. "Lane....."

"I love hearing you say my name, baby," he growls. "Say it again."

I say, "Lane," again, but I don't mean it that way. "We can't."

"Why can't we?"

"Because.....you're my boss."

"Don't worry about that."

"How can I not worry about it? We're going to be working together. This is totally inappropriate."

He starts burrowing his way down between my legs. "That's what makes it so hot."

I try to push him away by his shoulders, but my heart isn't it. I really want him to.

"Lane....seriously. We can't."

He finally leans back. He lies across my lap with his hair all messed up. He looks more like the boy in his mugshot like this—not like a high-powered CEO, but just like a normal guy who's enjoying himself.

He studies me for a second and then sniffs. "All right. If it bothers you that much, we don't have to."

"It doesn't bother me. It's just....you know....reality."

He keeps staring at me for a minute before he threads his fingers into my hair and pulls me down. "Kiss me."

I kiss him. That kiss gets stronger. His tongue sizzles in my mouth. He definitely means it like that.

I don't know how long he keeps kissing me, but he breaks off after a while and sits up on the couch. The bedspread is only big enough to surround both of us if we stay sitting right next to each other.

He pushes it aside and I use it to wrap around my shoulders. I don't like seeing myself insulating myself from him, but he doesn't seem to notice.

He picks up his pants and starts straightening them out to put them on.

"Look, let's just forget last night ever happened and go on working together the way we were before," I tell him.

He barely glances at me. "If that's the way you want it, we can do it that way."

"What other way is there?"

He shrugs. "I don't know, but if I've learned one thing in life, it's that there is always more than one way to do everything."

"You don't actually mean.....that we would keep doing this, do you? Do you realize how sleazy that would be—us doing it on the side while we're running a company together?"

He looks up at me one more time and then goes back to putting on his pants. "Where's your bathroom?"

"There's one right over there." I point across the living room.

He takes his T-shirt and business shirt over there and goes into the bathroom. Right before he shuts the door, I catch a glimpse of him from behind with his pants on and no shirt.

His back rises from his narrow waist to a broad, chiseled fortress of muscle. His neck slopes out of that up to his messed-up hair.

He's magnetically hot, but that only makes him so much farther out of reach.

Only now, when he walks away, do I realize how cold and empty my body feels without him under this bedspread with me.

I had him in full body contact with me just now. He fell asleep with his arms around me. Now he's gone.

I should get up, take a shower, and get dressed for work, but I don't move. I stay wrapped in the bedspread until he comes back.

I don't want to feel the world outside. I want to hold onto this warmth—his warmth. I want to keep feeling this silky sensation of his skin against mine. I don't want that to end.

It will end the minute I take a shower—the minute I get out of this bedspread. I'll wash it away and put on my clothes and become a corporate shark just like him.

What a hollow way to live. I never saw it until right now, but I don't have time to think about it before he comes out of the bathroom wearing his shirt.

He buttons it up and tucks it into his waistband. He doesn't show any sign of surprise or disgust that I'm sitting here wrapped in a bedspread.

I realize I'm sitting in the same place I was the night of the carjacking—except that I'm naked under this bedspread.

He could take the bedspread off and everything we did last night would start back up again. I know that. He's only getting dressed to leave right now because I told him I wanted him to.

I don't want him to. God, what is wrong with me?

He sits down next to me on the couch. Does he see how devastated I feel about him leaving?

He leans in close and scratches my back through the bedspread—just like he did that night. "It's going to be all right," he murmurs. "Don't worry about this. It's okay."

I can't speak. I wish like anything I could believe that. I have to believe it because he's the one saying it.

He always tells me that. He's the only person who can make me believe it. Everything is always okay when he's around.

"I'll see you later, okay?" he murmurs and kisses me on the side of the head. "Don't worry about a thing. Everything is going to work out. You'll see. Have a good day, okay?"

I can only nod before he grabs his phone and lets himself out of my apartment. I buckle under the weight of despair as soon as he leaves.

What the hell did I just do? He always acts so gentle and caring. How could I throw that away by hooking up with him?

I feel like a tramp for not keeping it professional with him, but I guess the horse left the barn on that one a long time ago.

I shut my eyes and pass my hands across my eyes, but that doesn't help. I wind up sinking back down on the couch.

As soon as I get into that position, I feel Lane's arms around me. He's lying right behind me under this bedspread. His heat pulses into me from behind so I don't get cold.

He would still be here if I let him stay. He wanted to stay here with me.

I shut my eyes and wrap the bedspread tighter around my shoulders and body—just to trap that feeling near me for one more minute before I get up and wash it all away.

That little bubble of calm and protection gives me the strength I need to stand up and start my day.

# Chapter 22: Samantha

T he Titanium Finance building hums with a new kind of energy. All the same buzz of voices and activity fill each room, office, and workspace, but this is different.

A new zing of excitement fills the air. It reminds me of the early days when we first started out. We all felt like we were building something historic then.

The same breathless, infectious sense of urgent excitement crackles in every room. A lot more people smile at me when we get into the elevator.

Their cheeks flush with anticipation for the day ahead and their eyes sparkle with new enthusiasm. We're doing something great here. I just know it.

I have to pass Derek's office on the way across the executive suite, but he isn't here. Reese McCall isn't here, either.

I check my appointments. Ethan Rosch isn't scheduled to come over until eleven o'clock. That isn't a very good start to his first day as acting CMO, but who am I to judge?

I get started on my appointments and emails when Spencer Holt sends me a message.

*We're having a cascading server failure on our investment platform. I'm working to contain it by switching temporarily to an alternate server, but I need authorization for payment. It's a $10k deposit to handle our rate of traffic. Derek would usually handle this, but he isn't here. I don't know who else to ask.*

I make a snap decision and text him back. *Do it. Consider the funds authorized. Do I need to contact the company to transfer payment? I don't care what you have to do. Just get the servers running so the platform keeps functioning. We'll iron out the details later.*

He writes back right away. *Thank you so much, Samantha. I was going crazy.*

*No problem. Just do it. Get our platform running no matter what.*

*Thank you,* he replies again. *I'll have the server provider send you the invoice right away.*

I get off the chat with him and immediately call down to customer service to inform them of the problem.

It takes me a while to spread the word. The phone and internet reps are already fielding angry calls and messages from clients and customers about the platform not working.

I get the invoice, pay it, and tell Spencer that the payment is on its way right now. He's profusely grateful.

I try to get back on track with my own work only for Bradley to burst into my office next. "We got a massive problem, Samantha."

"Spencer already told me about the servers. We're taking care of it."

"I don't know about that. We just got slapped with an SEC audit. They want to go through every page of our books starting this morning."

My head shoots up....and then I relax. "Okay. Let them."

His eyes drop out of their sockets. "Really? You don't care?"

"Who's the investigator doing the audit?" I turn back to my laptop. "I didn't get any notification about this."

"It came through Derek's work email. He isn't here, so his assistant just told me."

I only nod. "Forward me the email. I'll handle it."

He blinks at me again. "You will? But you aren't the CEO."

"I'm the CFO. Who better to handle an SEC audit? Besides, I have access to all the documentation. Just forward me the email. I'll take it from there."

He pulls out his phone and frowns down at it. "I don't know about this."

"You don't know about what?"

"You taking over as CEO in Derek's place. How do you know you're authorized to do it?"

"Who the hell cares if I'm authorized to do it? Someone has to deal with the SEC. Do you want to handle it instead?"

"Hell no!" he exclaims. "My department is operations. You won't catch me anywhere within ten miles of a spreadsheet."

I laugh at him. "Then that leaves me, doesn't it? Spencer is in the middle of a massive computer failure and Cesar is a people person. Don't worry. We have nothing to worry about from the SEC."

He frowns again. "Are you sure?"

I make a face at him. "I practically have the company books memorized. Who would know better than I would?"

"I'll trust you." He puts his phone back in his pocket and turns to leave my office. "You should have the email by now."

"Thanks, Bradley. You're doing great work here."

He turns back and frowns at me over his shoulder. "Thanks, Samantha. That means a lot coming from you. I always thought you should have been the CEO running this company."

He walks out with those words hanging in the air. It sure looks like I am the CEO running this company—for now, at least.

I contact the SEC, find out what documents they need, and forward everything over there right away.

The investigator is a petite, bubbly, Legally-Blonde young woman named Evie Knight. She couldn't be more helpful, not to mention delighted to be investigating Titanium Finance.

She chirps in my ear like we're best friends now. "It's so great that you're being so cooperative and helpful with this audit. Most people kick and scream and slam the door in my face."

I chuckle to myself when I get off the phone with her. I'm just turning back to my computer when Ethan Rosch, Marshall Weiss, and Russel Shauer come in.

I expected just Ethan, but all three of them invade the place and start going through the building department by department. I'm too busy with the SEC audit to notice until three employees from the accounting department come up to see me.

"Marshall Weiss is down in accounting raising hell about the charges from the new server provider," one of the women whispers under her breath. She glances over her shoulder toward the door. "He told Spencer Holt he'd get fired as soon as Lane Prince found out about the IT department going behind his back."

"Weiss wants us to cancel the payment," another woman murmurs. "What should we do?"

"Don't do anything," I tell them. "Just go ahead with the payment."

Just then, Ethan comes to my office door and overhears this. I guess I can't say he overheard it since the door is open.

He shoves past the employees shooting daggers back and forth between them and me. "You're telling them to override Marshall's orders? You don't have the authority to do that, Samantha."

I wave the accounting employees away. "You can all go back to work. I'll handle this—and make sure that payment goes through. We need those servers."

They make a speedy escape. I'm left dealing with Ethan.

I start by trying to pretend he isn't there, but he gets in my face. "I ask you a question, Samantha. You can't authorize a payment that big without getting clearance from us—or at least from Lane."

I don't even look at him. I pretend to click on my computer. "The last time I checked, you were coming over here to fill in for Reese McCall as the Chief Marketing Officer. No one invited any of you to get all up on our accounting business."

"I'm a member of the Apico executive board!" he snaps. "I have as much right to get all up in your accounting business as anyone."

"Then you can pull your head out of your ass and realize that Apico just bought a massive lemon without that server. We don't have a business at all without that server. Can I make it any clearer for you? I saved your company by authorizing that payment—but you're too stupid even to realize that. Now get the hell out of my office."

Just then, Marshall Weiss and Russel Shauer storm in. "What the hell are you doing sending documents to the SEC for?" Marshall demands. "Do you realize the damage you could have caused?"

I heave a massive sigh and roll my eyes to Heaven. "If I withheld the documents, it would have made us look guilty of something. It's an audit—that's all. The SEC is empowered to audit our books whenever they want and so what if they do? We have nothing to hide."

"I hope you've enjoyed being CFO of this company, Samantha," Russel growls. "You'll be out the door by the end of the day."

"Then I won't have to deal with your bullshit anymore," I mutter under my breath. "I have better things to do than explain myself to you. Ethan, if you aren't going to go do your job by running the marketing department, then all three of you can go back to Apico because you're useless to us here. We need a marketing exec, not a bunch of whiners."

I deliberately turn back to my computer and put them out of my mind. I don't need this shit. This is not what I or any other Titanium employee signed up for. This isn't what I gave that speech about to get the Titanium staff on board. Seriously.

The three of them stand there staring at me with their mouths open. Apparently no one has ever talked to them like this before. They better get the hell used to it 'cuz my mama didn't raise me to put up with this crap.

They finally leave and I turn back to my computer. Before I can even put my hands on the mouse, Bradley hustles in.

"Oh, my God, Samantha! You are my new hero!" he whispers. "That was absolutely the ballsiest thing I have ever heard! Holy shit!" He burst out in nervous giggles like a little boy. "'We need a marketing exec, not a bunch of whiners.' Just wait until I tell the guys downstairs!"

He rushes around my desk and kisses me on the side of the head. "You're the best!" He races away still cackling to himself.

I try not to smirk. At least some around here appreciates what I do.

We all get back to work the way we're supposed to. I double- and triple-check to make sure that, (1) Evie Knight got all our documents, and (2) the server company got our payment and the new server is up and online.

It is. Our traffic is going through the new server, and a few hours later, Spencer tells me our investment platform is back in business while the techs downstairs straighten out our old server.

Ethan, Russel, and Marshall don't show their faces for the rest of the day. I don't hear anyone else complaining about them interfering, either.

At two o'clock, Spencer texts me to say that the new server will use up all our available traffic allowance and we'll need more. I authorize payment on that, too, and then, just because, I send through the payment ahead of time so we don't suffer any break in service.

I'm just settling down at my computer to finish reading and sending all the emails I should have finished this morning. It's been a big day.

Then I remember. Lane will have to approve everything I've done today. If he doesn't, I could be out on my ass exactly the way Russel says.

Then I won't have to worry about the fact that I hooked up with him. The whole thing will disappear into the past and we can forget it ever happened.

# Chapter 23: Lane

I get off the phone with my legal team and go through the documents finalizing Apico Acquisitions' takeover of Titanium Finance. Everything looks good.

I open my accounting software program to check the numbers on both companies when Russel Shauer, Ethan Rosch, and Marshall Weiss storm into my office without knocking.

"That rotten bitch screwed us over!" Russel snaps.

"Um....what rotten bitch?" I ask.

"Samantha Mulholland," Marshall growls. "She's over there tearing Titanium apart behind our backs."

I take a second to squash my temper. They did not come in here calling Samantha a rotten bitch. I have to deal with this like a grownup. "What is she doing?"

"She spent ten thousand dollars on some tech glitch," Ethan tells me, "and on the way over here, we got a notification that she authorized another twenty for the same thing! We told her she didn't have the authority to make that kind of decision on behalf of a company she barely even runs anyway."

I frown at them. "What are you talking about?"

Marshall either doesn't hear me or he was winding up to say something before he walked in here. "And she went and dumped a whole truckload of documents on the SEC without even checking them first. She could wind up ruining not just Titanium but all of Apico into the bargain."

Now I'm really confused. "Hold on a second. She spent ten thousand dollars on a tech glitch? Why?"

"The Titanium investment platform server went down and she rerouted all their traffic through an alternate server."

"Well, what the hell else was she supposed to do?" I tell him. "Titanium isn't even a business without that server."

Marshall stares at me in shock. "You're....you're actually defending her?"

"We would be watching our money go straight down the drain right now without a working server. What did you think she was going to do—sit on her hands and wait for us to tell her what to do? She did the right thing. She took the initiative. She probably saved the company. In fact, I'm certain she did."

"You can't be seriously defending her," Ethan counters. "You should have heard the way she talked to us. She's rude."

"What did she say?"

The three of them exchange glances. I really wish I could have been there to hear it, but they'll probably never tell me the truth.

"She said I had to go take care of the marketing department and get the hell out of her office," Ethan grumbles.

"Well, that is why we sent you over there—not to supervise her decisions. Now you're in here bitching to me about her while Titanium is running without a marketing exec."

His face goes dark. Now I know for certain she told him exactly the same thing.

Steam starts whistling out of his ears, so I hold up my hand. "Just tell me if Derek Salazar is over there."

"No, he isn't," Russel replies. "Apparently, he's been out of contact and no one knows where he is. Bradley Lenz found out about the SEC audit and forwarded the whole thing to Samantha."

My eyebrows shoot up. "SEC audit! She dumped documents on the SEC to comply with an audit?"

"She should at least have checked with us first," Marshall counters. "There could have been something incriminating in those documents."

"Please, Marshall," I sneer. "We value her for her competence and excellence as CFO. No one would know better than she would if there was something incriminating in those documents. I'm sure she has nothing to hide."

They look at each other again. So she must have told them that, too. What a pack of idiots.

I shut my eyes and make a command decision. When I open them again, I wave all three of them out of the room. "You three stay here at Apico from now on. I don't want any of you setting foot in the Titanium building again. Is that clear?"

"You can't do that!" Ethan roars.

"So now you're telling me what I can and can't do? Your interference could have cost us the company and gotten us into trouble with the SEC. You three are staying here from now on. I'll assign someone else to run the Titanium marketing department."

"But what are you going to do about Samantha?" Marshall asks. "You can't just leave her over there running the whole company by herself."

My head shoots up. What a great idea. "Why can't I?"

"Because....." he blusters. "Because....because she's only one person."

"She has Cesar Pound, Bradley Lenz, and Spencer Holt working with her. In fact....." I bend over my computer and start clicking. "I think I'll tell her to promote a new CMO from within. I'm sure she knows who at Titanium is the best qualified....."

"You're making a big mistake," Russel tells me.

"My mistake was thinking I could send outsiders into that company and expect them to do as good a job as the people who made it successful in the first place. This is what we agreed and this is exactly what we asked her to do—to keep the company running the way it ran before we took over. She's the best person for that right now."

They look at each other some more. I pretend to concentrate on my computer so I don't see them leaving my office with their tails between their legs. What a bunch of dopes.

I go over a few more items, but the idea won't leave me alone. I really could leave her over there to run Titanium by herself. God knows she'd do a better job than anyone from Apico. Not even I could do it as well as she can.

I finish what I'm doing and Eddie drives me to the Titanium Finance building. I get a thrill when I know I'm on my way over there to see her.

I can't help fantasizing about last night. Her scent hovers in my nostrils. The delicious sensation of her satin petals clinging to my shaft still electrifies my nerves when I think about it.

I have to stop myself from thinking about it or I'll get hard right now. I try to block out the memory of her sex-drunk eyes floating in front of me, but all those sights and sensations, the sounds of her screams, the feel of her thighs slapping against me when I drill her—they intoxicate me out of my mind.

Is she thinking about me like that? Do thoughts of me kissing her and holding her down distract her from her work?

Does she feel my skin pressed into her back and my leg between her thighs? Does she drift off and stare out the window thinking about me sleeping behind her with my arms around her?

I love the smell of her hair in my nose while I sleep. I love the soft, warm heat radiating off her back. That turns me on as much as everything else about her.

Her magnificent breasts spilling out of her bra......her hard little nipples twitching when I pinch them.....her inner muscles spasming around my shaft as I draw it out of her saturated, quivering channel......the blessed waves of ecstasy spreading outward from her sweet flower to the rest of her body.

And those eyes! The eyes I can never forget. I never want to stop looking into those eyes....unless she's so dopey with orgasms that she can't hold eye contact anymore.

I smile to myself thinking about it, but I really am getting hard now. I have to adjust my package in my shorts when I get out of the limo.

I can't wait to see her and talk to her. She's perfect—but I already knew that.

I'm just about to enter the building when I stop on the sidewalk. Derek Salazar comes toward me from the other end of the block. He narrows his eyes at me as we size each other up.

"Where have you been today, Derek?" I ask.

"That's none of your business," he snaps. "I don't answer to you."

"Does that mean you plan to quit Titanium Finance?"

"This is my company!" he fires back. "What I do or don't do is none of your business. I run this place—not you."

"No, you don't. You've been AWOL all day while your employees run this place without you. The whole company could have gone up in smoke while you've been out there sulking."

"What the hell are you talking about? I've never done anything but help this company. I built this company—not you."

I purse my lips. This is going nowhere. "You have two choices, Derek. You can go inside and start cooperating with the transition as a member of the Apico conglomerate or you can walk away right now. No one will miss you, I promise. These people can run the company just fine without you—maybe even better. You're an Apico employee now. If you don't accept that, then you won't be an Apico employee and you can go work somewhere else. It's your choice."

I walk away. I don't have time to deal with him anymore. He left the company at its most crucial time. The company could have suffered because he got too emotional about the takeover.

I go into the lobby and half the people there greet me by name. "Good afternoon, Mr. Prince," Jennifer tells me.

"Good afternoon."

"Welcome back, Mr. Prince," some guy tells me on his way out the entrance doors.

It feels good to walk into a place where everyone knows me and everyone treats me like the boss. I take the elevator upstairs to the executive suite.

I get another stomach load of adrenaline on my way to Samantha's office. I'd like to bang her into the desk, but that can wait.....until when? When would I ever get a chance to do that?

She'll always be my subordinate and I'll always be the boss just like she says. That will never change unless something catastrophic happens like she stops working for Titanium.

I would do anything to prevent that, which means she'll always be my subordinate.

She's right that us doing it is inappropriate and even kinda sleazy. I don't like to think that way, but it's true.

And I was right that those are the things that make it the hottest. I love thinking about doing her in the boardroom or her office or the elevator—anywhere in this building or in a business setting. It all makes it so much riskier and trashier.

I shouldn't be thinking of her and trashy in the same thought, but it still turns me on to think that way. Does it turn her on—or does she just see it as sleazy and trashy?

I wouldn't want her to think I'm disrespecting her because I think she's dynamite.

Bradley Lenz comes out of his office just as I'm walking past. He jumps a foot in the air when he sees me. "Welcome back, Mr. Prince."

"Thank you, Bradley. How has your day been so far?"

"It's been great." He starts walking backward in front of me to keep pace with me. "Are you here to bust Samantha for authorizing the new server?"

"I'm not here to bust anyone for anything, Bradley. Don't you have work to do?"

He grins at me. "You should have heard her ball out the Apico execs. She told Ethan Rosch we needed a marketing exec and not a bunch of whiners." He bursts out in maniacal laughter. "It was priceless! Then she told them to pull their heads out of their asses and get the hell out of her office."

I have to stop myself from smiling. Good for her.

I'm almost at her office. I don't want her to overhear my conversation with Bradley—or for Bradley to overhear my conversation with her.

I stop in the middle of the floor and turn to him. "You and the rest of the Titanium personnel don't have to worry about anyone from Apico coming over here anymore, Bradley. You can all go on with your work the way Samantha said."

He raises his eyebrows. "Really? What made you decide that?"

"Never mind. You can pass the word to everyone that no one from Apico will interfere with Titanium again."

"What about you?" he asks. "You're still here."

Now I really do smile. "I'm not here. You can't see me. This is all a figment of your fevered imagination."

He laughs again. "Oh, yeah. Right. Got it. I must have been smoking the tailpipe a little too much." He turns away smirking. "See you around, Mr. Prince."

# Chapter 24: Lane

S amantha shoots out of her chair the minute I walk into her office. A million questions race past her eyes. Does she think I'm here to bust her?

I shut the door and sit down in the chair across from her desk. She studies me from behind her defenses. "Can I help you with something?" she asks.

I wave at her desk chair. "Sit down. I want to talk to you."

"If this is about what I said to Ethan Rosch...."

"Will you please sit down? I just want to talk."

She hesitates before she finally sits down. "What do you want to talk about?"

"I want you to run Titanium on your own from now on. I want you to work with Spencer, Bradley, and Cesar to keep the wheels turning the way they were under Derek. I want you to make decisions exactly the way you made them this morning without answering to anyone. If you absolutely have to promote a new CMO, you can bring someone up internally from the marketing department. I'm sure you have someone in mind already."

She blinks at me. "Are you serious? You want *me*.....to run Titani um.....by myself?"

"With Spencer, Bradley, Cesar, and anyone you promote from the marketing department."

"So......you don't have any problem with what I did this morning?"

I try to shrug that away. "I don't want you to make every decision thinking about whether or not I'd have a problem with it. I just want you to do it without second-guessing anything. Just do what you think is right. I'm sure you can get everyone else around here on board with that. They adore you."

She turns bright red and looks away. "I don't know about that."

"I do. You're fantastic."

Her eyes shoot back to me. Those eyes! My God, she makes my nuts ache when she looks at me like that.

"Are you sure you aren't doing this because of what's going on between us?" she asks.

I pretend to raise my eyebrows like I'm really surprised by that question. I'm not. I expected it.

"What *is* going on between us?" I ask.

"That's what I want to know. I don't want you giving me special treatment because we're......" She breaks off and doesn't say it.

I take a flying leap. "Have dinner with me tonight."

She colors even more. "I don't think that's a good idea."

"We can call it a professional dinner between colleagues. We can even talk about business if it makes you feel better."

"Will we be talking about business or will we be talking about what's going on between us?"

"What's the difference? Just have dinner with me. It doesn't have to be a lifetime commitment."

"Are you sure?" she asks.

Now it's my turn to blush. "We can talk about what's going on between us much better over dinner than we can here."

She snorts. "You're on drugs if you think that."

I can't help grinning at her. She's too smart for her own good. "So can we at least agree on you running Titanium by yourself—with your other four execs? Are you at least comfortable doing that much?"

"I will if you want me to. I thought you were coming over here to bust me downtown."

"Not at all. I think you made excellent decisions—even better than Derek. You should have been running this place all along."

She looks away and the color spreads from her cheeks to her ears and neck. That neck! I want to sink my teeth into it and breathe my hot breath in her ear right now.

"I'll need you to report to me—say once a week," I go on, "but I meant what I said. I don't want you to make decisions based on what you think I would want you to do. I want you to run this company according to the principles you mentioned at the meeting. I want you to run this place the way it should be run for the good of the whole company. Can you do that?"

"I can do it. I just find it hard to believe you're doing this for some reason other than what happened last night."

Now it's my turn to snort. "I'm quite sure I would be doing this even if nothing happened last night. You're the best we have for this job. You're the best thing for Titanium right now—even better than Derek. You proved that today."

"So.....so this is all strictly business."

"Absolutely. Now about having dinner with me......"

"Are you sure that's strictly business, too?"

I spread my hands in front of her. "Whatever is going on between us affects our business, so yes, talking about it is important to our business. It's important that we discuss whatever it is and get clear on exactly what we're doing. Don't you agree?"

"I guess so. I just don't see why we have to go to dinner instead of talking about it here."

I burst out in another smirk. I'd like to tell her that having dinner with me will be a better way to discuss it than me bending her over her desk and filling the building with her screams.

I decide not to say that, though. I can still behave myself in public when I absolutely have to.

Instead, I say, "I'm sure I'd be asking you to have dinner with me if nothing happened last night. I'd be asking you as a colleague and a valued employee. It's just dinner. If it really bothers you that much, I'll promise that nothing will happen afterward. I'll drive you home and....."

"And?" she interrupts.

I burst out laughing. I can't help but blush. She really is a treasure. "And then I'll go home to my place and it never has to happen again."

Right in front of my eyes, she compresses her lips and gulps. Does that gulp mean she wants it to happen again? The thought makes my stomach flip.

"All right," she finally agrees. "I'll have dinner only if you swear on your honor that nothing will happen afterward."

I raise my right hand, but I can't wipe this stupid grin off my face. Everything she does charms me out of my pants—literally. "I swear on my honor nothing will happen afterward."

She finally allows the tiniest smile to tug the corners of her lips. Those lips! "All right. I'll have dinner with you, then."

"Great. I'll pick you up at your place at seven." I stand up. I really, really don't want to leave.

I head for the door. Maybe lightning will strike and she'll wind up in my arms anyway.

"Lane?" she calls after me.

I turn around, but she isn't in my arms. She's over there behind her desk.

The eyes say it all, though. She *is* thinking about it.

"Thank you," she tells me.

"What for? I should be the one thanking you for saving this outfit."

"Thank you for believing in me," she blurts out. "No one has ever believed in me before—not like this. I've never had a boss who thought I could run the whole show by myself."

"Well, you can. You proved that today." I point at her. "Just keep doing it."

# Chapter 25: Samantha

I really have to stop checking my appearance in the mirror while I wait for Lane to show up. He's taking me to dinner, but he insists this is strictly business and he swears we won't do anything afterward.

I have to choose my outfit carefully. I don't want to wear a business suit. I should. If this is strictly business, then I should wear a business suit, shouldn't I?

I don't wear a suit, though. I don't want to wear anything too attractive, either. I don't want to make this into a date when it isn't one.

I go for a plain, elegant, knee-length black dress with simple gold jewelry and no other accessories besides my handbag. I wear heels, but I keep them mid-range instead of sky-high.

I look like I'm going to a funeral instead of a business dinner, but this isn't really a business dinner. Lane and I....we've already done it once.

Well, not exactly once. We did it more than once. We just did it all on the same night.

I really need to stop thinking like that. This is not a date.

At least we'll be able to clear the air tonight. Then we can get back to work. I won't have to live wondering what it meant or if it meant anything or when he'll come around expecting it to mean something different than what I expect it to mean.

He's right about that. We need to get clear on this now. This will be the best thing for the business.

I smooth down my dress and check my teeth one last time. It's almost time for him to pick me up.

I get another flashback of making out with him in the limo. Making out with him in the limo would be even hotter if I was wearing this dress.

I can just imagine him sliding his hand between my knees and up under my dress....and he would be able to feel my body more easily through this dress than a suit.

I'm just putting my phone, keys, and a packet of tissues in my handbag when he knocks on the door. I have to stop myself from charging over there and ripping the door off its hinges.

He bursts into a huge grin when he sees my outfit. "Stunning as usual," he remarks.

"You said you would keep it strictly business."

"This is strictly business. You're always stunning during business hours, too. In fact, you're stunning outside of business hours now that I think of it...."

"Stop it," I tell him. "Let's go."

I step out of the apartment. I feel his eyes on me as I lock the door. I turn around to leave.....and find him standing right there.

He doesn't move for a second. He just stands there staring at me like.....Does he want to kiss me right now?

The feeling of his arms and hands slipping around me overpowers my senses....and then he turns away to head for the elevator.

He doesn't take my hand tonight. He would on any other night, even before anything happened between us. He would have taken my hand right after the carjacking. He's been doing stuff like that all along.

He doesn't do it now, though. We ride down the elevator in silence.

Now I realize what a bad idea this was. He stands there simmering with barely concealed pressure. The tension mounts to the breaking point.

He'll grab me any second now and start kissing me and groping me and making me moan.

He doesn't, though. Just standing this close to him drives me crazy. He wants to. He barely holds himself back—or maybe he doesn't. Maybe he finds it easy to tempt me and test my resolve to resist him.

Maybe he enjoys making me tremble with desire for him—except that I'm the one who said we can't. He would do it in a heartbeat if I said I wanted to.

I do want to. That's the problem. This is going to be the hardest dinner of my life.

Things escalate to a whole new dimension when we get downstairs. He holds the limo door open for me to get in. Then he gets in after me and the limo pulls away.

I have to struggle to sit still on the seat. I keep slipping into fantasies about him touching me and fingering me and pulling me onto his lap in the back of this limo. I'll never be able to ride in this car without thinking about that.

The tension coming from Lane makes me shiver in my seat. I glance over and see him staring straight ahead. He doesn't look at me, but he might as well be.

He smolders away over there like a volcano ready to blow. One look and it would be all over. Jesus, what was I thinking agreeing to this?

I don't even trust myself to get through tonight without starting something.

He won't, though. He gave his word and he won't do anything with me. He probably wouldn't do it even if I said I wanted to.

He would probably control himself and the situation even if I started kissing him and slipping my hand between his legs. That's just the way he's made.

The limo pulls up in front of Salvini's, the same place where he ran into me last time.

He was with some of his board members then. Maybe this is his go-to spot for business dinners. He really is taking this seriously. I shouldn't have expected anything less.

I half-expect him to put his arm behind my back on our way inside, but he doesn't. He hovers near enough to make me feel his presence, but he always holds off just enough to stop himself from actually touching me.

We get a table for two by the windows. This is definitely more romantic than getting a table on the mezzanine.

He pulls out my chair for me just like we're on a real date. As soon as we sit down and his eyes lock on me across the table, all thought that this could be strictly business goes out the window.

This was never going to be about business. That's impossible. I'm not even sure if anything can ever be strictly business between us ever again.

The way he looks at me definitely isn't strictly business—or any other kind of business. This is pure romance.

He bites back another grin and his eyes sparkle. "So...."

"So?" I ask.

"You wanted to discuss what's going on between us," he reminds me.

"So did you. You said it was important for us to get clear on exactly what we're doing."

"Right. So what exactly are we doing?"

"It looks like we're having dinner together."

He nods. "Very astute."

"Like I said, it was probably a mistake. We should just forget it so we can keep working together. That would be best for both companies, don't you think? It isn't like anything could ever happen between us."

"What makes you say that?"

"Because...." I have to check myself. "Because you're my boss. Because you own the company I work for." I open my mouth a second time and the words die on my lips. "You....you actually want something to happen between us? Are you insane?"

"I don't see what's so insane about it. I think you're terrific."

"But....don't you think it's terrible business practice to sleep with your subordinates—especially when the relationship between Apico and Titanium is still so tenuous? Jesus, what am I saying? It would have been outrageous for us to sleep together anytime—anytime I was working for you."

He only shrugs. "I don't know about that....."

"You don't know about that! Are you saying you think it's okay—for either of us? It's....it's tasteless. It's creepy."

"Who's being tasteless and creepy—you for sleeping with the boss or me for sleeping with an employee?"

"Both!" I reply. "You know I'm right."

He sits there regarding me across the table. "It sounds that way when you say it like that, but I can't see anything tasteless or tacky or creepy or dirty about what we did last night. I want more of it—not less—and not in a trashy, boss-sleeps-with-his-secretary way. I want .....you."

My jaw drops. "You can't be serious!"

"Why can't I? If you tell me you really don't want to, then I'll have no choice but to accept it, but something tells me you do really want it. I saw you last night. You want it as much as I do."

I shut my mouth and look away. He didn't just say that.

He's right about one thing. I could never think of last night as trashy or dirty or low. It was just....beautiful.

The connection between us is beyond anything I ever thought possible. Doing it with him is beautiful because I know the person he is. I know what he's worth. I want the person he is even more than I want his body.

I know he feels the same way about me. He thinks I'm gorgeous, but he really wants the person that I am. That's what he really craves.

He slides his hand across the table and leaves it lying palm up where I can see it. It lies there inviting me to place my hand in his.

All the voices in my head tell me not to touch him, but I can't ignore that hand.

I put my hand in his and blissful warmth floods me. It's the warmth of a man who always takes care of me. It's the warmth of a man who protects me, looks out for me, defends me, and believes in me.

He squeezes and that radiant heat rushes over me. God, how I wish I was in his arms right now feeling that heat in every pore and crevice. What am I thinking by pushing him away?

He lowers his voice to a barely audible murmur. "What are you thinking right now?"

I have to swallow to get my throat working. "I mean....how would it work? Everyone would find out."

"Just tell me you want it. Tell me to my face that you want it and you don't really just want to forget it like it never happened."

"Of course I do. I only said that because....well.....I mean.....it could never work out, could it? It's impossible."

"Nothing is impossible, sweetheart," he breathes. "You should know that."

That voice makes me want to cry, but it also feels like dissolving in a river of pure passion. He caresses his thumb across my knuckles. Everything he does soothes me into a trance.

Just then, our server comes to take our order. We have to scramble to figure out what we're going to order.

Lane doesn't put his hand back on the table after the server leaves.

"Let's change the subject and talk about business," he suggests.

"Um....okay, but we haven't clarified....the other thing."

He bites back another smirk. "Let's just leave it on the table for now."

"But wasn't the whole point to clarify where we stand and what we're doing?"

"We clarified that we both want it," he points out. "That's enough for me right now."

"But....so what are we doing?"

"We're leaving it on the table and changing the subject."

I squirm in my seat. "Uh...okay. What do you want to talk about?"

"What made you go into finance?" he asks.

"I didn't. I worked at a machine factory in south Maine before I moved to New York."

He nods. "Oh, yeah. Griswold & Sons. I remember now. So you didn't do accounting for them?"

"I started in HR. I got a job there while I was in college studying business administration. The lady who always did payroll at Griswold got sick and I was the most junior person in the department. No one else wanted to do it, so I got stuck doing it. I actually liked it and I got really good at it.....and then everybody kinda noticed and started dumping all this other accounting work on my desk. I eventually moved up and became the head of the accounting department. That's when I moved to New York and started up with Derek." I flinch. "Sorry. I shouldn't mention him."

"Go ahead and mention him."

"Anyway, he gave me a chance. No one else would have made me CFO of a major corporation."

"But Titanium Finance wasn't a major corporation then," he points out. "The company was still small. You grew with it and became CFO."

I nod. "Yeah. That's what happened. Derek was the one who made that happen for me. I wouldn't be where I am right now if not for him. He's right about that."

"I understand why you feel loyal to him, but you're selling yourself short. You're where you are right now because of your own dedication and hard work. If you only cared about being loyal to him, you would be on the street right now the same as he is."

I feel the color drain from my face. "Is that where he is—on the street? Did you punt him?"

He has to stop himself from laughing. "Of course not. I told him he had a choice—either to become a contributing member of Apico or not. Apico owns Titanium now. He's either an employee like the rest of us or he isn't. It's as simple as that. Come on. You know he always had a choice. He could have walked away ten times richer if he'd only accepted my offer. All of you could have. He chose to be selfish instead."

I can't hold eye contact with Lane because he's right. Derek could have sold Titanium to Apico, made a mint, and invested the money in an even richer company.

All the rest of us could have been laughing all the way to the bank, too. He robbed us of that. God only knows why I still feel anything for him at all after the way he botched this.

Just then, the server comes with our food. This topic is making me uncomfortable, so I decide to change the subject. "What did you want to be when you were growing up—before you went into business?"

"I wanted to be one of those guys who does maintenance on the bridges of New York," he replies.

My head shoots up and I stop dead with a mouthful of food. "No way!"

He nods, but he won't stop blushing. "I heard they made good money. That was the best I could imagine then. I thought if I could just get a decent job and live in a decent neighborhood, that I would have it made." He shakes his head and laughs over his food. "What an idiot I was back then."

"So what happened—apart from you going to jail? You could have gotten out and gotten a maintenance job. You probably could have gotten your mom and sister out of the ghetto on that salary."

"I'm sure I could have, but I couldn't have sent my sister to college—and I definitely couldn't have bought my mother's apartment building. I didn't graduate from high school, so I got my GED while I was inside."

I stare at him across the table. Every word out of his mouth rings like a big, deafening bell in my head. He really is amazing if he overcame all these challenges and obstacles.

He doesn't notice me staring at him.

"I started studying business because I thought it would help me make more money. After I got out, I got a job in the call center of an insurance company sales room. Then I found out how much the execs of that company were making and it was all over."

"That's incredible. It seems unbelievable that you came from where you did and now you're here. It doesn't seem real."

He beams at my reaction. "Thank you. I suppose I have a right to be proud of myself."

"You do," I murmur and I mean it.

We finish eating and go back outside to the limo. Riding back to my place feels different this time.

Neither of us simmers with passion about to drive us out of control. Neither of us is any danger of ripping the other person's clothes off.

This feels easy. This feels normal.

I've been spending so much time with him lately. He seems to have moved into my life. I don't see how it's possible anymore for him to move out of it. He's just....here. He's a part of my life already whether I want him to be or not.

Going out to dinner with him.....it doesn't feel wrong or out of line or inappropriate. Quite the opposite. It feels perfectly appropriate, natural, and such an obvious solution to....something. I don't know what problem it's the obvious solution to, but it is.

He gets out of the limo, tells Eddie to wait for him, and walks me up to my apartment.

He grabs my hand outside the door and eases in to kiss me. "Good night," he murmurs.

"Good night," I whisper back. "Thank you for the wonderful dinner."

"See you tomorrow, okay?" he replies.

I nod and find myself smiling up at him. If this is what leaving it on the table means, then I can live with that.

# Chapter 26: Samantha

I lean forward and extend my hand across the seat to hand the cab driver my cash. "Thank you," I tell him. "Keep it."

"Thank you, Ma'am!" he calls back and I get out of the cab.

Driving by myself still doesn't feel safe, so I've been taking cabs to and from the office. I'll get back on the horse—someday.

I swing the door to slam it shut and turn toward my apartment building. I dig into my handbag looking for my apartment keys when someone comes up behind me.

A strong hand grabs my shoulder. "Samantha!"

I jump out of my skin and spin around thinking someone is about to attack me. I gasp out loud when I see that it's Derek.

He doesn't notice my reaction. "I've been looking for you," he tells me. "I need to talk to you."

I don't want to talk to Derek, especially after he scared me on a street corner in the middle of the night. "You didn't have to ambush me here. You could have called me. You have my number."

"I wanted to see you."

"What about?" I ask over my shoulder. He's the last person I want to talk to right now. I want to get off the street, go inside, and barricade myself in my apartment.

I'm okay most of the time. I can get through my normal workday and go about my normal routine. My face is starting to turn back to its normal color, too.

Times like this bring it all back—all the terror of that night. I don't like being outside on the street at night or any loud noises or people surprising me with anything.

Anthony, the doorman of my building, stands at the outer door. He would normally open the door for me to enter.

He moves over to open it, but he gives Derek a dirty look. Anthony is too observant not to notice my reaction. I don't want Derek to come inside the building.

Anthony will stop him if I ask him to, but I feel bad about kicking Derek in the teeth when he's already down.

"I heard you're running Titanium Finance now," he begins. "Is that true? Are you helping those sharks tear my company apart?"

"I'm running the company because you were too self-absorbed to do it, Derek," I snap over my shoulder. "You could have ruined the company by not selling to Apico when you had the chance...."

"You actually wanted me to sell out to Lane Prince?! Are you nuts? The guy is a cannibal."

"I don't care if he's Hannibal Lecter, Derek! You had a duty to your employees to do the best thing for all of us. You didn't do that because you only cared about keeping your precious company for yourself. You should have done the right thing by sticking around and smoothing over the transition, but you couldn't even do that. You're out because you failed. Admit it. You never cared about any of us the way you said you did. You only cared about making yourself look good."

He doesn't hear a word I say. "Just tell me if you're running the company or not. That's all I want to know."

"Well, someone had to when you stopped showing up for work. Someone had to handle the SEC audit that wound up in your email inbox and you weren't answering your messages—so yes, someone had to step in and I did it. The rest of us are surviving without you. Sorry to hurt your feelings, but the world didn't stop just because you decided not to show up at the office."

I catch Anthony listening to our conversation. I've never been so grateful to have him there. He'll step in if I really need to get rid of Derek.

"You don't understand!" he raves. "I can't get anything started! I lost something when I lost Titanium. I can't seem to pull it together."

I soften. Poor guy. He had something good and now he's adrift. "Look, things will turn around for you. You're on the ropes right now, but you'll come back. You're smart. Something will turn up."

He takes a step closer to me. "I always thought we had something special...." He raises his hand toward my face.

I see him about to make a move on me and I react without thinking. I might have reacted more than I should have, but I can't stand here and let him get the wrong idea.

I jerk my head away before he can touch me and swipe my arm to knock his hand aside. I take five quick strides toward the door.

Good old Anthony opens it for me to enter and then sidesteps behind me to block Derek from following me.

My heart won't stop pounding. I hustle over to the elevator. My hands shake when I press the button. Derek did not just try to make a pass at me. Hell no.

I have to stop myself from pushing the button again and again and again to get the elevator to come faster. I hear Anthony and Derek talking outside. I don't want to think about what either of them is saying.

The elevator takes too long to come. I'm getting just desperate enough to take the stairs when the doors finally open.

I dive inside and have to go through another flurry of restraining myself not to push the button a million times on the inside. The elevator doors close and I collapse against the wall fighting to breathe. I'm safe. I'm okay. I'm inside and he's out there. He can't get to me.

I go to my apartment, lock the door, and collapse on the couch. The down bedspread is still here. I sleep down here now. I feel safer here.

This bedspread smells like Lane. I wrap it around myself without taking my clothes off and stretch out on the couch. I'm okay now because he's here—or I can pretend he is.

Pretending isn't enough—not tonight. I shiver thinking about Derek coming up behind me just now. I need Lane—but I can't have him. He's out of reach—and yet he isn't.

I attack my handbag and pull out my phone. My hands are still shaking when I navigate to his contact.

I've been talking to him all week about Titanium business. I check in with him multiple times a day even though he lets me make my own decisions.

I tap his contact and hold my breath while I listen to the phone ring. I really need him to answer right now.

I shut my eyes and wince thinking he might be busy, but it doesn't switch to voicemail.

My heart leaps when he answers. His voice tells me he's happy to hear from me. "Hey, sweetheart!" he exclaims. "What a surprise. Shouldn't you be in bed?"

I find myself laughing with thrilling relief. He's here. "I am in bed. I just wanted to hear your voice."

He hesitates way too long. "Is something wrong? You sound a little shaky."

Of course he knows. Of course he can tell.

"It's just....someone came up to me....just now....on the street....and started me. I just....." I take a deep, shuddering breath and blurt out the truth. "I guess I just never feel safe except when you're around."

"Aw!" he murmurs. "You're really sweet."

I curl deeper into the bedspread. "I miss you."

"I'm happy you feel that way about me, but you know we could never build a relationship on that. You need to start feeling safe on your own. It would never work for you to become dependent on me. You know?"

I wince and tears sting my eyes. Of course he understands that, too.

"You know how I feel about you," he goes on. "You know I'll always protect you and support you in whatever you need, but you need to get stronger before you get together with anybody, no matter who it is. It would be especially important if you got together with me because we have this history of me taking care of you. You know what I mean? This is way more important than us being boss and employee. We could overcome that. We can't overcome this—not until you start feeling stronger." He pauses. "Are you hearing me?"

I let out a long, shuddering sigh. "Yeah. I hear you."

"Do you agree?" he asks. "You know I'm right. Right?"

"Yeah," I mumble. "I just.....I just miss you. I miss you being here."

"Aw. I miss being there, too, sweetie. I miss everything about you. Are you gonna be okay tonight?"

"Yeah. I just needed to talk to you."

"How did your day go today?"

I shrug at nothing. I don't want to tell Lane about Derek. "It was good. The SEC auditor is really nice. She's been very reassuring that she hasn't found anything concerning in our document submission."

"You did the right thing giving her the documents when you did. Is there any further sign of problems with the server?"

"Yeah, that was the other thing I meant to tell you. The server went down again today. We diverted again the way we did last time. We still had a credit with the new server company, so we got back online much quicker this time. Spencer is looking for a new long-term server provider because the old one is just too unreliable."

"You could use U-Tech Hosting," he suggests. "That's what Apico uses. If Titanium came under the Apico account, Apico would cover the expense as part of our umbrella corporate costs. Then you wouldn't have the expense on the Titanium books."

"You would do that?!" I exclaim. "That would be great!"

"We can start organizing it tomorrow. You can divert from the temporary server to U-Tech with no interruption in service. Then you won't have to worry about fixing whatever is wrong with the old server."

"Thank you so much! That is awesome. I can't wait to tell Spencer."

He chuckles. "Anytime. That's what Apico is here for. If we can make Titanium run any more smoothly, you only have to tell us."

I want to thank him again, but I sense this conversation coming to an end. "Thank you for talking to me. I feel better now."

"Of course, sweetheart. You know I always want to talk to you. Are you tired enough to go to sleep now?"

"Yes. Thank you again."

"Go get in bed and go to sleep. I'll talk to you tomorrow."

"Okay. Good night."

"Good night, sweetheart," he breathes. "Sleep tight and have sweet dreams."

He hangs up.

I shut my eyes, pull the bedspread over my head, and huddle there hugging my phone. What a gentleman he is for holding off on us getting involved.

Of course I'm not strong enough to get involved with anyone, especially not with him. Becoming dependent on him would be the worst thing for me—for both of us.

I'm already dependent on him. Of course he realizes that.

Just don't ask me how I'm going to get strong enough to ever get involved with him or anyone else. I can't even fall asleep without thinking about him.

I need to take the first step right now. I sit up and get to my feet.

I fold up the bedspread and take it back to the guest room. I don't need it. I won't use it again.

I need to get back in the habit of sleeping alone in my own bed. Lane isn't here, which means I have to take care of myself.

He's still with me. He's still guarding me and protecting me from the other side of town.

I go upstairs, change into my pajamas, get in bed, and pull the covers over my head. I can fantasize about Lane here.

That's what I'm doing—fantasizing about him. I'm fantasizing about him holding me while we sleep....and making out with him in the limo....and the way he looked at me across the table at the restaurant.

I'm fantasizing about holding his hand.....and about his deep, warm, soft voice murmuring in my ear through my phone.

He misses me. He wants to be here with me. Those words give me such a rush of emotion and warmth.

I curl up in bed hugging my phone. I'm safe because he's here. He's with me.

He's thinking of me and missing me. He's wrapping his arms around me right now and holding me close. Nothing can happen to me as long as I'm with him.

# Chapter 27: Lane

I feel an instant chill when I walk into The Billionaires' Club. A bunch of people stop what they're doing to turn around and stare at me. I must have the Scarlet Letter branded on my forehead.

It's been like this ever since Derek Salazar dropped the bomb about me having a criminal record. I really don't care. I just wish the rest of the world would get the hell over it already.

I've done business with half the men in here. I'm still the same person I was then. I didn't just wake up one morning and have a criminal record appear out of nowhere.

No one else seems to see it that way. I'm suddenly the worst monster that ever walked the face of the Earth. Even people who were semi-okay with my acquisition tactics now whisper behind my back and even outright glare at me.

That isn't true. A few people still stick by me. Jackson Metcalf, Dante Helme, and Judah Hayes make a point of coming over to me.

"I knew you'd be the best thing for Titanium Finance," Judah tells me. "Everything you touch turns to gold."

"Thanks, man," I murmur. "Thanks for sticking up for me."

"Forget all that." He claps me on the shoulder and doesn't let go. He steers me over to the buffet, but I don't see him, Dante, or Jackson eating.

For all I know Judah has a criminal record, too. People treated him like he had one when he first joined the club. Apparently being the only black man in the room makes people instantly assume you have a criminal record.

Maybe he's secretly relieved that someone around here actually has one so everyone can start hating me instead.

The weird thing is that no one in the whole club has ever actually asked me about my record. They all just automatically fall on one side or the other—either supporting me or shunning me. None of them needs any evidence to make their decision before they do one or the other.

"You really got yourself a winner with that Samantha Mulholland running Titanium for you," Jackson tells me. "I'll give you one thing, man. You know your people. You really know how to bet on a horse and let them win."

"Hey, if it ain't broke, why fix it?" I ask.

"You got that right," Dante agrees. "The company is more profitable than ever—and the share price has never been higher. Maybe Titanium needed to cut the chaff, you know what I mean?"

I don't ask who he means. I can see Derek Salazar glaring at me from across the room.

He stands with five other guys all murmuring in each other's ears. I don't have to wonder what they're talking about because they keep glancing in my direction.

Dante draws my attention away from them to refocus it on the people who actually matter. "So what's your next move? What do you have your eye on next?"

"Nothing yet. I'm still consolidating Titanium. We've had a few hiccups to iron out—and a few wrinkles between Titanium and Apico."

"It can't have been anything serious," Jackson chimes in. "I can't imagine Samantha having a problem with anybody."

"She wasn't the problem. A few people had problems with her. That's why I put her in charge of Titanium without any Apico involvement. She wasn't running Titanium before, but she knew exactly what to say to the employees to get them back on track. We needed someone in-house for that—and I guess it just became obvious that we needed someone in-house to run the whole shebang. So it all made sense in the end."

Dante nods, but before he can answer, Niko Holloway sits down on one of the big plush leather couches, props his feet on the coffee table, and flips on the big screen TV.

Niko is the youngest member of the club. He's only twenty-seven, tall and strapping, with short, curly brown hair, tiger-brown eyes, and bursting at the seams with alpha confidence. The guy owns a room the minute he walks into it.

He made his money in trucking—and he still does. He's the modern equivalent of Jimmy Hoffa but with way better manners.

If you want something done, all you have to do is ask Niko and it will be done. The guy is a goddamn steamroller.

He owned The Billionaires' Club the minute he walked into it, too. He treats the club like his own personal penthouse apartment. He does what he pleases and never asks anyone for permission to do anything.

He never once doubted he would get in. He just basically moved in on us even though he's so much younger than the rest of us.

He throws his arm over the back of the couch and surfs to the news. The announcer is reading out the results of the Department of Agriculture report on crop yields.

The other club members fall silent to listen. Most of this information affects stock prices and at least some aspect of their businesses.

It doesn't affect mine, but Dante and Judah both turn around to listen, too. I wait for the segment to finish.

The announcement ends and some of the members turn back to their conversations. Niko picks up the remote to turn off the TV, but at that moment, the program switches.

It shows a reporter standing on a street somewhere in the Bowery. It isn't my old neighborhood, but it might as well be.

The hair on the back of my neck rises when I hear my own name.

"In tonight's local interest segment, we feature New York native business magnate Lane Prince and his epic rise from the mean streets of New York to the halls of corporate power. Born the son of a poor single mother and raised in the Bowery projects, young Lane flunked out of high school and got in trouble with the law for protecting his sister from a life of forced prostitution in a local gang. When the gang leader in question tried to force Lane's sister to work for him, Lane hunted the man down, threatened him with a firearm, and put him in the hospital."

Dead silence falls over the room. Everyone listens. No one even breathes.

Out of that silence, Judah's hand lands on my shoulder again and he squeezes. That tight grip sends another shiver up my spine. Everyone knows now.

The reporter passes down the block and stops in front of another building before he starts talking again.

"Lane gained his GED while serving two years in a juvenile corrections facility. When he came out, he worked here, at Sentinel Insurance, starting as a junior phone sales operator. It was while he worked at Sentinel Insurance that he developed a software service known as GaleQuip, an AI-based robotics programming platform that revolutionized the industry for thousands of businesses. He sold the company for millions less than three years later. Since then, the man who would become known as one of New York's fiercest business leaders has acquired more than fifty companies and continues to...."

Niko switches the TV off in the middle of the rest of the story. Everyone here knows the rest.

Niko shoots me a wild grin over the back of the couch, juts his chin at me, and nods in approval.

"You're the man, Lane," Jackson mutters in my ear. "Good for you."

I can't stop the blood from rushing to my cheeks. These men will always have my back. They stood by me even before they knew the truth. They're the ones standing by me again now that they know.

The tension in the room dissolves and everyone goes back to what they were doing. They don't glare at me or stare at me or whisper behind my back. The ones that did pretend they never were.

I can forget it. I can be gracious, now that I've been vindicated. I don't need to rub it in their faces.

I'm sure some of them are feeling pretty damn stupid right about now. Good. They should feel stupid for assuming. If someone has a problem with me, they better say it to my face.

Things heat up between Derek and the other members, though. He tries to talk to them, but they either shake their heads or wave him away. Is he trying to convince them that I really am the lowlife he says I am?

He tries talking to someone else. When he doesn't get the response he wants, he blows up and gets in his companion's face.

The other guy raises his hands and tries to back away. Other members step in to pull them apart, but Derek shakes them off, too.

His voice starts rising. "You have to listen to me, man! Don't you understand? This is not what we signed up for."

He spins around to confront the people holding onto him. They have to back off real quick. Is this gonna turn into a fight right here in The Billionaires' Club? That would be a first.

Before the situation can disintegrate any further and possibly turn to bloodshed, Kevin Drake walks over there. Thank the stars he's the club's membership officer. A lesser man wouldn't be able to pull this off.

"Excuse me, Mr. Salazar," Kevin says in his kindest, gentlest tone. This is definitely the first time I've ever heard Kevin refer to any club member by their last name. He's on a first-name basis with all of us, including Derek.

Not anymore.

"I'm afraid I'm going to have to ask you to leave," Kevin goes on in the same gentle murmur. "Your net worth has fallen below a billion dollars. You no longer qualify for membership in The Billionaires' Club."

Another dangerous silence falls over the room. Derek whips around the other way to stare at Kevin. "What?!"

Kevin waves toward the exit. "I'm very sorry, but we have a standard for membership and you no longer qualify. I'm afraid I have to ask you to leave. Please. Don't make me call security."

Derek glares at him just as hard....and then Derek's eyes glance around the room. He sees everyone staring at him and listening. No one moves.

His expression changes from stunned disbelief to pure, shocked horror when he realizes exactly what Kevin just said.

I cringe inwardly. This would be the worst humiliation ever. Thank the gods above this isn't happening to me.

I have to feel sorry for the guy when he clamps his mouth shut, bends his head to look down at the floor, and strides out of the room.

No one moves until he leaves. Kevin follows him out.

The first whispers spread through the room as people start talking again, but Judah, Jackson, Dante, and I don't.

I feel like I've just witnessed a death of some kind—or maybe attended a funeral. Poor Derek. The guy might have shot himself in the foot, but no one deserves this.

He might have spared himself the indignation if he hadn't been so bent on getting back at me. Kevin could have approached Derek in a private moment and broken the news.

Derek had to go making a spectacle of himself in public. He had to go getting in people's faces and maybe even resorting to violence on the club floor.

He forced Kevin's hand. Of course Kevin had to step in.

The four of us are still standing there wondering how to break the uncomfortable silence when old Saul Gottlieb walks in.

He smiles when he sees us, comes over, shakes hands with all four of us, and then he and Dante start talking about some business venture they plan to do together.

Niko Holloway stands up from the couch and sees me watching him while he buttons his jacket. He holds eye contact for a minute and then walks out.

# Chapter 28: Samantha

B radley comes into my office and slaps a stack of file folders down on my desk. "This is all the operations reports for the last five years that you asked for."

"Thanks, pumpkin," I reply without looking up.

He laughs. "Just don't start calling me munchkin. I couldn't stand that."

I shoot him a grin and start flipping through the files.

"Why did you want this, anyway?" he asks.

"No reason," I lie. "Thank you again. I'll see you tomorrow."

"See you around. Don't work too late. Oh, what am I saying? You always work late."

"I get on my hamster wheel power generator and run all night long." He laughs on his way to the door and I yell a little louder as he walks out of my office. "How do you think we can afford to keep the lights on?"

His laughter fades down the hall moving toward the elevator. He didn't shut my office door, so I stand up and do it before I sit down and study the files in front of me.

My phone rings and I switch it to video chat. Lane shows up on the screen. "Hey, sweetheart," he greets me. "What did you find out?"

I prop the phone against my laptop so I can talk hands-free. "I got the personnel files from Bradley. I just got rid of him, so I'm looking through them now."

"Look for someone with computer expertise," he tells me.

I make a face. "We're talking about the whole IT department. They all have computer expertise."

"Then someone especially devoted to Derek....or someone with exceptional computer knowledge. I'm telling you there is no way our U-Tech server just happened to go down exactly the way the Titanium server did. Someone is screwing with us."

"I know, but it's gonna take me some time to go through all these files. I'll take them home and go over them tonight...."

"No, you won't!" he snaps. "It's already almost eight o'clock. Leave the files in your office and go home and get some sleep. You can work on this tomorrow."

I smile at him through the screen. "You're so sweet."

"I mean it. If someone is sabotaging us, we can take our time finding the sucker. Your health is more important."

"I don't feel right about leaving the files lying out for anyone to see. It's bad enough Bradley knows I asked for these."

"Can you store them somewhere more secure—a safe or something?"

I snort. "A safe? What do you think I am—some kind of Teamsters boss? I'm a glorified accountant."

"You can take them home with you if you swear to me on your father's grave that you won't even look at them before tomorrow morning."

I beam at him. He knows me so well. "I promise. I'll leave them locked in the trunk of my car. Is that secure enough for you?"

"Fine." He bursts into a grin. "I really appreciate your hard work. I feel so much better knowing you're over there handling Titanium for me so I don't have to come in there and crack heads myself."

I laugh. "If anyone needs their head cracked, I'll be the one to crack it."

"I know you're a badass. Do you need anything else tonight?"

"I'm all good. I'll talk to you tomorrow. Hopefully, I'll know something more about this by then."

"Okay, sweetheart. Good night."

We hang up.

It's been a week since Lane left me in charge of Titanium Finance. We talk on video chat all the time—multiple times a day—but it's always business.

He never mentions taking our relationship to another level. I'm not even sure we have a relationship. In fact, I'm sure we don't. I'm not ready for one yet.

Running Titanium on my own makes me feel stronger, though. I can survive without him. I can even drive my car to and from work by myself without freaking out.

I go through my computer and make sure all the other employees are out of the building. I don't want any of them to know I'm investigating the IT department for sabotaging our servers.

I log out of my computer, pick up my handbag and the stack of files, and leave the office. Jorge, the night cleaner is vacuuming the carpets.

He waves to me since we can't talk over the noise. I get in the elevator and ride down to the underground parking garage. My car is the only one still here.

I don't have any problem walking across the garage, unlocking my trunk, and locking the files inside. Walking through a deserted parking garage at eight o'clock at night would have given me a panic attack two weeks ago.

I have Lane to thank for this. Just knowing he supports me makes me stronger. He supports me enough to walk away from a relationship if that's what I need.

I get behind the wheel, start the motor, and drive up the ramp to street level. I have to stop there to wait for a break in the traffic.

Cars stream past me with their headlights blazing in the night. I glance left and right waiting for the traffic to ease.

That's when I see a scuffle in a ground-level parking lot right next to the Titanium Finance building.

A few different cars sit in the parking spaces. A woman and two men stand next to one of the cars, but these people aren't together—at least, they shouldn't be.

Goosebumps erupt on my skin when I see one of the men grab the woman by the hair. He slams her face down on the side of the car and the other guy jumps in to wave a gun in her face.

My heart stops when the first guy grabs for the woman's purse. These assholes are mugging this woman right in plain view.

Hell no. Not again. I won't just drive off and leave some other woman to go through what I went through or maybe even worse.

I don't wait for a break in the traffic. I yank my car out into the street and almost hit a few other cars.

They blare their horns at me, but I don't care. I whip around the corner and pull into the parking lot.

The guys are so busy attacking this poor woman that they don't hear my tires screeching or the horns squawking. I skid to a stop right next to the woman's car—at least I assume it's her car.

I make a split-second decision about what I'm gonna do, kick open my driver's door, rip my keys out the ignition, and storm over to them.

I unleash all the fury I wish I'd unleashed on my attacker. I want to pay him back for what he did to me. I'll just have to pay it forward by doing it to someone else who's already in the middle of an almost identical crime.

I flip my keys around and walk right up behind the second attacker—the one with the gun. I consider calling out to him to get his attention away from the woman, but I don't want him to turn the gun on me.

I go for the surprise attack instead, brace my keys between my fingers, and hit him as hard as I can right at the base of the skull. He has a buzz cut so I can see exactly where to hit him in the most sensitive spot.

He crumples at my feet and the other guy whips around to stare at me in stunned disbelief. So much for the element of surprise.

I'm just considering running for it when the woman strikes without mercy. I don't even see her until she lunges for the guy with one of those telescoping batons.

She nails him across the back of the skull, too, and he buckles on the spot.

I stare down at him and then I look at her. She stares back at me in breathless astonishment.

"Are you okay?" I gasp.

"Yeah!" she pants. "Thank you so much! I was so worried!"

"You were?" I look down at the second guy. He's out cold. "That was amazing!"

"You, too!" she exclaims. "I really thought I was a goner."

"Are you sure you're okay?" I want to pat her down. "We should call the Police."

"Yeah!" she gasps again and starts fumbling to get her phone out of her purse.

"Are you sure you're okay?" I ask again like an idiot. "We could call an ambulance."

"I'm okay." She bursts into a grin. "Thank you again for coming. It's so good to meet you."

I stick out my hand. She's already holding the phone to her ear. "I'm Samantha—Samantha Mulholland."

She has to quickly switch her phone to her left hand to shake mine, but she won't stop beaming at me. "I'm Katrina—Katrina Prince."

My world comes to a screeching halt when I hear that name. Katrina Prince. What are the odds?

She has brown hair—unlike Lane's—but they have the same blue eyes. She has a thin stature and a spare, lean look.

She doesn't notice anything unusual—of course not. The phone rings in her ear and I hear the operator come on the line.

"Hello!" Katrina yells way too loudly. "I...I just got attacked....in a parking lot. Two guys with a gun....tried to mug me.....and another woman came along and helped me. We knocked the guys out. They're still here. We need the Police right away."

She shoots me a grin while she listens to the operator. Nothing happens for a second before I hear a siren a few blocks away.

She says, "Okay, thank you," to the operator and hangs up. "There are two squad cars down the block. They're on their way over now."

Katrina and I stand there together until the cops show up. They cuff the attackers and then Katrina and I have to answer a million questions.

We stay standing side by side until Detective Beckett rolls up. He frowns at me. "Tell me you didn't get attacked again."

"I didn't. She did. I was pulling out of the garage right over there and I saw two guys holding her down and sticking a gun in her face. I came over and....." I trail off. Did I do something wrong by hitting that guy so hard?

"You did what?"

I try to shrug to take the pressure off myself. "I stuck my keys between my fingers and hit him in the back of the head to knock him out."

"And then I hit the other guy with my baton." Katrina holds it out to him. "Do you need to take it into evidence or anything?"

He scowls at the two of us and then goes over to one of the squad cars. He's on his way back with a plastic evidence bag when Katrina murmurs in my ear, "He looks mean."

"He's okay," I whisper back. "He's a good cop. He's just doing his job."

"Do you know him?" she breathes.

I shrug again. "Sort of."

He pulls up in front of us, opens the bag, and she sticks the end of the baton inside it. She compresses it down to its smallest size so it fits.

He seals the bag and puts it in his jacket pocket. "I'm gonna have to ask you ladies to come downtown and fill out full statements."

"No problem," I reply.

He gives me another sharp look. He really does look stern. Maybe he's just surprised that I'm not shaking like a leaf.

I find myself blinking at the surroundings in wonder. I can actually breathe. Hitting that guy and saving Katrina did something to me. It took back something I lost the night of the carjacking.

I feel pretty damn good right now. I don't mind going downtown to answer Detective Beckett's questions. I know now that I did the right thing.

Detective Beckett waves behind him at the many squad cars. "Come with me. I'll drive you to the station and bring you back when we're done. If you don't mind, I'd like to interview you both at the same time so we can compare your stories."

I see Katrina looking doubtful—or maybe scared.

"Okay, we'll do it," I tell the detective, "as long as we can ride together there and back."

He nods. "Done."

I turn to Katrina to explain that I'll be with her all the way, but she already looks relieved that she doesn't have to go alone.

Detective Beckett takes us to an unmarked car sitting at the curb. It's a good thing he's driving us because my car and Katrina's are completely blocked in by cop cars.

We both slide into the back seat. "It's okay," I whisper to Katrina. "This is just a formality. It's nothing to worry about."

She shoots me another relieved grin. "Thanks again."

"You did great," I tell her. "I was really worried about that second guy until you took care of him."

She bursts into an even bigger smile, but just then, Detective Beckett gets behind the wheel, starts the motor, and we head off into the night.

# Chapter 29: Lane

I walk into my penthouse apartment, toss my keys on the table by the door, and collapse on the couch. I scoot all the way down to rest my head on the cushion.

I'm beat, but at least I don't have to worry about Titanium Finance. That is one load off my mind, now that Samantha is on the ball.

I don't even really worry about whichever member of the Titanium IT team is sabotaging our server. She'll find the sucker. I don't envy him one bit when she does.

I can leave the whole company in her capable hands. I can't remember trusting anyone as much as I trust her.

It's almost better like this than if we did get involved. At least this way I know she's all right. We work so well together. I wouldn't want anything to damage the business—any of it.

I still think she's amazing, but she's out of reach—for now, at least.

Having all this responsibility taken off my hands leaves me plenty of time for doing nothing. I could go out....or order in. I can do whatever I want—until tomorrow.

I don't even have to worry about her checking those personnel files. She promised on her father's grave. There is no bond stronger than that.

I smile at the thought. She's so precious. She's going to make some guy very happy someday.

I kick back on the couch and switch on the TV. At least I don't have to worry about anyone running any more local interest stories on me. Now everyone can go back to thinking about someone else.

I switch to the news expecting the usual shootings, stabbings, wars, political intrigue, and election hijinks.

I shoot off the couch in big hurry when the top story comes on. "Two local businesswomen foiled an attempted mugging that could have turned into an abduction or worse. The second woman was pulling out of the parking garage right over there when she saw the victim being assaulting in the parking lot behind me. The second woman pulled her car in and knocked one assailant unconscious with a strike of her keys to the back of the attacker's head before the victim struck the second assailant with her baton. The women then called the Police and both suspects were apprehended. They are now in custody. If anyone witnessed any part of this crime or has any other information, they are encouraged to come forward and report to the Police immediately."

I stare at the screen in shock as a video camera follows Samantha Mulholland and my sister Katrina to Detective Beckett's car.

I see both women talking in the back seat as he drives them off. No damn way. I am not seeing this.

Katrina....and Samantha.

I can't sit still. I spring across the room, snatch my keys, and race downstairs, but I have to call Eddie to take me to the Police station.

He's already kicking back in his quarters downstairs from my apartment. It takes him a while to get his pants on and bring the car around.

He drops me off in front of the Police station and I tell him to drive around the block. I half-dread what I'll find once I get inside.

My heart won't stop racing. Katrina....and Samantha. The Fates must have brought them together....but why....and how?

The two sides of my world are colliding in the biggest possible way. Taking Samantha to meet my mom was one thing. This is on a whole new level.

Which one of them was the victim and which one was the super-hero who saved the day? I can't imagine.

I just pray to Almighty God that Samantha didn't get attacked again. She's been doing so good lately. I really thought she was coming out of this. I hope this didn't set her back again.

I walk into the Police station and immediately spot them sitting in the waiting room chairs. They sit side by side with their heads together. They hold a rapid, whispered conversation.

They're so riveted to each other that they don't see me. I stand across the room watching them. What are they talking about? Is Samantha telling Katrina how she knows me? That would be the icing on the damn cake.

I take a few steps into the waiting room. It isn't as packed with the walking dead as it was last time.

I halt halfway across the room. They still don't see me. Katrina laughs at something Samantha says and she lights up, too. These two—they were made for each other.

Seeing them together does something to me. I might have been okay with nothing happening between me and Samantha, but that was before. I'm not okay with it now.

This is meant to be—this right here. She belongs in my life. I know it now. I just have to win her back. I don't even know if I lost her or if she's already moved on.

Maybe she's strong enough now that she doesn't need me. How would I survive that?

I take a few more steps and Samantha looks up. Her eyes stab into my guts. She's still there. She still wants me. She's still waiting for me even if she doesn't know it.

"Lane!" she exclaims and Katrina spins around.

"Lane!" Katrina exclaims and they both stand up.

I look back and forth between them. I don't know which of them to talk to first. I don't want either of them to think I care more about the other.

Fortunately, Katrina saves the day by hugging me. That seems to set the avalanche in motion and I wind up hugging Samantha, too. "Are you two okay?" I ask. "I just saw the story on the news. Did either of you get hurt?"

"We're both okay," Samantha replies. "I got there before the guys did anything."

"She was a rock star," Katrina gushes. "I thought I was done for until she showed up."

I raise my eyebrows at Samantha. "You? You're the new dark avenger?"

She bursts into giggles, but just then, Detective Beckett comes out of the back. "Hello there, Mr. Prince. I was wondering when you'd make your appearance."

"This is my sister, Katrina. I just saw the story on the news."

"I gathered that much. I was just about to drive these two ladies back to their cars."

"I'll take them," I offer. "My car is right outside."

He nods. "Sounds good. You two ladies have a better evening than it has been. You both have my card. I'll be in touch if we need any further information."

"Thank you, Detective," Samantha tells him.

He smiles and leaves. That leaves me with the two super-heroines.

I look back and forth between them again. "So which one of you wants to explain yourselves first?"

Samantha giggles again. "You already saw it on the news, right? What else is there to explain?"

"Nothing, I guess. Come on. You two are late for bed."

I lead the way outside just as Eddie pulls up to the curb. Samantha and Katrina jabber the whole way out of the station.

"The guy with the gun had a tattoo on his neck. Did you see that?" Katrina asks. "I think he might be Russian bratva."

"Really?" Samantha asks. "How do you know? Did you recognize it? Have you had cases with them before?"

"I haven't, but one of our partners actually represented one of them in a legal dispute with another bratva. We had these big, beefy, tattooed Russian bruisers coming and going in and out of the firm all day long. I got to see more of them than I wanted to see."

"Wow, my job seems so tame by comparison," Samantha exclaims.

"Sometimes you really would rather have tame, wouldn't you?" Katrina laughs.

Neither of them seems to notice when I open the door for them to get into the limo.

They sit together on one seat talking their heads off. I sit on the other seat listening.

"Tell me about some of your other cases," Samantha tells Katrina. "It sounds so interesting."

"That was a unique case. Most of being a lawyer is sitting around in the library. I'm sure being a captain of industry like you are is much more interesting."

Samantha snorts. "I'm the CFO. My job is spreadsheets. My job doesn't get interesting."

"Come on," Katina chides. "You were just telling me earlier that you averted a major disaster by funding an alternate server to keep the whole company going. That sounds exciting."

"It was exciting in a I-pushed-a-button-on-my-mouse kind of way," Samantha replies.

Katrina explodes with laughter and they launch into another exchange about some aspect of Samantha's role at Titanium.

I look back and forth between the two of them. Neither of them asks me a single goddamn thing. Should I be worried about this?

I don't say a word all the way back to Samantha's building. "We're here, Mr. Prince," Eddie tells me through the window.

Samantha looks outside. "I need to go back to the parking lot to get my car." She shoots me the wickedest, most devilish grin I've ever seen. That grin gives me a stomach load of butterflies. "We wouldn't want anyone to steal our secret stash, would we?"

"What secret stash?" Katrina asks.

"If I told you that, I'd have to kill you," Samantha replies and makes Katrina laugh again.

Samantha jumps a foot in the air again. Her eyes fly open and she points at Katrina. "Oh! I could tell you about that! You would find that interesting—almost as interesting as representing the Russian bratva." Her face falls and she glances at me. "Or maybe I shouldn't."

"Tell me what?" Katrina asks.

"Go ahead and tell her," I interject for the first time. "We need something to talk about on our way back to the parking lot. No one here will spill Titanium Finance's company secrets."

I give Eddie directions back to the parking lot while Samantha launches into the whole story about the servers going down, us switching Titanium to the Apico U-Tech server, and then the same thing happening to our server.

She talks at length about the people in the IT department she likes as the prime suspects for our saboteur.

I fall silent again while she and Katrina yap away like they've known each other all their lives. I really don't want to find out what happens when we get to the parking lot.

Eddie pulls in. It's almost midnight, so Katrina's and Samantha's cars are the only ones still here.

I get out first and hold the door open while the two women get out. Silence falls between the three of us as we come face to face with each other.

I have no flippin' clue what to say to either of them. How much does Katrina know about my checkered history with Samantha? I hate to think.

Katrina will be the first to find out if it works out between me and Samantha. Am I really thinking that—that things might work out between me and Samantha?

If she's out there rescuing random strangers from getting mugged, then she's a lot stronger than I thought—a lot stronger than she was.

Tonight certainly boosted her confidence. She smiles more than I've ever seen. I never would have pictured her talking away to someone she just met like she talks to Katrina.

Tonight must have bonded them. I should be happy about that. I should be happy that they like each other and they're already making friends. I am happy about it. I just don't know what to do with myself.

Katrina rocks on her heels grinning like a fool. "So….."

Samantha squeezes my arm. "I should probably get the evidence off the street. I'll see you tomorrow, okay?"

I give her quick hug. "Good night. I'll see you tomorrow."

She beams at me, gets in her car, and drives away. She smiles at us and waves as she pulls out into traffic.

Now I'm alone with my sister. I turn back to find her still grinning at me.

"So......how much did she tell you?" I ask.

"She told me everything." Now it's Katrina's turn to squeeze my arm. "You're a hero. I'm proud of you." She leaps forward and gives me a quick hug. "She's really sweet. I'm happy for you."

She goes to her car, gets in, and drives off into the night. So she knows everything. At least I don't have to explain it. I would hate that.

# Chapter 30:
# Samantha

I ride down the elevator with Bradley, Spencer, Cesar, and our new CMO, Austin Reinhart. He's a young, burly guy with wild, curly blonde hair and a big, infectious personality.

He gets along with everyone so he's perfect for marketing. He's been rising through the ranks at Titanium Finance for years, so he was our top pick to replace Reese.

All five of us stop dead in our tracks when we leave the building and find a magnificent stretch limo waiting for us outside.

"Whoa!" Austin breathes. "We are NOT riding upstate in *that.*"

The driver gets out and opens the back door for us.

"It looks like we are," I reply.

"Mr. Prince sent me over to take you upstate," the driver tells us. "All your luggage is already on the way up to the resort. Are you ready to go?"

I thank him and get in. All this riding around in a limo with Lane has prepared me for this. The four guys take longer to work up the courage to get in.

We find a small fridge full of drinks and a huge basket of snacks waiting for us inside. The guys take in every detail and the limo pulls away from the curb.

"Have you ever been to Black Oak Estates, Samantha?" Austin asks me.

"We've been there four times," I reply. "Titanium sends a team up there every two years to network and pitch new investors and high-ticket clients. So we've been planning this convention for two years."

"And we'll start planning the next one as soon as we get back," Cesar adds. "This is your big chance to shine, Austin. You can knock everyone's socks off with your winning personality."

He lets out his big, rolling laugh. "Just don't tell me what any of the clients' net worths are. I'm not used to this."

I find myself grinning at him. "Just wait 'til you see the resort. It's time you moved up in the world."

He shakes his head, but he's more interested in the snacks. He has to try hard to be polite and share them with the rest of us.

The novelty of riding in a limo wears off pretty soon and we all just sit around for the rest of the four-hour trip north to Upstate New York.

The limo finally pulls into a long, curving wooded driveway. It opens into sprawling, rolling fields surrounded by dense, dark woods.

We stop outside a gargantuan five-story building perched at the edge of a glassy lake stretching into the sunset.

"Wow," Austin breathes.

I pat him on the shoulder. "Your suite overlooks the lake. You can gaze at it all you want."

"When you aren't talking to clients," Cesar corrects. "Come on, big guy. Let's go check in."

We walk into a towering lobby with massive timber beams rising to a cathedral ceiling set with skylight windows.

A giant fireplace occupies the center of the lobby with flames cracking around a stack of logs. The fire fills the lobby with warm, inviting ambiance.

Austin stares at everything while Bradley, Cesar, Spencer, and I check in. Then I make Austin check in.

"The lounge is over there." I point past the fireplace to another luxurious sitting area overlooking the lake and an expansive deck.

A disappearing swimming pool, hot tub, and tennis court extend out to the edge of the lake and lead the viewer's eye to the sinking pastel colors of the setting sun.

I show Austin where the dining room and bar are and then where our rooms are. "And this is the convention hall." I lead him into a converted ballroom the size of a gymnasium. "This is where everyone will gather to network and see and discuss each other's offerings."

"Where is everyone?" he asks. "I thought the other attendees were coming tonight just like we are. I thought they'd meet us here."

"They're already here. I saw a few of them in the bar and the lounge. I'm going to my room for a few minutes. I'll meet you back here and introduce you to some of them."

I go to my room. My luggage is already there, including my laptop and the display I'll use at the convention to talk about Titanium Finance's offerings and investment opportunities.

My room is a giant open square with a huge bed in one corner, a magnificent bathroom with a walk-in wet-floor shower, a deep modern square tub, its own sauna, and a second tub for cold plunges.

There's also another indoor hot tub near the sliding nested glass doors leading out to the deck. This would be the most romantic room to share with someone special if I only had someone to share it with.

I leave the cover on the hot tub. I can use the tub in the bathroom if I really need to.

I stand at the windows and gaze out at the lake. I can finally relax after weeks of work getting ready for this convention—not to mention tracking down our mystery saboteur.

Fortunately, it was no one important to the company's long-term survival. It turned out to be a young computer programmer named Rex Martin. He only worked for Titanium for five weeks. For some reason, he got some crazy idea about ruining Apico by spoiling the takeover.

Now he's in jail after pleading guilty to willful destruction of property, fraud, and a raft of other charges.

Our SEC audit came back clean, so I can finally enjoy myself here away from the hustle and bustle of New York. This convention has always been a happy, easy, relaxing time for me—one of the highlights of my work year.

I go back to the lobby and meet up with the guys. Bradley is already talking to four other convention regulars and Austin is up to his neck making another three laugh. The grass doesn't grow under that guy's feet.

I go to the bar to get myself a drink and find myself standing next to Lane Prince. "What are you doing here?" I exclaim. "I didn't know you were coming."

"I wasn't planning to. I just came to see how things were going with you five."

"We haven't even started the convention yet. Things aren't going anywhere with us."

He only smiles at me. This is one of the few times he's seen me wearing anything other than a business suit.

I'm wearing a casual knee-length skirt and a beige linen blazer over a white T-shirt. I feel shorter in flat white sneakers instead of heels.

He seems so much taller like this. He has to look down at me. It makes him seem stronger, more powerful, and more commanding, but somehow kinder and even more protective than usual.

"It's good to see you letting your hair down," he tells me. "I hoped getting you out of town would take the pressure off you."

"I'm glad I got all those other projects off my shoulders before I came here. Now I don't have to worry about anything but enjoying the convention."

The bartender brings my drink and we turn around to watch the other attendees. "Come sit down and talk to me," he tells me. "I never get to see you anymore."

"We see each other every day."

"That's just business. I want to talk to you in a purely social setting."

"This is business, too, remember?"

He sits down on one of the couches in the lounge. This one has another enormous fireplace.

I sit down next to him, and just because this is so casual, I wind up tucking one leg under me.

"So tell me about this convention," he begins. "I don't know anything about it. I've never been here before. You have."

"It's really more a family atmosphere. Everyone who comes here on a regular basis already knows everyone else who comes here on a regular basis."

"What's the point of pitching anybody if they already know everything about you?"

I find myself laughing. "A lot can change in two years. Titanium is owned by another company now. Derek always came with us before. He isn't here anymore. You are."

His eyes take on an even deeper level of intensity. "Have dinner with me tonight."

I raise one eyebrow. "Is that a good idea?"

"Have dinner with me in a strictly professional capacity."

I guffaw in his face and roll my eyes. "Please."

"It's just dinner. You would be eating dinner in the dining room over there even if I wasn't here."

"I would be eating with the guys. We really would be talking about the company. We wouldn't be gazing longingly into each other's eyes and thinking about....other stuff."

Now it's his turn to laugh. "Okay, you got me. If that's the way you feel, you can tell them that I'm here to give you a performance evaluation and that's why we need a table to ourselves."

I open my mouth to say something and change my mind.

"What?" he asks.

"I was just going to suggest something, but maybe that's not such a good idea, either."

"What is it?"

"Well.....this resort offers dinner on the deck. We could eat out there.....alone."

His eyebrows shoot up. "That sounds great."

I turn bright red and look away. "I'm going to regret this."

"Do I have to arrange it with the concierge or something?"

I nod. "Yep."

"I'll do go that now. So....what time?"

"How about eight? The guys will be in the dining room then."

"Okay." He shoots me a smirk. "See you then."

He leaves for the lobby and I wilt on the couch. What in the world am I thinking? This can only end one way, but it sure looks like we're going there.

# Chapter 31: Lane

I make sure to dress up in my best suit to have dinner with Samantha. I can't believe my luck that she actually suggested we eat alone on the deck. This should be perfect—perfectly romantic.

I've been racking my brain to come up with a way to restart things with her.

The hard part is that things are going so well at work. I don't want to mess that up.

Talking to her is so effortless. It's just easier to keep things the way they are.

I don't want to keep things the way they are—not after what I saw when she met Katrina. I want this. I just don't know how to get it.

Tonight is the first step.

I stop by her room and knock on the door at thirty seconds before eight. She answers wearing a painted-on black evening dress that plunges between her luscious, tempting cleavage.

Just in case I forgot to look down there, she also wears a drooping gold chain knotted below her collarbones. The long end trails between her breasts and rides there on two heavenly pillows pushed up on either side by her strapless shelf bra.

The dress's spaghetti straps leave her arms and shoulders bare—perfect for kissing and sinking my teeth into. This is going to be the hardest dinner of my life.

She wears her hair swept up in a coil on the back of her hair with two curling locks framing her face. Long, gold, dangling chain earrings sway against her neck. That neck!

A gold chain bracelet surrounds her delicate wrist and she's wearing heels again—high heels with black pantyhose.

My jaw drops when I see her. I really want to tackle her back into that room and never let her leave. I never want to let any other man see her like this.

That's what this dinner is all about. It's about me making my move to get her into my life as something other than an exec in one of my companies. I have to get through this dinner to make that happen—and I don't even know if she wants it to happen.

She does want it to happen. That's what this dress means. She dressed up for me. She made herself so stunningly attractive that I would never be able to resist her. She wants this. She wants it as much as I do.

I hold out my arm and she beams at me with those glowing warm brown eyes of hers. "Hi," she murmurs.

"Show me where we're supposed to go."

She glides down the corridor to its far end. She doesn't go back through the lobby. She passes through a side door leading onto the deck.

We find a private table set with candles. We're the only people out here. Almost everyone else at the convention is male, so they don't have dates.

A waiter in a tuxedo pulls out her chair for her and we sit down. He pours the wine I ordered and then leaves us alone.

I allow my eyes to dip back to her body. Her clothes leave absolutely nothing to the imagination—and yet they leave everything to the imagination. "That is not what I call professional attire," I tease.

She laughs. "You didn't actually expect me to believe this was going to be a professional dinner, did you?"

"I guess not."

"Did you come up here just to see me?" she asks. "Tell the truth."

I can't even blush at the way she's looking at me. She looks absolutely mouth-watering. "I didn't, but I would have if I'd known I was going to see you like *that.*"

She does blush. Holy smokes, she's gorgeous!

"So what did you want to talk to me about in a professional capacity?" she asks.

"This." I stretch my hand across the table. "I don't want to talk about us in a professional capacity. Or I guess it would be more accurate to say that I want to talk about us in a *not* professional capacity. Or rather I don't want us to be talked about in a professional capacity."

She laughs. Her whole expression lights up like that was the best, funniest, most excellent thing I could have said. If my wit charms her that much, maybe I actually stand a chance here.

I glance down at my hand. It still lies facing palm up on the tablecloth right in front of her. She doesn't take it. Will she?

"I thought we were both clear that we weren't going to do anything to jeopardize our working relationship," she replies. "What happened to that?"

I can't help letting my hungry eyes trail down to her neck, her cleavage, and her bare shoulders. "I'm pretty sure it already has been jeopardized."

"Did my dress jeopardize it or was it something else?"

Now it's my turn to laugh. "The dress definitely drove the nail into the coffin, but I would say it was everything else. It seems like everything jeopardizes our working relationship including our working relationship. It doesn't seem like we do anything in a professional capacity anymore. Don't you think?" I hesitate and then blurt out, "Are you gonna hold my hand or just leave me hanging here?"

She bursts into another blushing smile and places her hand in mine. Her slender fingers feel magical.

I want to crawl my hand up my arm to the rest of her, but I can wait. I've waited this long. Why rush it when this is so good?

"You still haven't solved the fundamental problem of you being my boss and me being your subordinate," she points out.

"But we both want to. We both want this. We both admit we want more than just a working relationship—and it seems like we already have one. You're much more than an employee to me and I know I'm much more than a boss to you. We wouldn't be sitting here right now if we were."

"I agree the relationship evolved over time, but how do you plan to overcome that problem? It doesn't seem like we can go forward with anything until we solve it. We could stay exactly the way we are now without developing it any further. Things are pretty good the way they are now...."

"No," I tell her. "I don't want things to stay the way they are now. I want them to develop. We've been like this for too long already."

"What do you propose, then? How do you suggest we develop? I don't see that it's possible when we have this professional obligation standing in our way."

I shrug that off. "If it worked out between us, I could make you joint CEO of Titanium—or just CEO of Titanium. Then we would be equally ranked and both subordinate to the Apico Acquisitions

Board of Directors. Then I wouldn't be your boss and you wouldn't be my subordinate anymore."

Her jaw drops and her smile drains away. "You couldn't do that!"

"Why not?"

"Because! We haven't even dated! We aren't even in a relationship. You're talking about.....you're talking about......."

I squeeze her hand. "I'm serious about this. I want this to develop and I want it to develop seriously. I want us to go all the way if we can. How will we know if we don't at least try it?"

She gapes at me with her mouth open. "You're serious!"

"Absolutely. Tell me this. Do you have any objection to us getting serious with each other—apart from the whole boss-employee thing? If I wasn't your boss and we weren't working together, would you have any objection to getting involved with me?"

"Of course not!" she exclaims. "But that doesn't mean anything. We *are* boss and employee."

"But that could change. We could come up with some other solution where one of us stopped being the boss and one of us stopped being the employee. Then there would be no problem. Am I right?"

She blinks at me in speechless shock.

"Hello?" I ask. "Do you have any argument against that?"

"I just....." She gulps and takes a slug from her water glass. "I had no idea you were so serious about us."

"Well, I am."

Her eyes dart toward the resort building and her expression changes again. "I.....I don't know if I can. I mean....I don't want to do something unethical by sleeping with my boss at a business convention. It seems so......so low."

I squeeze her hand and I don't let go. I massage her knuckles just enough to get her attention back on me. "Then don't sleep with me.

Let's just agree that we're doing this. We'll move forward and see where it goes. We don't have to sleep together."

"You mean....we don't have to sleep together right now....but we will. We will at some time in the future."

I can't help but lower my eyes and blush. "I suppose that's what we would be agreeing to—that it would lead to that."

She opens her mouth to say something else, but just then, our server comes out with our food. Our hands separate, but starting our meal gives me plenty of time to feast my eyes on her sitting across the table from me.

We're doing this. I'm going to have this woman if it's the last thing I ever do. Nothing will ever stop me. She's too priceless. I can't let her slip away.

I don't bring it up again during dinner. I turn the conversation to other things and so does she.

"How's Katrina doing?" she asks me. "I haven't heard from her."

"I'm surprised. I thought you two would become besties after your shared adventure."

She laughs. "We did hit it off, didn't we? I guess we've both been busy."

"She was really impressed by you.....and so was I. When I said you needed to get stronger, I didn't mean like that."

She beams at me. "Thanks. I'm proud of the way I handled it."

I take a minute to let that sink in. She did more than handle it and she's more than strong enough for a relationship now.

She's the one who keeps pointing out all the reasons we shouldn't get into a relationship. She's strong enough now. She doesn't need me anymore.

Knowing that somehow makes her a thousand times more attractive. She's an independent woman with her own career, her own money, and her own life.

She does still need me, though. She needs me for something more than that—something more than protecting her from all the monsters out there.

The server takes our dishes away and we sit holding hands, sipping our wine, and gazing out at the lake—or pretending to gaze out at the lake. I spend pretty much the whole time gazing at her.

My attention doesn't make her uncomfortable, though. It doesn't bother her anymore that we're sitting here in such a romantic setting, holding hands, drinking wine, and talking about having a serious relationship.

Oh, what the hell am I saying? We're already in a serious relationship. I can't imagine anything more serious than this.

She's already such a big part of my life. She's the only woman in my life. Every other woman fades into the past. They all seem like I was just wasting my time with them until I found her.

After way too long of just sitting here murmuring to each other about whatever random shit happens to pass through our minds, a chilly breeze blows over the lake. She shivers.

"Would you like to go inside and sit by the fire?" I ask.

"I should probably call it a night. I have to be ready for the convention tomorrow—and I would have to change if I went anywhere the guys might see me."

I nod. Of course.

I stand up and use her hand to help her stand up—like she needs my help.

She follows my direction perfectly. She doesn't let go of my hand on our way inside. "I had a nice time tonight. Thank you."

I pull her hand through my arm and press it into my sleeve. I really want to kiss her right now, but I settle for just bending close to her. "I would do it every night. You know that."

She blushes and looks away. "Neither of us would get any sleep if we did that."

"Eventually we would get exhausted enough to pass out."

She laughs. "How long are you staying at the convention?"

"I'll definitely stay tomorrow just to see how it all works and talk to anyone who needs talking to. I don't know about after that."

We stop in front of her room. Now I can turn to look down at her. She radiates beauty, grace, confidence, and charm. Every minute in her presence is an exquisite pleasure—almost as much of a pleasure as her body itself.

Time stands still when I cup her chin in one hand and lift those sweet lips to mine. I kiss her as deeply as I want. I don't have to hide how I feel about her.

We aren't colleagues or co-workers or any other professional anything anymore. This is way more and now we both know it. We're doing this no matter what it takes.

She glides both her satin arms around my neck and sinks into that kiss. I only hope that kiss goes on and on forever and never ends.

# Chapter 32: Samantha

Lane straightens up and gazes down with me in pure blissful happiness. The glow in his eyes....I can only call it love.

I guess I knew before tonight that he loved me—and I love him. We've never said it, but now he's finally admitted that he wants something serious.

I guess I always wanted something serious, too. I just never believed it was possible.

I still don't. I still don't see how it would work, but I guess we just have to try it and find out.

He squeezes my hand once and lets his fingertips trail down my cheek. "Good night," he whispers and backs away to leave me at my hotel room for the night.

"Good night," I murmur back. "Thank you again for the wonderful dinner."

He smiles, nods, and starts to pull away. He dives back in for one last quick kiss and takes a step back. Our hands slip out of each other.

Our hands come within inches of breaking contact before he spins around, grabs me, and sweeps me off my feet kissing me fast and hard. His arms clamp around my body.

I gasp for breath trying to keep up with these ravaging kisses. One of his hands sweeps up my back to my neck.

That feeling of his fingers gripping the back of my neck—it shocks me into gasping again. He wants it. He wants it right now—not sometime in the future.

He steps forward and pins me against the door of my room. His weight falls against me and I feel him getting hard under his clothes.

He won't stop devouring my mouth. His tongue blasts into mine and he snatches the breath from my lungs. I can't help but moan.

He eases his weight off just enough to lower my feet to the ground, but he doesn't back off. His hands cover every inch of me from my shoulders and arms, down my back, around my waist, and up to my breasts.

This dress leaves so little between me and his overpowering hands. Every touch sets my skin on fire. My body trembles at the intensity of his desire. His mouth consumes me to my core.

He squeezes one of my breasts and that one act blasts him into a new frenzy of rabid passion. He grabs me again, scoops me up, and supports me with one arm under my ass.

He holds me off the ground where he can bury his face in my cleavage. His hot breath sizzles on my skin. He leaves scorching hot kisses and bites back and forth from one breast to the other.

He keeps crawling lower and nudges his way right inside my bra. He doesn't let up until he finds my nipple and inhales it into his mouth.

I gasp again and that gasp turns into a moan. I'm going to start screaming any second now.

Then the whole resort will know what's going on, but in some way I can't explain, it really does make it hotter this way.

I'm doing it with him right here—right against the door of my hotel room. My colleagues and fellow execs are right down the hall.

This wasn't how I planned to proceed with him, but then again, nothing is.

We both want it, so why do we keep holding ourselves back? Why do I keep holding myself back?

I want him. Holy Christ, do I want him!

My body detonates in an unholy storm of desire for him. I've been hiding this even from myself.

All these weeks we've been working together kept it buried, but it started even before that.

Depending on him, needing him, making myself vulnerable to him, and leaning on him—all those things actually kept me from him. They stopped me from really meeting him the way I need to—like this.

I couldn't unleash this passion before. I needed him too much.

Now nothing can stop me. He sets me down and leans his weight against me kissing me just as deep. He doesn't try to stop me from feeling how throbbing hard he is. He wants me to feel it. He wants me to know how much he wants to ravage me.

I scramble to get my room key out of my handbag in between kisses. He doesn't make it easy. He might even be trying to make it harder by mauling my mouth so I can't see what I'm doing.

His hands drive me out of my mind by groping my breasts and crushing my ass through my dress. He grabs me behind my thighs and pumps into me in lifting motions that stop just short of lifting my feet and legs off the ground.

Those movements match exactly how he plans to pump into me just as soon as he gets his hands on me—just as soon as I can get this damn door open.

I finally get my key and tear away from him to turn around and unlock the door, but he attacks me from behind. Now he can see that

I'm trying to get the room open so we can go inside. We both know what will happen in there.

I fumble with the key as his weight crushes me from behind. I can't breathe.

He jams both hands down my thighs from the front, rakes his fingernails up my legs, and then both his hands slide inward to the center.

He scoops up between my legs and that pressure skyrockets me into a dizzy trance of pleasure and desire. His hard prick digs into my ass each time he pumps against me.

His hot mouth pants in my ear and then his blistering lips drag down my neck to my bare shoulder.

I spasm at the intensity of his teeth sinking into my shoulder. He gnaws across my back, up the back of my neck, and around to my other shoulder while he keeps driving into my ass from behind.

I moan every time he plows into me. I feel him trying to take me, but my flimsy dress stops him. He lets it stop him.

He keeps scooping his hands up between my legs, pulling my thighs apart just enough to spiral me out of this world, and drilling into me from behind exactly the way he's going to when he gets me inside this room.

A door slams down the hall somewhere. Are the rest of the Titanium execs watching us right now? How long will it take for one of them to come around that corner and see us?

I try one last time to get the key into the hole. The lock pops.

Lane lunges for the handle, pushes it down, and our combined weight stumbles into the room.

He spins me backward and pushes me face down against the wall. He's on top of me in an instant, shoves into me from behind one more time, and pulls away just as fast.

He flips me around to face, wraps one arm around my waist, and pulls me toward the bed.

His eyes gleam in the light coming from outside. There is no other light in this room except the starlight shining off his eyes.

He slows down now that we're actually in this room alone together. He keeps kissing me, but he does it softly, passionately, gently as he backs toward the bed.

He sits down on it and now I know he can take all the time he wants. He draws me between his knees and looks up at me from below while we kiss.

I find myself stroking his cheeks and forehead to push his hair back. He's all I've ever wanted.

I can forget in this room that I work for him—that I really am sleeping with the boss at an out-of-town convention the way I always said I didn't want to.

No part of his eyes or face tells me he's thinking about that, either. This is so much bigger than that.

He drags his sultry fingertips down my dress, down my stomach, down my hips, down my thighs, and past my knees.

He very slowly lifts the dress. Its satin fabric shimmers on my skin as he glides it up and pushes it over my head.

He doesn't even look at my body when he takes it off. His eyes remained locked on me forever while he unclips my bra and slides my panties down.

Standing naked in front of him completes something that was broken before. How can something be so meant to be? How can it make so much sense?

This has been coming for a long time. Doing it with him before meant nothing. This is when it really happens—right now.

He won't let go of my eyes while he pulls off his jacket and shirt. He throws them away and keeps staring deep into my soul while he tears his fly open and kicks off his pants.

Of course we have to be naked together. How else would we be? We belong like this.

Does he see the happiness radiating out of my eyes? Does he see the cosmic perfection of me just finally accepting that we're supposed to be this way?

He wraps his arms around my waist and his heat blasts me apart. He pulls me down to straddle his lap and our bodies lock together like they were made this way—because they were.

Everything fits from our lips to our arms wrapped around each other to my muscles clasping him deep inside me to our eyes swimming in this endless cosmos of each other.

His warm hand drags up my back to my neck again. My hair comes loose and spills over my face and his. My hair hides us both in this little world where nothing exists but us.

I could stay like this forever. I *will* stay like this forever. I don't see how this can ever end.

Then he starts pumping into me. His shaft swells with every stroke and bursts me at the seams. I gasp and those tortured moans rise to groans of excruciating passion.

"Yes!" he whispers in my ear. "Yes, baby! Come on. That's right. That's so good. Come on."

I whimper as the first torturous wave breaks through me and over me. It destroys the walls holding me in. I can't contain all this energy building inside me. I can't contain myself.

He tightens his grip around my body. His fingers clamp a little tighter on the back of my neck.

My body succumbs to his direction as he pulls me into each commanding thrust. Each deep, thumping beat explodes me to smithereens.

I hear myself screaming in rapture. His fingers close the rest of the way into a fist in my hair. His biceps strain from the effort of holding me in position. He moves me against him faster and deeper and stronger. I can't resist where he's taking me.

He pulls my head back and blasting hot kisses burst down my neck to my chest, across my shoulders, and down to my breasts.

This is all part of it. This is all part of my surrender to the inevitable. He has me now. Who knows where it will end?

His other hand migrates down to the small curve of my back. That hand guides me down on him as my deepest essence floods over his rock-solid shaft.

He leans a little farther back to get a better angle. He arches upward and pulls me down on top of him.

As soon as I get into that position, some animal ruptures out of me and I pounce on him. I attack him much harder than he's been holding me until now.

I bite down on his mouth and hurl myself onto his greedy spike for all I'm worth. I brace my arms and legs and slam backward to drive him in even harder. Nothing he does will ever be hard enough. I need all of him. I need him as deep inside me as I can get him.

I can't even kiss him anymore. I husk in grunting, rutting passion taking him all the way, but he only contracts his muscles to drill me just as hard.

He snarls at me with every thrust. His lip curls back and he bares his teeth. He holds onto my hair. I sense him holding me the way the carjacker did, but this is nothing like that. This isn't even on the same planet as that.

Lane seizes one of my breasts in a crushing grip. I feel him pinching my nipples and then squeezing my ass and thighs.

I want to be wild like this. I want to attack him and take what I want even though I know he wants it, too.

"Fuck, yes, baby!" he growls. "Come on! Give it to me!"

Those words send me crashing over the edge. I can't stop. I slam back on him and the dam breaks. I collapse face down on his chest screaming in broken ecstasy. I can't stop driving down on him again and again. I can never stop.

His breath floats into my ear and hair. "That's right," he whispers. "That's right. You're all mine, aren't you? Yeah. That's so good."

The epic surges of power charging through me slow down eventually, but I still don't stop stroking on him. My channel becomes ultra-sensitive with quivering spasms racing upward and into my deepest being.

I slow down a little more trying to cope with the sheer electric thrills of those sensations.

As soon as I start to slow, Lane picks up the pace. He consolidates his grip and pumps into me from below. I scream again trying to survive all this, but he's moving too fast to stop.

He rolls me over onto my back, pivots onto his knees between my legs, and drives up into me while he inhales every brutal kiss from my lips.

He only keeps me like that for a second before he slides out and uses one of my legs to roll me onto my stomach.

I think he's going to slam into me from behind, but he doesn't do that. He props one knee forward so he can pump into me from the side.....and then he rolls onto his side to pull me against him.

His arms wrap around me and he draws me against his body—where I belong. He buries his face in the back of my neck and every part of his warm, beautiful body touches every part of mine from our heads down to our knees.

He keeps moving inside me with one leg raised to give himself enough room. That undulating wave of bliss surrounds me in rapture. Nothing can ever be wrong because now I'm in his arms where I should have been all along.

# Chapter 33: Lane

Sunshine streaming through the window stabs me in the eyes. I squint....and see the lake outside Samantha's hotel room.

I collapse on the pillow. She lies asleep in my arms with her magnificent ass tucked against my hips. I have to seriously restrain myself to stop myself from touching her right now.

I start to get hard when I think about clasping her breasts from behind, but right then, I hear my phone buzzing down on the floor. It's in my jacket pocket where I left it last night.

I look over at it and Samantha stirs in my arms. She groans once and that groan turns into a whimper.

That sound shoots straight to my guts. God, I want to make her whimper like that all the time. Am I really thinking that? Am I thinking I want her all the time?

Hell yes. I'm doing a hell of a lot more than thinking it. I'm planning it and talking to her about it.

I'm gonna make this happen. I never let a little thing like circumstances hold me back from anything I wanted before. I won't let circumstances hold me back from this, either—not something as good as this. It's too good.

I heave out of bed just enough to grab my jacket, yank it toward me, and crash back on the pillow to check my phone. It's a notification from Ethan. I don't read anything beyond that. He can wait.

Samantha stretches and squirms, but she doesn't try to get out of my arms. She tries to scoot back against me and weasel her way back to where she was before.

Looking at my phone definitely shows me what time it is, though.

I wrap my body around hers and feel her melt. Holy shit. I have to have this woman. I have to have her in every possible way, every day, forever. I won't accept any other outcome.

I bury my face in her neck and she sucks her breath through her teeth. She arches her head back and stretches her neck under my mouth.

She twists in my arms trying to get me to touch her and hold her and fondle her the way I did last night. Jesus Christ, I love feeling her like this! I love feeling how much she wants me to own her.

My hands close on her breasts and that sweet, smoking-hot, pathetic little whimper lights me up all over again. I glide my hand down her stomach toward her thighs.

"It's six o'clock, baby," I whisper in her ear. "You have to be down on the convention floor in two hours, which means you need to take a shower, get dressed, and eat breakfast before then. You need to meet up with your guys and prepare—which means I need to be down on the convention floor in two hours."

She responds by grabbing my wrist and shoving my hand the rest of the way down between her legs. I can't keep my hands off her, but I have to be careful.

If I start something with her now, I could get caught here along with her. Then we'd both be late and the game would be up. The game might be up already.

I rub her swelling flesh, but I do it gently and I keep my hand on the outside—just enough to turn her on. Her heat dissolves in my arms and she moans a little louder. I have to stop this now before it goes any further.

I lean back, roll her toward me, and rotate onto my hands and knees above her. She's all messy with pillow creases on her face and her eyes still puffy with sleep.

I bend over her and kiss her long and deep. I want to fall into her arms and feel her wind her legs around me to pull me in, but that will have to wait for another day.

"I'll leave first," I whisper between kisses. "I'll go back to my room and we can go to breakfast separately. I'll see you on the convention floor. Okay?"

She doesn't answer except to keep kissing me. She really isn't making this easy.

I let my lips slip off her mouth.....and then I see her eyes. This woman is mine. I'll never let anyone else near her. I'll never let her look at anyone like that again—except maybe if she has my baby. I could live with that.

Right in that moment, I want to tell her I love her. The words come into my mind without me even trying. *I love you.*

I can only stand to tear myself away from her because I know I'll see her downstairs in a few minutes. I'll see her every day from now on in one capacity or another. Life would be intolerable without her.

I don't say that, though. I should, but this feeling inside me—those words don't do that feeling justice. The only words that do it justice are, *Marry me.*

I could live with that, too. I could do a hell of a lot more than live with it. I want it. I want to take her all the way.

I want everyone downstairs to know we're together for life. I want the whole damn world to know how much I love her, want her, need her, crave her, demand her.

I can't say any of that now. I settle for saying, "I'll see you down there," and I get out of bed.

She stays where she is while I get dressed. I just have to make myself presentable enough to get to my room so I can take a shower and change. I don't have to think about anything else.

She breaks the silence by asking, "Are you still planning to stay for the rest of the convention?"

"We'll see how it goes or if anything comes up in New York that I have to go back for," I reply over my shoulder and make another snap decision. "How about we have dinner again tonight—this time really in a professional capacity—like down in the dining room in our business suits where everyone can see us?"

She smirks at me. "That will throw them off our trail."

That smirk makes me grin back. I kiss her one more time, say, "See you down there," again, and slip out of the room.

I don't see anyone all the way back to my room. I strip, get in the shower, get dressed, and check to make sure no one can tell from the outside that I spent the night with her.

I wish they could. I wish they could see her essence branded into my skin. I wish they could see the surge of confidence it gives me to know that I can walk up to her, kiss her, and roll her in bed anytime I want to

.

I know that now. She feels the same way about me. She might not feel the same way about spending the rest of her life with me, but she wants us to work toward that.

Actually, she does feel the same way about spending the rest of her life with me. She might be holding back right now because we still work together, but we can fix that.

I make any last-minute adjustments to my suit and make sure my hair looks right before I leave my room.

I'm just putting my phone in my jacket pocket when Ethan walks up to me from farther down the corridor. "What are you doing here?" I ask. "You never said anything about coming to this convention."

"Where have you been?" he demands.

I do my best to play it off and act casual. "What are you talking about? I've been right here all night."

"I've been texting and calling you for hours trying to find you. I told you in a million texts that I was coming up here to check on the Titanium presentation. If you were here all night, you would have seen my texts."

"Well, I have been here all night, but I haven't stayed glued to my phone the whole time. I just got out of the shower. I must have missed it."

He narrows his eyes at me. Does he realize?

I have been here all night. I've just been in another room on the other side of the resort. I haven't lied to him—yet.

He tightens his lips. He definitely has something up his ass, either about me or something else. "I want to talk to you about the Titanium situation before the convention opens this morning."

"Can we talk on the way to breakfast?" I ask. "I'm really hungry."

He compresses his lips again and falls in next to me on our way down the hall.

"The rest of the board and I have a problem with Samantha running Titanium by herself," he begins.

"Are you sure it's the rest of the board and you or is it just you that has a problem with her running it by herself?" I ask over my shoulder. I should have known this would come back to haunt me.

"It doesn't matter because it's a problem. We need to seriously evaluate if she's qualified to make these decisions on her own."

"She isn't making them on her own and she isn't running Titanium by herself. She's running it with Bradley, Cesar, Spencer, and Austin. Are you seriously suggesting we replace all of them? We would wind up with exactly the same problem. We can't run Titanium from the Apico boardroom. Titanium needs its own executive team and we all agreed these people were the best for the job."

"You decided that," he counters. "We didn't."

I stop in my tracks and study him. What is this really about? Is this about Samantha—or Titanium?

The fact that he's questioning my judgment is bad enough. Now he's making this personal about Samantha. He doesn't say that, but I am definitely reading that vibe in his pitch.

"She's too unconventional to put in charge of the company," he goes on. "We need to hire our own man to take over as the new Titanium CEO. Then she can go back to being CFO and the rest of them can go back to being whatever they are. None of them is qualified to be that one number one person."

"Are you sure about that? Can you think of anyone in the whole industry better qualified than she is? I can't. I don't see any problem with her decisions."

"You have to admit you have a blind spot where she's concerned," he counters. "You wouldn't see any problem with anything she did no matter what it was."

# Chapter 34: Lane

I walk away from Ethan so he won't see me smirking. He got one thing right. I definitely have a blind spot where Samantha is concerned. I think everything she does is perfect.

The business side of my brain doesn't see anything wrong with what she does, either. That's the weird part. I know business. If she was too unconventional or whatever the hell he's saying about her, I would know it. I would see it.

I would never let her do anything to jeopardize my business. She never does. That's the thing. She does everything exceptionally well. I would pay a lot to get a CEO as good as she is in charge of Titanium.

I don't have to pay a lot because she's already there. She does the job better than anyone.

The numbers don't lie, either. Titanium's profits are up and so is the share price since she took over. The place runs better than when Derek was in charge.

I don't see how Ethan or anyone else on the Apico executive can have a problem with anything she does—unless it's personal.

That doesn't make sense, either. They were all thrilled to have her on the team when we first acquired the company. What changed?

Maybe they see me giving her special treatment—but it isn't like she doesn't earn it. I would treat her the same way even if I wasn't involved with her and planning to keep her as my own.

The thing is I did all this when we weren't involved. I put her in charge thinking nothing would ever happen between us—or prepared for nothing to happen between us.

I would have done everything the same way even if I'd never seen that carjacking, never helped her, never spent all that time in her apartment, never touched her like that, and never slept with her.

I can't explain any of that to Ethan, but the good news is I don't have to. I don't have to explain myself to him or anyone else.

He hustles after me yapping in my ear. "What are you going to do about this?"

"I'm going to eat breakfast and then I'm going to the convention. We can't do anything about it from here—and while we're at it, you're going to have to come up with something more compelling to show me that we really do need to do anything about this. You're going to have your work cut out for you if you want to convince me there is anything wrong with her work, her decision-making, or her leadership. Now, if you don't mind, I'm hungry. Was there anything else you wanted to talk to me about?"

He stops outside the dining room. Why isn't he eating breakfast?

He shuffles his feet in front of me and mumbles, I guess not." Is he squirming? Now I'm really curious why.

I walk away from him. Bradley, Cesar, Austin, and Spencer are already in there, so I sit down with them.

They laugh, joke, and shoot remarks back and forth about clients they've already secured even though the convention hasn't even started. They're all so much more relaxed here.

Did Apico do this? Did Apico cast a shadow over Titanium?

These people are only capable of this kind of enthusiasm when they get out of the office. I'm definitely under-utilizing them. I'll have to change that, but not the way Ethan says.

They make a big deal about me eating with them, and a few minutes later, Samantha shows up. She doesn't look happy.

"Is something wrong?" I ask her as professionally as I can.

"Ethan Rosch is here," she murmurs under her breath and her eyes dart sideways. "He just talked to me out in the hall." She opens her mouth to say something else, but she stops herself.

My blood starts to boil. He better not have gotten in her face about anything she's doing here.

I keep my tone flat. "What did he say?"

She opens her mouth and falters again. Whatever Ethan said must have been bad. "I don't think I should tell you here."

I stand up. I want to take her hand, but I can't do that in front of the guys.

I motion her back toward the lobby so I can confront her. "What did he say, Samantha?"

"He said....." She has to struggle over the words. "He said he would be watching us at the convention today. He said if he sees us do anything that violates Apico policy, he'll pull us all from the convention and send us back to New York right away."

I stiffen and do my best not to snarl at her. "You do exactly what you planned to do at the convention. Don't worry about him. I'll take care of him."

"Listen to me, Lane," she blurts out. "We can't do this with him hovering over our heads, breathing down our necks, and watching our every move. We're here to relax and so are all our clients. This looks incredibly bad for Apico. It doesn't make Titanium look bad because we already know these people. It makes Apico look terrible and now everyone knows that Apico owns Titanium. If these clients sense him stalking us down and scrutinizing every detail of our business, they'll just leave. They won't think less of us. They'll think less of Apico. Do you understand that?"

I clench my teeth holding back all the things I really want to say to her. "Yes, I understand that, sweetheart. I understand it perfectly well. Now go eat breakfast. I want you ready to rock and roll on the convention floor and you need food for that. Go in there and coordinate with your guys. I'll deal with Ethan."

"What are you going to do?"

"You don't worry about that. I promise he won't bother you today. You won't ever see his face. Now go on. Really. I mean it."

I push her back toward the dining room. I want to kiss her, but this is more important.

I watch her go inside and sit down next to Bradley. She still looks nervous, but she shakes it off so she can banter and joke with her team. That's good. She'll be fine today as long as she doesn't have anyone stressing her out.

Ethan makes it super easy for me to find him. He strolls right up to the dining room.

"Go back to New York, Ethan," I tell him.

He jumps out of his skin and spins around. "What?"

"I said go back to New York, Ethan. Get in your car and drive back to New York. There's nothing more you can do here."

He stiffens. "I'm afraid you have this all wrong....."

"No, you're the one who has it all wrong. I'm going to be at the convention today. If I see your face anywhere in the hall—at any time—even once—you're fired. Is that clear? You'll be out of Apico and on your ass. You can walk back to New York for all I care. Do NOT let me see you at the convention today. Don't let me see you talking to anybody. Don't let me see you watching from afar. Don't let me see that you exist. You can lock yourself in your room if you absolutely have to stay here, but you will NOT go onto the convention floor—and don't let me find out you were talking to any of the potential clients outside the convention, either. Are we clear? Did you understand all that?"

His features harden, but they also twitch back and forth between resolve, fury, and something else—something like fear. He knows exactly who he's dealing with.

I stay there just long enough to make sure he heard me and he understands. Then I walk back into the dining room and sit down with the others.

The only seat left is next to Samantha. How convenient.

I make a point of keeping the conversation light. I catch her giving me questioning looks, but I only smile at her.

I would rub her back to reassure her, but I hope I accomplish the same thing with my eyes. I can't have her worrying about anything while the convention is going on.

# Chapter 35:
# Samantha

I step into the convention hall and look around, but I don't see Ethan Rosch anywhere. His presence definitely throws a bucket of cold water over what should be a fun, relaxing time with my team and my potential clients.

I have to do this, though. I want to do it. I've been looking forward to this for two years. This is my moment—or it should be.

I walk into the hall and three young resort workers come over to me. "This is your table here, Ms. Mulholland. Can we help you set up? Do you need anything for your speech this afternoon?"

I smile at them. I know them all. They always help me every time I come here. "I have everything I need. Thank you for all your hard work. I just need to set up."

They go off to help the other presenters. Bradley shows up to help me arrange our display on the table.

We set up display boards, fliers, and brochures about our products. We include a bunch of new printed material about the Apico takeover and the new changes we're making to comply with Apico's policies.

Cesar and Spencer come in a minute later, but Austin gets waylaid by four clients he talked to last night. They all start laughing and living it up the way they were before. Austin is really coming into his own here.

The convention kicks off and all five of us get flooded by people talking to us about Titanium. Everyone wants to know about the Apico takeover, what we've been doing since, how we're doing things differently, and how things will change in the future.

I explain it all as calmly as I can. I see Lane wandering through the hall, but he always seems to be paying attention to everyone else. He doesn't come near the Titanium Finance table.

Halfway through the morning, Saul Gottlieb comes over to me. He's a billionaire trade tycoon with an international import company bringing in goods from markets all over the world.

He smiles at me. "Always a pleasure to see you here, Samantha."

I hug him. "Hey! You made it back. I thought you'd be jetting off to Mumbai or somewhere like that."

He laughs. "I just got back from Shanghai, actually." He turns to study my display. "Always a top-notch display and presentation from Titanium. I'm impressed."

I blush. "Don't be. I have a cast of thousands pulling my puppet strings from out of sight."

"Don't we all? I've been meaning to ask you about Derek Salazar's exit from the company."

I try not to bristle at the name. This is nothing I haven't been talking about all morning. "What would you like to know?"

"His exit seems to have turned much more hostile than I would have expected—no pun intended."

I don't smile. Derek's situation is nothing to joke about and Saul obviously isn't joking about it.

"I wish I could help you," I tell him. "I don't know anything about the circumstances of Derek's departure except that he just stopped showing up for work. He took the takeover pretty hard—as you can imagine. Lane Prince is right over there. You should ask him about it. I'm sure he knows more than I do."

"I was just wondering about the transition you made from CFO to CEO," Saul goes on. "How did it happen that you started running the company yourself in Derek's place?"

"I'm not CEO. I'm still officially CFO, so I'm no higher ranked than any of the other executives. I don't see my role as running the company and I definitely don't see myself taking Derek's place. No one can do that."

"But you must admit you're the one making most or all of the executive decisions. Is that correct?"

I shift my weight to my other foot. "I wouldn't say that."

He lays his hand on my arm and leans a little closer. "I don't mean to pry, my dear. I'm simply curious how it happened."

"It happened because, like I said, Derek just stopped showing up for work. He stopped answering messages from anyone. Important emails about an SEC audit were sitting unopened in his inbox, so his assistant and the other executives forwarded them to me in my role as CFO. I made decisions about that—and I also made decisions about the allocation of funds to deal with hardware malfunctions that were threatening our company. That's all I did. Then Apico asked me to step in and run the company with the rest of the executive team—but only because I understand the company's internal culture and staff better than they do. Lane Prince asked me to hire internally to replace our CMO—only because I knew the people better and I could do it quickly. That's all that happened. I definitely didn't replace Derek. No one could ever take his place. He was Titanium's north star for so lon g."

He smiles at me and his expression clears. "I see. Thank you for explaining it to me. I've been so worried about him lately."

"Who—Derek? Why are you worried about him?"

"He disappeared. He vanished out of New York. No one knows where he is or what happened to him. Some of us wanted to help him out—give him a hand up, as it were—help him get back on his feet. Now we can't find him and no one knows how to contact him."

I frown. "That's weird. I would have thought he'd turn to his friends for support."

"That's what we thought, but we can't support him if we can't find him." He squeezes my arm again and his smile radiates warmth. "It's so nice to hear someone speak highly of him. He's a good man and a good businessman even if he is under a cloud at the moment. It can happen to the best of us. It's no reflection on his abilities."

"Of course not. I always admired Derek. I gave him the best years of my working life and I would do it again. I really hope he gets back on his feet somehow....but maybe that's asking too much."

"Let's hope not."

He turns away with a satisfied smile and I see some other potential clients moving in to take his place. I know them from previous conventions. They're all as enthusiastic to talk to me as I am to talk to them.

One of them is Diego Espinosa, a European billionaire who made his money in international military contracts. I also spot Giovanni Nowaczyk, the entertainment tycoon. I know both of them and I've pitched to them before.

Both of them have expressed interest in investing in Titanium Finance and they both know Derek. It would be a feather in my cap if I could get even one of them to invest.

Before they can get near me, Ethan bursts out of nowhere and storms up to me. "You had no business talking to Mr. Gottlieb or anyone else about Apico taking over Titanium Finance or Derek Salazar's relationship with Apico."

I gasp at his audacity, especially since all the conference attendees can hear him. "What are you talking about?!" I counter. "Talking about Apico taking over Titanium Finance is what I'm here for. I couldn't pitch our company without talking about it."

"You've been stepping out of line ever since the takeover. You can't just run Titanium the way you see fit."

"That's what Lane told me to do. That's what the whole Apico board told me to do."

"That doesn't matter. You're in no position to discuss Derek Salazar or any other internal matter with anyone outside the company. All of that is proprietary company information. You could lose your position for broadcasting it all over the country."

"Proprietary!" I gasp. "Are you out of your mind? Are you actually suggesting I keep critical information on our financial position from potential investors and clients?"

"I'm talking about Apico, Samantha!" he snaps. "You aren't in any position to make executive decisions on behalf of Apico Acquisitions...."

"I'm not. I was talking about Titanium and my personal relationship with Derek Salazar who happens to be a mutual acquaintance of mine and Mr. Gottlieb's—and yes, it is necessary for our clients and potential investors to understand the nature of the takeover, Titanium's internal workings, and the company's financial health. It amazes me that you would actually consider concealing this information from any potential client or investor."

Someone calls out of the crowd, "You tell him, Samantha!" I recognize the voice, but I can't see anyone with Ethan in the way.

I become aware of people gathering around to listen. This is turning into a situation I never anticipated.

Ethan has his back to the room. He doesn't see all the investors and clients we're supposed to be pitching standing around listening to every damn word. Would he say these things if he realized they could hear him?

"You aren't authorized to discuss the takeover, Titanium's internal workings, or the company's financial health with anyone!" he snaps. "Just do your job and stick to the plan or you'll be....."

At that moment, without any warning, Lane materializes out of thin air, grabs Ethan's elbow, and drags him away. Lane steers Ethan out of sight.

I'm left standing there staring at thirty people—mostly men. I know all of them. They stare back at me with plenty of sympathy and righteous indignation that Ethan actually had the rudeness to bitch me out in front of the whole convention.

Diego Espinosa comes up to me and pats me on the shoulder. "Don't think anything of it, Samantha. Lane will handle this. None of us thinks any less of you for supporting Derek."

I look away, but I can't stop my cheeks from burning. "Thank you. I'm sorry you all had to hear that."

"We think more of you for supporting Derek," Giovanni tells me. "Whoever that asshole is sure is making Apico Acquisitions look bad."

"But that doesn't matter because you're the one running Titanium Finance, not him," Diego goes on. "If we invested in the company, we would be doing it because of you. We know you wouldn't withhold information from us."

"No, never. I would never do that.....but I don't know if I'll be running Titanium Finance for very much longer. If Ethan has his way, I might not have a job at all when this is over."

# Chapter 36: Lane

I pull Ethan into a side hall away from the convention. No one can overhear us here, which is a good thing because I'm about to tear this fool a new one.

I make sure to keep my voice low. I don't want anyone to hear me. "What are you thinking—criticizing Samantha in front of all those people?! I told you not to set foot in the convention hall."

"I don't take orders from you, Lane," he fires back. "You didn't hear her. She was out there blabbing to everyone..."

"I heard everything she said, Ethan! She was completely right and you were completely wrong. Now you went and embarrassed Apico in front of all our potential clients and investors. You're the one who damaged Apico today—not her."

"I didn't damage anything. I told you this morning you have a blind spot where she's concerned...."

"And I told you this morning that if you set foot in the convention or showed your face to anyone that you would be out on your ass." I feel my temper rising. "This has nothing to do with Samantha. You made a fool of yourself and you made Apico look terrible."

"That's nothing compared to what you're doing," he counters. "Do you think I don't know what you're doing up here?"

"I'm pitching clients and trying to make them see that Apico is worth investing in—which is more than I can say for you."

"You're up here screwing around with Samantha," he blurts out. "I know you had dinner with her on the deck last night and I know you spent the night in her room last night. Really, Lane. Don't you have enough floozies running after you? You didn't have to shit in your own bed by knocking over one of your own executives—but don't worry. As soon as you get back to New York, I'll be drawing up termination papers for both of you. You'll be out the door and none of us will ever have to deal with you or your bullshit ever again."

He walks off and leaves me stunned. This is what Samantha warned me about. Now she'll suffer along with me.

I go off by myself, but not before I glance into the convention hall. She's over there by the table talking to Diego Espinosa and Giovanni Nowaczyk. They all look relaxed and Giovanni laughs at something she says.

She always bounces back. I just wish I could protect her from all of this. She's likely to hear a lot of this as long as she and I are involved with each other.

I don't want anyone talking to her the way Ethan just talked to me. I could break his face for calling her a floozy and saying I knocked her over. That was just foul.

Of course someone would see it that way. A lot of people will probably see it that way. They don't know how I feel about her and I don't even necessarily want them to. This is mine. I don't want to share it with anyone but her.

She spots me watching her. She casts one questioning glance my way and goes back to her conversation. She's too responsible to flub the rest of the convention because Ethan can't keep his mouth shut. At least she doesn't know what he just said.

I don't want it to ruin the rest of the convention for her, so I leave and walk around the estate grounds for a while. I don't go back to my room until late afternoon.

At seven o'clock, I cross to the other side of the resort and knock on Samantha's door. She freezes like a deer in the headlights when she sees me. "Um...hello," she stammers.

"Hello. Are you ready to go to the dining room?"

She glances both ways down the hall. "Um....why are we going to the dining room?"

"You said you'd have dinner with me in a professional capacity."

She bursts out laughing. "Aren't you the one who said nothing we do is in a professional capacity anymore?"

I have to grin at her. "I did say that, but you did say you would have dinner with me."

"Are you sure that's a good idea?" She glances to the left again. "Is Ethan still lurking around?"

"He isn't lurking. He's circling—and yes, he's still here. He won't bother us, though. Come on. I'm hungry."

She makes a face. "Something tells me you're always hungry."

"I am." I grab her, scoop my arm behind her back, and pull her in for one hard, quick kiss. "I definitely am."

Her lips compress against mine and she starts to open her mouth. Mmmm. I could get a lot more of that, but business comes first.

She goes back inside her room, sticks her feet into her shoes, and gathers her room key, phone, and a few other things into her purse before she steps out into the hall.

She locks the room behind her and blushes up at me. "I guess we shouldn't hold hands."

"I'd like to, but we can save it for another time. It will be nice to save things like that for special times just between us."

She looks up at me with such a deep, passionate glance that I want to attack her right here in the hall. My fingers automatically migrate to hers, but just then, we turn the corner into the lobby. We have to separate.

We sit down together at a table in the dining room. Austin and Bradley stand at the bar out in the lounge with five other convention attendees. They talk and laugh loudly. I don't see Spencer or Cesar anywhere—or Ethan for that matter.

Samantha blushes at me across the table. "This is all so civilized."

"How did the rest of your day go at the convention—after Ethan left?"

She makes a face. "The other attendees were very supportive. They all know Derek."

"Did you make any progress with Diego Espinosa?"

"Naw. He's too rich for us. He invests his money in bigger positions overseas—positions Titanium Finance can't even hope to compete with. That guy is a giant."

"I know," I murmur. I don't tell her I know him from The Billionaires' Club.

"He was very supportive, though. They all said they think better of me for speaking up on Derek's behalf."

"What about Giovanni Nowaczyk?" I ask. "He's domestic."

"He came much closer to actually signing. He invests elsewhere, but he said he could be interested in investing with us, too. I'm going to meet him later this month and talk about it in more depth."

I raise my eyebrows and nod. "Good for you. Just be careful and don't let him hit on you. He can't walk into a room with a woman without hitting on her."

She turns bright red. "He tried to hit on me earlier."

I furrow my brow. "He did, did he? I might have to kick his ass."

She laughs, but right then, our good buddy Ethan makes another appearance. He pauses at the dining room door to look around, spots us, and comes straight over to us.

"Oh, no!" Samantha breathes.

"Just relax, sweetheart," I tell her. "There's nothing to worry about."

"How can I not worry?"

Ethan stops next to our table and sneers down at us with a self-satisfied grin. "Defiant as always, aren't you, Lane? I'm happy to inform you—and you, Ms. Mulholland—that you're both now unemployed."

Samantha gasps, but I remain calm. "I'm glad you came over here to tell us that, Ethan. It gives me the perfect opportunity to give you this."

I pull a sealed white, unmarked envelope out of my inner jacket pocket and hold it out to him.

He takes it, flips it over, and waves it at me when he doesn't see any writing on it. "What the hell is this?"

"It's your letter of resignation."

He glares at me and then slits his finger under the flap to tear the envelope open. He rips out the folded letter inside, reads it, and I get a thrill when all the color drains from his face.

I'm just deciding how to humiliate him in front of Samantha the way he humiliated her, but he runs off before I can say anything.

"What did you just do?" she whispers. "What was in that letter?"

"Never mind. He won't bother us again. I'll just have to start looking for his replacement when I get back to New York." I lean across the table and take her hand. "Now I want to talk about you—and us."

Her eyes swivel sideways. "This is supposed to be a professional dinner, remember?"

"I don't want to hide what's going on between us anymore. I want the world to know. I don't want to sneak around acting like we're doing something shameful. I want to do it right out in public so everyone knows we're official."

Her eyes widen. "Official? As in—official?"

"Yes, official. I want you to stay here with me for a few days—just you and me—after the rest of your team goes back to New York."

"Won't that make it kind of obvious what we're doing? They'll realize when I don't get into the limo to go back with them."

"Tell them you have some business to wrap up and you'll see them first thing Monday morning—which you will. You can check out of that room you're in and stay in mine."

She blushes and looks away. "It sounds nice."

"Come on. This will be the first time we've been able to spend some time together just the two of us with no outside obligations. It will be like a mini-honeymoon before the honeymoon."

She bursts out laughing and her cheeks color. "You are NOT using that word—not this soon."

"Why is it soon? We've been through enough together. We know each other. It isn't like either of us is living under any illusions about who and what the other person is. We know each other's deepest, darkest secrets and we still want to be together." I hesitate. "You want to be with me, don't you?"

She nods and stares up at me with huge eyes. Her lips tremble.

I squeeze her hand a little tighter. "I want to be with you, too. I know my most dangerous secrets are safe with you just as yours are with me. I can't think of any better foundation for a relationship than that. I trust you with my life."

She gulps, compresses her lips, and looks down at our hands clasped on the table. If anyone on her team walks into the dining room right now, they'll see us holding hands in front of God and everyone.

I hope they do see. I hope they see and understand that Samantha and I are for real.

Just then, the server comes and places a basket of garlic bread and two bowls of salad in front of me and Samantha. We have to take our hands off the table to make room for everything.

Then the server takes our order. We could go back to holding hands, but she starts eating her salad instead.

I let the matter go for now, but I have no intention of letting it go entirely—or at all for that matter. I already know what I'm going to do.

We go through the whole meal talking about the other conference attendees and the leads and clients she already secured. I knew she'd do well.

"And don't even get me started on all the leads and promises Austin got," she finishes. "That guy is worth his weight in gold."

I have to beam at her. "I knew you'd hire the right person."

"Don't ask me how someone can be that outgoing. He can talk to anyone. He's a social magnet."

We stand up to leave the restaurant and I take her hand even though people can see us. I'm all finished playing games here.

I feel her tense, but she doesn't let go. She's right here with me in this.

I lead her out of the dining room. I don't look to see if any of her fellow executives are watching when I lead her through the lobby and down the corridor—to my room.

# Chapter 37: Samantha

I come out of the bathroom in Lane's apartment. His room at the Black Oak Estates resort is much bigger than mine. His room occupies the end of one wing with a huge, curved bank of bay windows looking out over the landscape.

We can't see any of the rest of the resort from here. We're all alone with the countryside. We've been here two days—at least, we've been here alone for two days.

The rest of the Titanium Finance executive team went back to New York on Friday. Lane and I have been here alone ever since.

Now it's Sunday morning. We'll go back to New York this afternoon—as soon as we check out of here. Then we'll be back in public.

We haven't talked about what happens after that. Neither of us wants to spoil this blissful escape from reality.

Lane hasn't told me if he's checked his phone to see what's happening with Ethan. I don't ask.

Lane lies asleep on the bed at one end of his palatial apartment room. The bedroom is just as big as the living room next door with broad, eggshell-grey tile, another indoor jacuzzi, and a collection of leather couches and armchairs surrounding a coffee table by the windows.

The living room is almost as big as my whole apartment back in New York with an open plan kitchen, sunken sitting area, and its own private deck with a private pool.

None of that fascinates me as much as the man in the bed across the room. The white sheet covers him from his stomach down to one knee. The sheet reveals the shape of his body underneath.

He lies with one arm stretched above his head and his face turned aside. He looks chiseled out of marble like this—like someone painted a picture of the most perfect man asleep in bed.

That's the body that gives me so much pleasure—his mouth, his hands, his arms, his chest, his stomach, his ass.....everything about him.

As soon as he wakes up, he'll want to do it all over again, but that's not why I'm standing here across the room watching him.

My heart cracks with emotion for him. I love him. I know that now. I love him for everything he is and everything he's ever done for me. I love that he wants to get serious about us.....and it also scares the shit out of me.

As soon as he wakes up, we both have to face the fact that we're going back to New York today. Knowing that will color the rest of our time in this room. Nothing will ever be the same even before we leave to go back to New York.

Life, business, family, all our connections—they'll all call on us with their obligations and demands. They'll leave less time for me and Lane to be together—and then we have to deal with everyone's reaction to our relationship.

I don't worry about his family or my family. The only person on my side who could possibly object would be Casey.

All I have to do is tell him about Lane foiling that carjacking. Then Casey will be fine with me going out with Lane or even getting serious about Lane. Casey's good that way. He only cares about protecting me and taking care of me.

I already get along with Lane's mother and sister. It's the rest of the world I have to worry about—the rest of the business world.

I don't want to let those thoughts interfere with the few precious hours Lane and I have left, but those thoughts are already interfering.

I do my best to shake them off and cross back to the bed. The early dawn light casts little shadows in the furrows between Lane's muscles. His chest rises and falls in sleep when I gaze down at him.

I could stand here gazing for the rest of eternity. When will I ever get a chance to watch him like this again? Maybe never.

I don't want to spend the time watching him. I pull the sheet off slowly, crawl on top of him, and draw the sheet over both of us.

I drag my breasts, thighs, and lips over that body—the body that sends me to the stars.

Every inch of his skin turns me on. I straddle him and nibble my way up his sternum to his neck, then to his ears, and finally to his mouth.

He lets out a deep groan of delight and his hands close behind me, but he doesn't open his eyes. His grip tightens when I start to rock on him.

His package stiffens and I screw my hips down on top of him. "Oh.....yeah......" he husks.

I love that sound. He clenches my ass in both hands and follows my rhythm in slow beats picking up speed.

A rush of heat and pleasure charges through me. I throw my head back with a moaning gasp and arch higher to take him deeper.

He takes that signal to grab my breast in his mouth. Now I can't escape. I yelp and then scream as the energy spikes. The feeling of him sucking my nipple translates down to my inner muscles. They clamp around his shaft and I explode out of control.

I throw myself down on him and feel his thick rod breaking me apart all over again. The last three nights together have left my tissues extra sensitive. The slightest stimulation skyrockets me out of this world.

He closes both arms behind my back to push me down and then releases me so he can lie all the way back on the bed.

His deep blue eyes float open to gaze up at me and both his hands massage my breasts.

He pushes me upright so he can see me riding him in mortal ecstasy. I can only see him for moments between waves of delirious passion that make my vision blur.

His chest and stomach feel so strong under my fingers. He flexes his abs each time he drills into me. He fills me to bursting and sends me reeling away into the clouds of glory again and again.

He throws back his head as the wave rises. His veins strain inside me as my inner muscles stroke every drop of juicy essence from his shaft.

He arches back and every muscle tenses to the breaking point. His lips curl away from his teeth and he shuts his eyes roaring as he erupts inside me. That feeling of completion brings one last scream from my lips before I collapse on top of him.

Sweat strings his skin all over his chest. His neck tastes salty when I kiss him.

He groans and his fingers thread into my hair when he holds me down. He shudders and whispers sultry curses in my ears.

"Fuck, baby, that is so damn good. You don't know how good that feels."

I know because he makes me feel just as good. I can't get enough of him.

Straddling him like this only makes me want him more, but this day demands too much from us. Those demands won't be denied.

I lift up just enough to start kissing him again, but the look in his eyes tells me he knows it, too. Life is still out there waiting for us. It won't go away.

He finally flips me onto my back, kisses down my chest and stomach to each of my thighs, takes one long, luscious bite from my dripping petals, and sits back on his heels. "It's time to get up, sweetheart. We have to check out in an hour."

I stay where I am with my arms above my head, my breasts exposed, and my legs spread. I smirk up at him daring him to walk away from me.

"Don't look at me like that," he tells me. "Come on. Get up. If you really have to, I'll stop by the side of the road and bang you over the hood of my car."

I laugh at him. "You really would, wouldn't you?"

"You're damn right I would. I would do it right there on the shoulder where everyone can see your breasts slapping against the metal. Now get up and don't give me any trouble."

I laugh and pry myself out of bed. I don't want any of that kind of trouble.

We take a shower together, but we have to continuously stop ourselves from groping each other.

He starts out by washing my body....and his soapy hands wind up between my legs. Then it's my turn and he starts getting hard when I wash him down.

We eventually drag ourselves and our luggage to the front desk and check out. I don't find out until we get there that Lane has arranged with the concierge for us to eat breakfast in the dining room even though it's past the time when they usually serve breakfast.

We have the whole resort to ourselves. We're the only ones still here besides the staff—which is good. I would have been keeping everyone awake for the last three days with my screaming.

We don't talk while we eat breakfast. I don't know what to say. I have no idea what will happen when we get back to New York.

I see Lane eyeing me across the table with the same questions hanging over his head.

I see plenty of certainty in those eyes, too. He doesn't question us—not ever. He's planning how he's going to do this. He's deciding how to proceed so he makes sure we're together.

I feel better knowing he's thinking about it and working on it. At least someone has an idea of what to do and how to do it.

We still have to deal with the Apico Acquisitions executive board—and the rest of the business world. What will *my* executive team say when they find out?

We finish eating and go out front to leave the resort. I don't have a ride since the rest of my team rode back to New York in the limo.

I expect Lane to ride back to town in a limo, too. I stand on the resort steps in shock when the valet brings over a long, low, black Ferrari with swooping, sexy curves.

It hugs the ground and its lever doors fold up toward the hood. "Get in," Lane tells me.

I can't stop staring at the car. "We....we aren't riding in that."

"Sure we are." He takes my suitcase and puts it into a white van parked at the curb. "The resort will send our luggage back to town for us. Come on." He shoots me a wild grin. "Let's have some fun."

I don't know what to think. The doors fold open to reveal two low leather seats practically sitting on the ground. The car's front end looks like some kind of predatory animal on the prowl.

Lane takes my hand to help lower me into the seat. He won't stop grinning.

He makes sure I'm sitting all the way down in there before he gets behind the wheel. He pushes a button to close both doors at the same time.

"Are you sure you know how to drive this?" I ask.

"Of course I do. This is my car."

I glance over at him, but he's already adjusting everything and starting the motor like a pro. He definitely knows what he's doing.

The engine roars to life. He shoots me one more crazy look, throws the car into first gear, and burns rubber out of the resort.

I have to hold onto the seat and the door. The G force of him cutting around tight corners plasters me back in the seat—and then he motors out onto the highway laying down the miles. I don't dare to check how fast he's going.

He keeps throwing the car into lower gears to blast around curves and to pass other motorists. Then he drops down into higher gears to put on speed on the straight-aways.

The thrill of doing something this dangerous gets the better of me and I laugh. He keeps smirking at me, but he has to pay attention to staying on the road.

# Chapter 38: Samantha

Lane's Ferrari flattens itself even lower as it picks up speed. The roaring engine sends quivering vibrations through me.

We cover the distance back to New York in no time. The distant skyline comes into view pretty soon. It casts a chill over both of us, but just then, his phone rings in his jacket pocket.

He pulls it out and hands it to me. "Could you see who it is?"

I check the screen. "It's Katrina."

"Answer it, will you please?"

I answer it and hold the phone to my ear. "Katrina—hi. It's me—Samantha Mulholland."

"Um...Samantha?" Katrina sounds shaky. I can barely understand her.

"What's wrong?" I ask her. "Did something happen? Are you okay?"

"I...I need to talk to Lane. I can hear that you're in the car. I need to talk to him. I'm sorry, but it's urgent. My mom is in the hospital."

Lane glances over at me and scowls. He doesn't smirk at all now.

"She needs you to pull over and talk to her," I tell him. "She says your mom is in the hospital."

He clenches his jaw, slows the car, and steers off into a rest area.

He takes the phone and says, "Hello," in a ruthless undertone.

Katrina's high-pitched wail comes through the line from the other end. She starts talking loud and fast. She practically shrieks into the phone.

He glares out at the highway in front of him. I hate to think of anything happening to his mother.

He finally says a curt, "Okay, I'm on my way right now," and hangs up.

He stuffs the phone in his pocket, puts the car in gear, and takes off down the highway driving even faster.

He keeps his teeth locked and his eyes narrowed. The muscle in his jaw tenses each time he grits his teeth.

I finally work up the nerve to ask, "Is your mom okay?"

"I don't know," he mutters. "I just have to get there as quick as I can. I'll drop you off and then I have to go straight to the hospital."

I lay my hand on his arm and squeeze, but his muscles feel as hard as rocks. He braces his arms against the steering wheel.

"Let me come with you," I tell him. "Let me support you."

He doesn't answer. He drives in silence for another hour until we get to New York.

He doesn't take me home. He drives straight to the hospital and parks in the underground garage before he shuts off the motor and turns to me. "Thank you," he croaks. "Thank you for coming."

"Of course. I want to be there for you. Let's go see what's going on."

We get out of the car. All our fun and connection from the resort evaporates in seconds as if it never happened.

Lane asks at the front desk and finds out his mother is in an emergency ICU unit waiting to go into surgery.

Lane walks extra fast on our way down the corridors. I have to jog to keep up with him, but I don't complain. I just hope nothing happened to his mother—nothing serious, at least.

We walk in to find Katrina sitting in a chair and holding her mother's hand. Anne lies on a rolling hospital bed with an IV in her arm and an oxygen mask over her face.

A fabric shower cap covers her hair. She looks really old like this.

Tears well up in Katrina's eyes the minute we walk in. Red blotches cover her cheeks like she's been crying a lot—like since before she called Lane.

Lane barely looks at her. He goes straight to his mother, takes her other hand, and bends his face extra close to hers.

He kisses her on the cheek. "Mama—I'm here," he breathes. "I came as soon as I could."

She comes to her senses and her expression clears when she looks up at him. She breaks into the same beaming smile she bestowed on him when he visited her in her apartment.

"My boy!" she rasps. "I'm so proud of you!"

He smiles, but his features wrench with buried pain. Tears swim in his eyes and he clasps her hand between both of his. "I love you," he whispers. "I love you more than anything."

"I love you," she replies and her voice breaks. "I love you and your sister more than you can ever know." Her expression goes dark. "You take care of your sister, son. Do you hear me?"

"You know I'll always take care of both of you, Mama. I'll never let anything happen to you—not ever again."

She starts to smile—and then her features freeze. Her eyes glaze and she stares through him at something beyond him.

Katrina reacts instantly, lunges for her mother, and shakes her by both shoulders. "Mom!!" Katrina bellows. "MOM!!"

Anne doesn't respond, and a second later, she collapses onto the pillow. Her eyes close and her head lolls to one side.

Katrina's yells spike to screeches. "MOMM!!" she shrieks. "MOM-MM!!"

Katrina charges out of the room and bellows down the corridor. "WE NEED SOME HELP IN HERE!!

She comes racing back and shakes her mother again, but Anne doesn't respond this time, either. She hardly seems to move at all. She isn't breathing.

Katrina jerks Anne's body one last time and explodes in a flood of tears. She falls on her mother's chest sobbing loud and hard.

I can't watch this, but I can't leave, either. Katrina's sobs make me tear up, too, and I barely knew Anne.

I lay my hand on Katrina's shoulder and she rips herself away from her mother's body, spins around, and collapses in my arms sobbing her eyes out. I can only hold her while she cries.

Lane stands there in stunned, silent shock. He doesn't even blink. He just stares down at his mother in frozen horror. It's all over even as he holds her hand in both of his. He hardly got a chance to say goodbye and now she's gone.

I put one arm around Katrina and slip my other hand onto his shoulder, but he doesn't respond. He feels wooden and half-dead himself.

Just then, a whole team of medical people rushes in with piles of equipment. They surround Anne's bed, but we already know what's going to happen. Nothing is going to happen. Anne is gone.

The medical people knock all of us out of the way. Katrina dissolves in even more wretched sobs. We can't even leave the room to avoid hearing all the medical people yelling orders back and forth.

They jostle Lane out of the way. He has to let go of Anne's hand. He finally turns away, staggers across the room, and rests his forehead against the wall with his eyes closed.

I want to go over there and touch him in some way, but I can't do that while I'm holding onto Katrina.

The medical people shoot Anne full of a bunch of drugs and defibrillate her a million times trying to get her heart going again, but nothing works.

Every shock sends Katrina reeling over the edge into another hysterical outburst of crying. I have to hold her with both arms until the medical people finally give up, declare Anne dead, and leave us alone in that terrible silence.

Katrina keeps bawling her eyes out. Lane doesn't move.

I can't keep standing here. This is like something out of nightmare. I can't let these two stay in the same room with their mother's body—not after what just happened.

I push Katrina off. "Come on," I tell her. "Let's get out of here."

She's sobbing too hard to protest—or to do anything else. I take her by one hand to lead her out of the room.

Lane hasn't moved. I'm not sure what to do about him, but I can't leave him like this, either.

I slip my other hand into his and say, "Come on, Lane. We're getting out of here."

He doesn't argue when I steer both of them back to the hospital lobby. I don't know what else to do with them, so I park them in a couple of chairs by the elevator.

Katrina covers her face with both hands and breaks down even more. Lane sits there staring straight in front of him. Did he break something just now?

Sitting in the hospital lobby feels almost worse than being in the same room with Anne's body. I call a taxi to take us to my place.

I don't know what else to do with these two, but at least we'll be comfortable there. I'll be able to give them something to drink and a place to lie down until the shock wears off.

I get off the phone and sit down in the chair next to Katrina. "I called a cab to take us to my place. We can relax there until we decide what to do next."

Lane doesn't respond at all. Did he even hear me?

Katrina looks up at me. Her swollen face is a mess of tears. "Sama ntha....."

"Yeah, sweetie." I stroke her hair and kiss her on the forehead. "Everything's gonna be all right. You'll see."

"I....I need.....to go....home....." She bursts into a fresh flood of tears. She keeps choking on the words. I have to concentrate to understand her. "I....I need.....to go....home....to my own home....."

"Are you sure? You're welcome to come stay with me. You don't have to be alone right now."

"I.....I need to be......alone......" Her mouth screws up in knots. "I need to......be...."

"Okay," I whisper. "Okay. Whatever you need."

"I'm sorry!" she howls. "I know I shouldn't....."

"Hey! Cut it out! You do whatever you need to do. You have my number, right? You go home. Let me know if you need anything from me. Okay?"

I put my arms around her and kiss her a few more times. I only wish I could do more.

She wails, "I'm sorry!" into my ear one more time. I shake my head, but nothing will make this better.

I don't blame her for needing to go hide somewhere. Maybe she needs to be away from Lane. Maybe his devastation is too much for Katrina to deal with right now. That's okay.

I take her outside and put her in the cab I ordered for all three of us. She sobs even harder when I tell her it's okay and everything will be all right in the end. Just don't ask me how.

She barely chokes out the address and the cab leaves. I wish I could help her, but maybe this is the best thing for her. Who would know that better than she would?

I make a mental note to give her twenty-four hours before I call her to find out if she's okay. Then I have to go back inside the lobby to deal with Lane.

# Chapter 39: Samantha

L ane still hasn't moved when I get back inside the hospital lobby. Is he even blinking?

I place my hand on his shoulder. "We're going home. Come on. Let's go."

He doesn't answer. He doesn't even look at me. His hand feels dead when I take it and pull him to his feet.

He stumbles after me to the parking garage. I take the keys out of his pocket, put him in the passenger seat, and drive the Ferrari back to my apartment.

I arrange with Anthony for an extra parking space in the underground garage to park the car next to mine.

Lane follows me upstairs. He just stands there in silence while I unlock the door. He lurches into the room and I push him down on the couch.

He folds into a slump on the cushions, but instead of looking straight ahead, he looks down at his hands.

He looks so destroyed like this. No one would believe he can command multiple billion-dollar companies. He can make the business world tremble with one flash of his sharp blue eyes.

That person isn't here. This is just a man who lost the most important person in his whole world. I can't let anything bad happen to him—not after this.

Trying to work out how our relationship is going to develop—it means nothing compared to this.

I leave him there, get the down bedspread from the guest room, and wrap it around his shoulders. I push him sideways, make him lie down, and tuck the bedspread around him. He can curl up here and do whatever he needs to do to deal with this.

I'm just tucking the bedspread under his chin and around his ears when his eyes catch mine. They don't look dull or dead or even shocked. They overflow with misery.

"Samantha?" he croaks.

I squat down in front of him and put my arm over his shoulders in a half-hug. "Yeah?" I ask.

He opens his mouth, and just like that, he breaks down sobbing his heart out. He turns his face downward into the couch cushion, buries his head in the bedspread, and quakes with racking, silent sobs.

I have to kiss him. The only part of him I can kiss is the side of his head, but that's enough.

I run my fingers through his hair and murmur in his ear. "It's all right, sweetheart. It's all right. Everything is going to be all right. She's safe now. She loved you more than anything and now nothing can harm her. She was so proud of you. You were everything a mother could ask of her son. You were there for her at the end. Everything's okay, sweetie. It's okay to cry. You're going to be all right. You'll see."

I don't know half of what I'm saying. It sure helped when he said those things to me. I just hope they help him some way or other.

I keep stroking him while he cries. He cries for a long time—almost as long as Katrina—but he does it silently. Maybe he had to get here, to my apartment, before he could let it out.

I wind up sitting on the floor with my arm around him. I rub his back and arms and pet his hair. I don't have to say anything. I just have to be here for him.

He eventually slows down enough to pry his face out of the cushion, but he doesn't look at me again. He wraps the bedspread tighter around his shoulders and glares into space through dull, bloodshot eyes.

I can live with that. I squeeze his shoulder, kiss him on the head, and go upstairs to my room where I sit on the bed and pull out my phone.

First, I call Steward Redmond, Lane's assistant. I've been video-chatting with Stewart on a daily basis for weeks about everything Titanium-related. We know each other pretty well by now.

He grins when he sees me. "You nailed your speech at the convention. I just watched the video the organizers posted on social media."

"Thanks. Listen, Stewart. I'm calling about Lane."

"What about him?"

"His mother died about an hour ago and he's a mess. He's gonna take some time off work for at least a few days, I'd say."

He frowns at me. "Oh. That's not good."

"Will you please inform all the rest of the Apico execs?"

Stewart picks up his phone. "I better call Lane and offer my condolences. Then he can tell me...."

"No, Stewart. Don't call him. Just leave him alone. He needs some time to get his life back together. It happened suddenly and he's not in any condition to deal with anyone right now. That's why I'm the one calling you instead of him."

He frowns even more. Does Stewart realize why Lane and I were together when this happened? Did Ethan spew the news all over town?

I realize in that moment that I really do not care what Ethan said about me and Lane. I really hope Ethan did broadcast it all over town. Then I won't have to explain it to anyone.

Lane and I are going to be together. Hell, we already are together. Why hide it?

"I'll call you tomorrow," I tell Stewart. "If you really need to contact Lane, call me first and I'll see if he's ready to talk to you."

"So.....is he with you now? Is that it?"

"I was with him when he got the call. He's in shock, so....." I decide to just bite the bullet and take the plunge. "I brought him to my apartment. He wasn't ready to deal with handling things on his own. So he's staying here for now until he's ready to leave."

He nods. I can just see him putting the puzzle pieces together. "Okay. Give him our best. Let him know I'll be waiting when he needs m e."

"Thanks, Stewart."

I get off the phone and call Marco Van Sant and the rest of the Titanium executive team. I tell them I'll be taking a few days off to deal with a family emergency. I don't tell them why. They don't need to know that.

I also tell them I'll be handling company business from home, so I won't leave the company high and dry in the meantime.

I go back downstairs to check on Lane. He's still lying in the same place, but he has his eyes closed now.

I leave him there and start making dinner. It's only four o'clock in the afternoon, but today felt like it lasted ten long, hard years.

I'm in the middle of straining the pasta when I get another call from Stewart. "I'm really sorry to bother you, but Lane had a bunch of accounts from the Cannon Summit accounting department. He was supposed to go over them and turn them in tomorrow morning."

"Do you want me to go over them? You can send them over to me. I know I'm not technically involved in Apico's other business, but...."

"Would you really? Oh, Samantha, you're a hero! Thank you so much!"

"Forget it. Does Lane have any other obligations coming up—like for the rest of the week? I'll deal with any you want me to deal with—just until he gets back on his feet."

"There's the Ashcroft contract. We just need him to sign it—but if he can't come into the office...."

"Send it over. I'll get his signature and I'll bring it by the office—or I can email you the signed copy."

He grins again. "You're awesome, Samantha."

"What about the rest of the Apico board?" I ask. "Will they be okay with all this?"

"I already talked to Marshall and Russel. They're just worried about Lane. They don't care about the work."

"Well, anything you need me to do, you only have to ask."

"Thanks a million. Oh, I meant to tell you Ethan Rosch resigned over the weekend. He didn't give any explanation. He's just out. So you don't have to inform him about Lane's absence."

I barely mumble, "Thanks." What was in that resignation letter? Lane must have had something serious on Ethan.

I get off the phone, finish making dinner, and then print out the Ashcroft contract that Stewart emails to me. I go through a dozen more emails from him, Marco, and Russel about other Apico business.

I pull up the Cannon Summit accounts next and scroll through them while I finish dinner. They're pretty complicated. I wind up leaning against the kitchen counter to finish reading them.

I finally put my phone down and plate up dinner to take over to Lane. I turn around and stop in my tracks when I see him sitting up on the couch.

He doesn't turn around to look at me. He sits there huddled under the bedspread. Poor guy. I know exactly how he feels.

I'm just about to walk over there and take him something to eat when my phone rings. It's Katrina.

"Hi, sweetie," I murmur when I pick it up. "How are you?"

"I'm fine," she chokes on the other end. I can still hear her crying. "I need....." She breaks down completely.

I hold the phone to my ear and listen to her sobbing her guts out. She sounds as bad as Lane.

I wait, but she doesn't stop. She keeps saying, "I need to...." and dissolving all over again.

I take the plate over to Lane and sit down on the coffee table in front of him. He keeps his eyes down.

I hold out the plate to him and he unwinds his arms so he can take it from me. He sits there in dull silence while he eats the food.

I listen to Katrina sobbing. "Are you sure you don't want to come over, sweetie?" I finally ask her. "Whatever it is, I can help you here. You don't have to stay alone."

She cries for a little longer and finally blurts out, "Maybe tomorrow."

"Okay, sweetheart. Whatever works for you. I'll be here all day.... and Lane is here. You can see him then. Okay?"

She barely husks out, "Okay," and hangs up.

I put the phone down. Lane still forks the food into his mouth without looking at me.

Out of nowhere, he rasps, "Thank you....for everything."

I shift over onto the couch next to him and rub his back. Then, because I can, I run my fingers through his hair. "Everything is gonna be all right. Do you want to sign the Ashcroft contract now? Then I can email it back to Stewart and you don't have to think about it anymore."

He nods at nothing.

I go get the contract, put it on a clipboard, and give him a pen to sign it. He does everything in a brutally robotic, resentful way.

The minute I take the clipboard out of his hands, he retreats into his down cocoon and tightens the bedspread around him.

It's almost painful to see myself reflected in his behavior. Now I know how much he cared about me when he played this role for me. He must have felt for me then the way I feel about him now.

I would do anything to protect him and make it all okay. It will be okay in time. It will be okay for him and Katrina the way he made it okay for me. He just has to get through it the way I did.

I get my own plate, sit down next to him on the couch, and pull him down to lay his head in my lap while I eat. Then I run my fingers through his hair and rub his back and shoulders while I finish going over the accounts on my phone.

Stewart sends me a bunch of other random busy work Lane was supposed to get done this coming week. I finish as much of it as I can so Lane doesn't have to come out of his stupor to think about it.

I check on him at ten o'clock. He hasn't moved and he's sound asleep in my lap.

I lean back on the couch, put my phone down, and shut my eyes. I don't want to disturb him.

# Chapter 40: Lane

**M**y eyes snap open. It takes me a split second to realize that I'm in Samantha's apartment again—and then I remember. My mother is dead.

The memory twists the knife deeper into my chest, but I can't even cry about that anymore. She's gone.

I always knew she'd die someday. Who doesn't?

I never wanted to think about what my life would be like without her in it. Now I have to face that long, dark road alone—except I'm not alone. Katrina still needs me.

I remember everything from the hospital. I could never forget that.

I also can't forget the way I completely let her down when she needed me. I was too destroyed myself even to hear her crying.

Samantha was the one Katrina leaned on. I'll never be able to live that down. I just hope Katrina understands.

She's coming over here today. I need to make up for it when she comes.

I need to be here for her the way I always have been. I need to be the strong one.

She deserves that. She doesn't have my mom to lean on anymore. I'm all she has left. That has to be enough.

I sit up. I need to pull myself together and start living my life. I have too many responsibilities to just fall apart like this.

I don't realize until I sit up that I fell asleep on Samantha's lap. She's asleep on the couch next to me, but she stirs when I move.

I blink at her stretching and groaning. She actually sat there all night so she wouldn't wake me up. She fell asleep in the most uncomfortable position—for me.

Overwhelming gratitude wrings my heart. This woman has been there for me through the worst night of my life.

She didn't have to do any of that. She could have just let me drop her off. Then she wouldn't have been there when my mom died. Samantha wouldn't have been there to take care of Katrina—and me.

She wouldn't be sitting here right now and neither would I. God only knows what would have happened to me and Katrina without Samantha there to carry both of us.

Samantha curls up on her end of the couch with her eyes shut. Her hair falls over her face. She's still wearing the same clothes she had on when we left the resort.

She's so beautiful. Her heart shines with inner splendor I can't even comprehend. How did I get so lucky as to win this woman?

She does all these things for me—and yet I know she thinks she's the lucky one for winning me. I can't even fathom that and yet I know it's true. I believe it with every ounce of my being.

I stand up and look down at her sleeping face. I want to kiss her, but she needs sleep more.

I still feel her fingers in my hair, her hand rubbing my back, and her soft voice murmuring in my ear, *Everything is going to be all right.* I believe it because she said it.

Now I know what a priceless gift I gave her when I took care of her. I didn't know it then.

I want to fall inside her and disappear. I want to turn my whole life over to her the way she turned hers over to me—but we can do this in a different way. We can become dependent on each other without robbing each other of what makes us who we are.

I'm going to marry this woman. That's all there is to it. There's nothing left to do but let the rest of the world know. Anyone who doesn't like it can sit on it.

I drape the bedspread over her to keep her warm and go into the kitchen to make coffee and breakfast. I'm in the middle of checking messages and emails when someone knocks on the door.

Samantha sits up and blinks at the living room trying to get her head back into gear. I answer the door not knowing what to expect.

Katrina bursts in, collapses on my chest, and breaks down sobbing again. It doesn't sound like she's stopped crying since yesterday.

Maybe she never will, but that's okay because I'm here now. I'm back. I can be here for her in ways I wasn't yesterday.

Samantha jumps up and hustles over to us. She rubs Katrina's back, strokes her hair, and kisses her on the temple while I hold her.

"Aw, sweetie!" Samantha murmurs. "Poor baby."

Samantha's care makes Katrina sob harder, but she needs that. Whatever she needs, she can get it here—from us.

Now I know there is an us. Me and Samantha—we're a unit now. Nothing will ever break us apart—definitely not anything like this.

I steer Katrina to the couch. Samantha rushes into the kitchen and comes back with a glass of juice and a box of tissues.

I sit down on the couch with my arms around Katrina. Samantha sits on the coffee table. That's where the caretaker sits. This is turning into a family tradition.

I kiss Katrina on the forehead in between bouts of crying. She cries for a long time before she can finally bring herself to speak.

"Did you get some breakfast?" Samantha asks. "Do you want to eat something?"

Katrina shakes her head. Her swollen lips and puffy cheeks flame with color and her hard eyes blur with tears. "I need to....we need to....talk about.....Mom's affairs."

"Okay. We can do that." I unwind my arms from around Katrina and take a gulp of the coffee Samantha puts in front of me. I made this coffee, but somehow, she's the one taking care of me and Katrina now.

"Mom....didn't have a will....."

I nod. "I know."

"You.....you owned her building...." Katrina goes on. "You paid all her bills. She didn't have anything."

I don't answer. This is nothing I didn't already know. My mom didn't have two pennies to rub together. Katrina and I grew up that w ay.

I paid all my mom's bills because she couldn't. I was the only reason she had a place to live at all. I don't say that out loud, though, because Katrina already knows.

Samantha must have already started to suspect. She doesn't make any noises of surprise when she hears the news. She saw firsthand where and how my mom lived.

"We should divide up her stuff....." Katrina start spasming again.

"Why should we divide up her stuff?" I ask. "Neither of us wants any of it."

"She had....family pictures....and stuff...." She loses the battle to hold back another wave of despair.

Now I know why she's so upset. She doesn't want to go into my mom's apartment.

No one in their right mind would want to wade through acres of ancient newspapers and rotten unfinished craft projects from thirty years ago to find the family pictures my mom might have hidden somewhere in there.

"I'll do it," I tell her. "I'll get the pictures. We can dump everything else."

She nods fast. That must be what she wants. That's probably all she wants—to ask me to do that so she doesn't have to.

I kiss her again. "You don't have to go. I'll get rid of all her stuff and then I'll sell the building. We don't ever have to go back there."

She breaks down sobbing again and I lean back on the couch to hold her on my chest.

She cries a lot harder and a lot longer this time. Now I understand.

Katrina must feel the same disgust and revulsion going back to that building—the same disgust and revulsion I feel going back to that building.

I never would have set foot in that building again as long as I lived. I only went back there because my mother lived there and she refused to leave.

She was too much of a packrat to leave. Now she's gone.

Katrina and I don't have to go back there to visit her, but that somehow makes it worse than reliving the bad memories of growing up in that building.

We won't be able to go back there to visit my mom anymore.

Death has torn that part of my life out of my chest and left this bloody hole I will never fill—except that I will fill it. I'll fill it with Samantha and the life we're going to build together.

She sits across from us watching us. She doesn't intervene and she doesn't say anything about me being there for Katrina. Samantha never inserts herself into our interaction.

"I'll go now," I tell Katrina. "I'll bring the pictures back here. Then you can have them. You can keep them for both of us."

She nods fast. She's crying too hard to answer.

I catch Samantha looking at me. She follows me to the door and slips my keys into my hand. "The car is downstairs in the underground garage—right next to my parking space. I don't know if you want to take it into your old neighborhood....."

"I'll deal with it." I pause there to take her hand and look deep into her eyes. "Thank you for this. Those words sound so pathetic compared to what you're doing."

"Stop it," she breathes. "Get out of here. I'll take care of her."

I slip out of the apartment. Of course Samantha will take care of Katrina. Samantha always takes care of everything. Katrina couldn't be safer with anyone.

I take the elevator to the building's lobby entrance, but I can't figure out how to find the underground parking garage. I ask Anthony, the doorman. He's seen me here enough times with Samantha.

He shows me to the garage and my car. I have to drop it off at *my* garage where it will be safe. I don't dare take it to the old neighborhood.

I don't want to deal with the locals, so I take a cab instead. No one notices me. They're all too used to seeing me pull up in the limo.

I go upstairs, but I have to fight down the urge to puke when I go into my mother's apartment. Thank the stars Katrina isn't seeing this.

My mom really let her hoarding tendencies run away with her these last few years. No way in hell would I ever keep this building.

I'll hire someone to come in here and haul every last scrap of this stuff to the landfill. That's the only place it belongs.

I go straight to the cabinet in my mother's bedroom. That's where she keeps all the family photo albums. Neither Katrina nor I give a hoot in hell about any of the rest of this shit.

# Chapter 41: Lane

I take another cab back to Samantha's apartment. Katrina breaks down again when I put the stack of albums on the coffee table in front of her.

She doesn't touch them or look through them. She just sits there staring at them and breaking down again and again and again.

Samantha sits next to her with her arm around Katrina's shoulders. I sit down on Katrina's other side and lay my hand on her back, but I don't talk. There's nothing to say.

These two women are my whole life now. Whatever happens to me will happen with them. I'll marry Samantha and Katrina will start going out with someone and get married.

Our families will grow up together and we'll grow old together. In thirty or forty years, we'll look back on today and realize it all started here—right here on this couch.

After a long while, Samantha picks up one of the albums and starts looking through it. She moves it closer to Katrina and points at one of the pictures. "Is that your dad?"

Katrina starts crying again, but she answers, "That's my grandfather—my mother's father. Her family lives in....in Saratoga, Florida. We never knew my father."

Samantha starts asking a million questions about all the people in the pictures. Katrina goes through the whole explanation of our family history. I don't say a word, but at least Katrina is talking again.

By afternoon, she seems to be coming out of her anguish. Samantha makes dinner for both of us and then I call Eddie to bring the limo around.

I put Katrina and the albums in the limo and take her home. I kiss her on the threshold. "Will you be okay?"

She looks up at me through tears. "I think I really need to get back to work tomorrow. All this sitting around feeling sad doesn't help. I'll go to the office tomorrow. That will help me start to function again."

"That's the way. You're gonna be all right. I'm certain of it." I kiss her on the forehead again.

She hugs me. "You really got yourself a prize with Samantha. You better marry her."

I bite back a grin—my first since my mom died. "I plan to."

"She's an angel. See you later."

I ride back to Samantha's apartment, but I tell Eddie to wait for me outside while I go in. She looks up at me. "Is Katrina okay?"

"Yes, she's fine. She plans to go to work tomorrow. She wants to get back into her old life."

"That's good." She cocks her head to study me. "What about you? How are you feeling?"

"I'm feeling like I want to get back into life, too, but not my old life."

She frowns. "What does that mean?"

I cross the room and take her hands. "I want you to come back to my place with me. I don't want to stay here anymore."

"But...I thought you were comfortable here. What's wrong with it?"

I rub her hands. I really want to kiss her right now, but I have to finish this now. "I want you to move in with me. I don't want you to stay here anymore—ever. I don't want to live without you. Come home with me—and stay there. This place.....it's very nice, but this isn't our future. Come on. Eddie is waiting for us downstairs."

Her eyes drop out of their sockets....and then she relaxes and smiles. That smile broadens wider and wider until it casts a blinding light over the whole world.

She barely whispers when she says, "All right. I'll come."

"So....do you need to pack up a few things or what?"

She bursts into an even bigger grin. "Okay. Give me a sec."

I sit down on the couch to wait while she goes upstairs to her bedroom. I can wait all damn night for this.

She comes down with a suitcase. Then she goes into her home office and comes out with another bag over her shoulder.

She stops in the living room and casts a glance around the room. Her eye settles on the picture of her father.

"Take it," I tell her. "Bring it with you."

She beams at me and her cheeks color. "Later. I'll come back and get the rest of what I need. I have a few other paintings I'd like to bring." She blushes again. "You might not like them."

"What are they—Pollock's?"

She laughs. "No, Malevich."

I join in the joke and take her luggage off her hands. She follows me to the door and pauses there to look back.

"You okay?" I ask. "We can wait if it's too sudden."

"No, I want to." She won't look at me. She keeps scanning the room. "I just....I just realized....I never really cared about this place. It's just a place. I just realized....I really don't care about leaving." She smiles up at me. "That's strange, isn't it?"'

"Maybe it would mean more to you if we stayed here."

"No. We should go to your place." She beams at me again. "Good idea. It's the perfect way to start over."

"Are you sure?"

She nods. "I'm sure. Let's go."

I wheel her suitcase to the door and carry the bag over my shoulder on our way to the elevator. She gives Anthony a massive hug. I'm not sure why, but he actually gets choked up when she tells him she's going to move out.

I finally put her and her luggage in the limo. Eddie drives us to my place.

Samantha and I hold hands on the way there. I could kiss her. I could grope her and rip her clothes off in the back of the limo.

This occasion means too much even for that. I don't know if ripping her clothes off will ever be appropriate again, but I'm okay with that.

This....whatever this is between us—it's bigger even than that. It's something even better than ripping her clothes off—which is saying a lot when it comes to her.

Eddie drops me, Samantha, and her luggage at the elevator in the underground parking garage of my building. She gives me an excited grin when I wheel her suitcase into the elevator. "Do I really want to know what your apartment looks like?"

"You're about to find out whether you want to or not. I gave you the option to back out. Don't worry. There isn't anything dangerous waiting for you up there."

She giggles. "Except you, right?"

I bite back a smirk. "Only if you want me to be."

She turns right red, but just then, the elevator stops.

It opens inside my apartment. Every floor of this building is one penthouse apartment owned by a single individual.

Most of them are owned by members of The Billionaires' Club, but they don't all live here all the time. They come and go when they feel like it or when they stay in town for business.

I wheel her suitcase inside and she steps out of the elevator, but she doesn't enter the apartment right away. She stands there taking it all in.

My apartment is bigger and nicer than hers, but it's still just a place to live.

Her eyes track to the long, rectangular sectional couch in front of a low flickering fireplace set into a wall of black stone.

Lever glass doors open onto the terrace with the trees surrounding the pool. A glass-paneled staircase rises to the bedrooms upstairs.

A fountain trickles down a wall of granite laced with vines and hanging plants in the middle of the living room.

I sit down on the couch here, too, and wait for her to migrate through the whole apartment looking at everything.

She goes from room to room and upstairs to the huge open bedroom.

I can just imagine her checking out the bed on a raised platform, the walk-in closet, and the bathroom with the big black stone jacuzzi tub and 360º shower.

Then she'll go out onto the other terrace on the second level with another pool, hot tub, and back downstairs to the indoor gym and racquetball court.

She finally comes downstairs, sits down next to me on the couch, and rests her elbows on her knees while she gazes into the flames flickering in the fireplace.

"What do you think?" I ask. "Do you think you could stay here? It isn't too big for you?"

She doesn't answer for a second before she glances over at me. Her eyes melt and her expression twists up with buried emotion. "You're here. Of course I want to stay here."

I have to kiss her. I slip my fingers into her hair, pull her into my mouth, and we both sink back on the couch.

Kissing her isn't good enough for this moment and she winds up falling onto my chest. I clutch her head against my heart.

This apartment doesn't mean shit without her in it. That's the truth. I don't care if we have to move back to the Bowery as long as we do it together.

She wraps her arms around me extra tight and squeezes. She feels the same thing. I don't even have to ask because she's here and she'll stay here from now on.

# Chapter 42: Samantha

I cross the Titanium Finance executive floor, smile and greet everyone, and enter my office. I didn't think I would get back to work this soon after Lane's mother passed away, but he and Katrina are both bouncing back better than I hoped.

Both of them have been back at work for a week. I haven't gone back to my apartment except to get my things.

Lane insists I hang the picture of my father in the living room. Lane even moved one of his other paintings so I could hang it up.

He's still deciding where to scatter my other artwork around his apartment. I thought it would take me years to get used to living in such an enormous penthouse, but for some reason, I'm getting used to that, too.

Lane and I just seem to fit together. Moving in together doesn't seem all that out of the ordinary.

We've already spent so much time together. We've been through a lot together. This feels easy by comparison.

I already cleaned out my old apartment and put it on the market. I don't have to go back there. Soon it will sell and someone else can enjoy it.

Lane has already sold his mother's building, too. He never wants to see it again. I honestly don't blame him.

I talk to Katrina every day, usually by video chat, just to make sure she's doing okay. We talk for a long time every time.

We get closer every day. I never thought I would get closer to anyone than I am to my own sister and brother.

Now Lane and Katrina are becoming like my second sister and brother—except that Lane and I are together. Now I just have to introduce Lane and Katrina to Casey and Olivia. Don't ask me how I'm going to swing that.

I sit down at my desk and open my computer. I'm just about to pull up my morning appointments when Bradley walks past my door.

He stops in his tracks and freezes when he sees me. "Samantha.... what are you doing here?"

I snort at him. "Um....I work here the last time I checked."

"You mean....you don't know?!"

"Know what? What am I supposed to know?"

He balks, glances up and down the hallway outside, and then hustles into my office. He bends over my desk talking low and fast. "You need to go over to the Apico Acquisitions head office right away! We all heard the word this morning..."

"What word?" I'm not sure I want to know. "Why do they want to see me at the head office?"

Bradly glances over his shoulder again and lowers his voice to a whisper. "You have to get out of here right now, Samantha! I don't know what's going on, but you need to go over to the Apico head office right now and deal with this."

"Deal with what? You're really scaring me, Bradley."

"Word went out this morning before anyone came into the office!" he whispers. "You're being accused of embezzlement. The Apico board is drawing up the paperwork right now to get you investigated and probably indicted."

I blink at him for a second. My brain won't accept that I actually heard him right.

A second later, my phone rings. It's Lane. He might call me this early in the morning for some minor detail of our joint business dealings, but the sound of my phone ringing gives me a very bad feeling.

I can't even get my voice to work well enough to answer him.

It doesn't matter because he starts blaring at me the instant I switch on the phone. "You need to get over here to the Apico head office right this minute, Samantha! Do you hear me?! I don't care if you have to charter a plane. Get over here right now—and don't talk to anyone. Understand?! Don't say a word to anyone. I don't care who it is or what they say to you. Just walk out the door, get in a cab, and come straight here. I'll meet you out front. Okay?"

My mouth moves, but I can't answer—not with those terrible words hanging over my head. I can't even more. I am NOT being charged with embezzlement. That isn't possible.

I can't even summon the willpower to get out of my chair. I look down at my phone. I should turn it off.

Bradley comes to my rescue by walking around my desk and taking hold of my elbow. Lane was talking loudly enough for Bradley to hear every word.

He takes hold of my arm and physically stands me up out of my chair. He murmurs, "Let's go," and marches me out of the office.

Everyone turns around to stare at me on our way to the elevator. Bradley doesn't let go of my arm all the way to the street.

He escorts me out to the curb, puts me in a cab, stuffs a wad of cash into the driver's hand, and gives the address for the Apico Acquisitions building.

I can't think or move or even breathe on my way there. This isn't happening.

I worked my ass off to make Titanium Finance work. I've given every ounce of my effort to Apico, too.

What possible evidence could they have that I ever embezzled anything? I've never embezzled in my life. I wouldn't even know where to begin.

I get out of the cab before I remember. My brother Casey is a lawyer. I should call him, but Lane rushes me before I can go anywhere.

He takes my elbow exactly the way Bradley did. Lane hisses low in my ear while marches me into the building. "You have to meet with the Board of Directors about the accusations, but at least we'll be able to see what evidence they have against you."

"What evidence *do* they have against me?" I croak.

"God only knows. This is our best way to find out. I already called Katrina. She's on her way over. I managed to stall the meeting until she gets here. No way in hell are you going in there without a lawyer."

That reminds me. I stop and look down at my phone. "I have to call Casey."

"Who's that?" he asks.

"He's my brother. He's a lawyer, too."

Lane frowns. "Oh." Then he shrugs. "Okay. Do it."

I tap Casey's contact, but when he answers and I hear his voice saying, "Hey, baby," on the other end, I lose it completely. I break down in tears. I can't stand Casey finding out about this, but he has to find out.

Lane puts his arms around me and I buckle on his chest. This isn't happening.

I hear Casey saying, "Baby girl? Are you there? What's wrong? Talk to me."

Lane takes my phone away from me. I start crying even harder when he puts the phone to his ear and starts talking to Casey in my place.

"Casey Mulholland?" Lane asks.

Casey changes his tone real quick. "Who the hell is this?"

"My name is Lane Prince. I'm the CEO of Apico Acquisitions."

"I know who the hell you are, jackass," Casey snaps. "Now tell me what the fuck you're doing with my sister's phone."

Lane gives him a quick rundown of the charges, where we are, the meeting that's about to happen, and that Lane has already called his sister Katrina to represent me. Lane then asks Casey to come over and help us and gives Casey the address.

Casey says a very curt, "I'm on my way," and hangs up.

Lane steers me to a bench in the Apico Acquisitions headquarters building lobby. The building is a big, luxurious, modern, glass office tower with beautiful sitting areas and a few indoor gardens in the lobby.

He pulls me down on one of the couches with his arm around my shoulder. "It's going to be all right. Casey and Katrina will straighten this whole thing out. Don't worry about it."

I struggle to pull myself together. I can't let the Apico Board of Directors see me getting upset over this. I need to go into this meeting composed so I can confront the charges rationally.

Katrina shows up first, sits down on my other side, and puts her arms around me, too. "We're gonna beat this thing," she murmurs in my ear. "You don't worry about this. Whatever they have on you can't be enough to stick. We'll beat it. You'll be back at work in no time. Don't worry."

I wish like anything I could believe that, but that awful word keeps ringing in my ears.

Embezzlement. I never thought I'd ever live to see the day when someone would say that about me.

Katrina turns to Lane and murmurs across me. "What do they have on her?"

"I have no idea," Lane murmurs back. "That's why we're having this meeting—so the board can show us why they even think she's guilty of this. I can't imagine what it might be."

"Wouldn't someone have noticed before now if anything was wrong with Titanium's books?" Katrina asks. "I thought you said everything was going well and Titanium's profits were up and everything since Samantha took over."

"They are. I just don't think there's any way...." He stops with his mouth open and his expression changes.

"What, Lane?" Katrina insists. "If you know something, you better tell me right now."

Before Lane can say anything, my brother Casey walks into the lobby. He spots the three of us from across the room.

He slows and then stops when he sees both Lane and Katrina with their arms around me. Casey's features harden into a wall of granite. He compresses his lips and grits his teeth before he comes over to us.

Lane and Katrina realize a second too late that Casey is standing right in front of us. He looks down at them talking across me to each other in this breathless murmur.

They both stand up way too fast. Lane tries to shake the tension out of his arms and holds out his hand to Casey. "Thanks for coming over so fast. We were just about to go into the meeting. This is my sister Katrina Prince. She's an attorney with Warner, Fitzgerald, and Palmer."

Katrina holds out her hand, too. "It's very nice to meet you. Your sister is very special to both of us. We're going to do everything possible to beat this thing."

Casey eyes them both, casts the most passing glance at their hands sticking out in his direction, and walks straight past both of them.

He sidesteps Lane, sits down next to me, puts his arm around my shoulders exactly the way Lane just did, and murmurs in my ear fast and low. "It's gonna be all right, baby. I'm here. I'm gonna take care of everything. Okay? Everything is gonna be all right. I'm gonna make it alright. Don't worry."

He flattens his hand to the other side of my face and kisses me on the cheekbone before he bothers even for a second to look at Lane and Katrina standing there.

I sense their discomfort that Casey is giving them the cold shoulder, but Lane and Katrina both shrug it off. "We should probably go upstairs," Lane suggests. "We're already late."

Casey looks up at him for the first time. "What do they have on her?"

"We don't know," Lane replies. "That's what we were hoping to find out in this meeting. I mean, they have to tell us what they have against her before they file any complaint. Right?

Casey skewers him with a brutal stare and then dips one nod. "All right. Let's go."

Casey takes my hand and pulls me to my feet. Lane doesn't try to come near me with Casey standing guard. He's always been protective. I guess Lane can respect that considering his history with Katrina.

Casey turns to me and uses his thumbs to wipe the tears off my face. "Come on and pull yourself together, baby girl. No crying in front of the enemy. Understand? Don't say a word in there. Let me do all the talking. Understand? You don't say a thing."

# Chapter 43:
# Samantha

L ane and Katrina lead the way to the elevator. Casey holds my hand and we ride up to the Apico Acquisitions executive floor in silence.

The tension in the elevator escalates to Armageddon level on the way there. The hostility between Casey and Lane is off the charts—or at least it is on Casey's side.

He doesn't say anything until we get to the executive floor. He leads me outside and lets go of my hand. "Here we go," he murmurs in my face. "Are you ready?"

I nod again. That's the best I can do under the circumstances.

Casey, Katrina, and I turn to follow Lane to the directors' boardroom, but Lane stops us there. "Wait a minute. You asked me downstairs if there was anything else...."

"You know something, don't you?" Katrina blurts out. "Tell me what it is. We need any ammunition we can get against these people."

"I don't know if it means anything....but this last weekend...."

"Spit it out, Lane," Katrina snaps. "We don't have time to tiptoe around. Just tell us."

"Samantha....and the Titanium Finance executive team.....they went to a convention upstate to network and court new clients and investors. I went up there to check it out....and...." Lane's eyes dart to Casey. "Things developed between me and Samantha."

"Is that all?" Katrina fires back. "Now is not the time to tell us that, Lane."

"You don't understand. One of the Apico execs showed up and started making trouble for Samantha."

"He did?" I blurt out. "You didn't tell me that."

"He started finding fault with your work....and you making decisions independently from the Apico executive. He wanted to either rein you in or get rid of you. Then, after he told you off in front of the whole convention, I took him aside and I was going to fire him. He told me he knew about us—that we were staying together at the convention. He said he was going to get both of us axed as soon as we got back to New York."

"But you gave him that letter—and he disappeared," I point out. "He resigned without any explanation before we even came back to New York."

"I know. I'm just saying...." Lane glances first at Katrina and then at Casey. Now Casey knows everything—as if he wasn't smart enough to figure it out already. "I'm just saying....he might have had something to do with this."

Katrina takes a deep breath. "All right. Now we know. Now let's get in there and find out who and what is really behind this." She glances at Casey. "Are you ready?"

Casey dips his chin one more time, but I definitely feel him seething with buried hostility toward Lane. This is not the way I planned to introduce them to each other.

Lane goes first followed by Katrina. Casey stays next to me and whispers in my ear again, "Everything is going to be all right. Don't worry about a thing."

I can half-believe that with him, Katrina, and Lane all supporting me. I couldn't do this alone.

Lane holds the door open for the rest of us and we file into the boardroom. Marshall Weiss, Marco Van Sant, Ricardo Thorn, and Russel Shauer sit off to one side.

A bunch of older executives sit at one end of the long table. This must be the Apico Acquisitions Board of Directors. I've never met any of them.

"You shouldn't be in here, Lane," an old man in the top chair begins. "Your involvement in this gives you a conflict of interest."

"That's exactly why I'm here," Lane replies. "I'm here to give Samantha my unconditional support. She's totally innocent of these crimes. If anything, she's being framed to drive her out of both Titanium Finance and Apico Acquisitions. These are her two attorneys, Katrina Prince of Warner, Fitzgerald, and Palmer and Casey Mulholland of Holden & Sons."

Casey looks up when Lane mentions which law firm Casey works for. Now Casey knows that Lane knows who Casey is, too. We're all on a level playing field here.

The old guy frowns and exchanges glances with his closest colleagues. "It isn't necessary for Ms. Mulholland to engage legal representation at this stage of the proceedings. I hope you realize how guilty this makes you look, Ms. Mulholland."

"You didn't think you were going to accuse her of embezzlement and threaten to get her indicted without her legal counsel present, did you?" Casey fires back. "You're the ones who look guilty by trying to entrap my client in a room by herself without representation. Now you better show us whatever evidence you have against her. Otherwise, we're done here."

"And it better be exceptional evidence," Katrina adds. "If it's as flimsy as I suspect, we'll be filing a counter harassment and specious prosecution complaint against Apico Acquisitions. I'm sure we can get a hefty settlement out of you to save whatever scraps will be left of your company's reputation."

The directors exchange more furtive glances. Now they really look nervous.

A middle-aged woman with streaks of grey in her hair stands up halfway down the table. She opens her laptop and turns it toward us on the table so we can see the screen.

"As you can see, funds have been disappearing from Titanium Finance accounts over the past month—all after Derek Salazar left. Samantha Mulholland was in charge of Titanium during the time period in question. She had sole access to these accounts and the money was all taken from special circumstances transfers specifically authorized by her alone."

I take a step forward to see the spreadsheets on the laptop screen. Casey shoots his arm across me to stop me.

"You will forward these documents to Ms. Prince and me immediately," he clips at the directors. "If we find out you filed any complaint against Ms. Mulholland before her legal team has had a chance to examine this evidence, you'll be opening yourself to another charge of malicious prosecution. Ms. Mulholland has a right to examine the evidence against her and answer the charges in her own defense."

"That's why we're initiating this investigation," the senior director points out. "We can't expect her closest supporters to carry out an unbiased investigation. We're turning everything over to the Police."

"If you really want to risk the public humiliation of bringing these charges only to have them disproved in a public forum, then you're too stupid to run this company or any other," Katrina cuts in. "If you were anywhere near as smart as you think you are, you would let us examine the evidence ourselves and find out who really embezzled the money before this blows up all over the internet where your clients and investors can see it."

"Or *we* can blow it up all over the internet for you," Casey replies. "We're going to get our hands on this evidence one way or the other. If you bring this complaint, we'll make sure you regret it for the rest of your days."

Lane interrupts for the first time. "Just forward us the documentation, Charles. You know you have to do it anyway. Don't smear the company's reputation by holding it back."

The old man sighs and waves to the woman. "Fine. Send it through."

"We'll examine this evidence and get back to you." Casey takes hold of my elbow and steers me toward the door. "If you have anything else to share, I strongly suggest you disclose it now. You'll all be much better off. Trust me."

He leads me out of the room. Katrina and Lane meet up with us outside.

A notification goes off on Lane's phone. "I got the file. I'm sending it to you, Katrina. What's your email address, man?"

Casey hesitates and then recites his email address. Lane works over his phone to send the document to all three of us. He pretends not to notice Casey acting like a volcano ready to blow his top.

"Now what do we do?" I ask.

"Now we go over those documents," Katrina tells me. "And we need to make sure you keep a clear head, Samantha, because you're the one who understands this stuff the best."

# Chapter 44: Lane

I let my head fall onto my arms on my desk. I really need to stop thinking about the charges against Samantha.

I look up, squint at my computer screen, and command myself to concentrate on my work, but the case keeps coming back to haunt me.

Casey and Katrina have been working around the clock trying to find some small detail that will clear Samantha's name.

Samantha and I have spent our every waking minute helping them, especially since, like Katrina says, Samantha understands these accounts so much better than we do.

Casey's threats did the trick. The Apico Acquisitions Board of Directors is letting Samantha continue working pending the outcome of the investigation.

That might be their way of sabotaging our case. Her working at Titanium while Casey and Katrina investigate the accounts only means she has even less time to help them comb through mountains of transactions.

Each of those transactions could be the clue that cracks this case—except that they couldn't *all* be the clue that cracks the case. That's the worst part about all of this.

Whoever did this targeted transactions she specifically authorized to deal with the server malfunctions. No one else had access to the funds between the Titanium Finance bank accounts and the server provider.

Whoever this embezzler is, he sure stitched up this case tight. None of us can find a single flaw in the whole thing.

I don't even really care that Casey Mulholland hates me and wants to kill me for hooking up with his sister. I understand how he feels. I would want to kill any man who looked at my sister like that, too.

I can live with him hating me as long as Samantha gets acquitted of these charges. I can live with everything else as long as she's okay.

My finger hovers over my mouse. The Ashcroft contract gleams out of my screen waiting for me to read it.

I could switch to the Titanium documents with one click of my mouse. Should I? I wouldn't see anything there that I haven't seen a thousand times before.

Just then, Marco Van Sant sticks his head into my office. "Hey! Why don't you knock off for the night? It's already nine o'clock. You'll go blind if you look at it any longer."

I sigh. "I'm not getting anything done here anyway. I might as well."

I switch off my computer, but the documentation still hovers in front of my eyes. I practically have all those entries memorized by now. There's nothing there for us to find.

I pull my jacket on and leave the office. Marco waits for me and walks next to me on our way to the elevator. He doesn't say anything while I text Eddie to come pick me up in the limo.

Samantha is working late, too. I know she has the same problem concentrating on work with this case weighing on her shoulders.

I'll pick her up in the limo and maybe take her out for a late dinner to take her mind off her problems.

A late dinner with me won't take her mind off the case. Staring at each other across the dinner table will only make us both think about it more.

I need to come up with a way to distract her, but I'll pick her up in the limo either way. At least we'll be able to spend a few minutes alone together before we go meet up with Casey and Katrina again.

Marco brings me back to the present. "Do you have any plans tonight?"

"Just going to meet up with my sister and Samantha's brother to go over the evidence against her for the embezzlement case." I pass my hand across my eyes. "I just wish we could find something."

"Maybe you aren't finding anything because there's nothing there to find."

"I know there's nothing there to find. That's the problem."

"And maybe there's nothing there to find because she really is guilty. Did you ever think of that?"

"No," I reply. "I honestly didn't."

He shakes his head. "You really got it bad for her, don't you? She was always going to be a problem for us. The company will be better off without her."

We both stop in front of the elevator. I don't answer.

I've heard it all before. I heard it from Ethan. I heard it from Marshall. I heard it from Russel.

Marco is the one person I have never heard it from. He has never said anything against Samantha—ever. So why is he saying it now?

The elevator doors open. I step inside and Marco steps in with me.

Marco Van Sant. He's the CFO of Apico Acquisitions and he's as solid as they come. He's one of the people around here that I trust most.

Why would he support Samantha in the beginning, only to turn against her now? Is it the embezzlement accusation? I find that impossible to believe.

We exit on the ground floor and walk outside together. Eddie stands next to my limo with the door open. Marco's limo sits behind mine. His driver opens the door for him.

"Try to take the night off for once in your life," Marco tells me. "You're gonna burn yourself out if you keep driving yourself like this."

I nod. "Thanks, man. I'll try."

He gets in his limo and I get in mine. Eddie shuts the door, gets behind the wheel, and pulls away from the curb. Marco's limo pulls out first and turns left.

"Drive around the block, Eddie," I tell him.

He cocks his head to study me through the rearview mirror. "I beg your pardon, Mr. Prince?"

"I said drive around the block. Drop me off in front of the Apico building....and leave the engine running."

"Yes, Sir," Eddie replies.

My mind starts racing on my way around the block. Marco Van Sant. He's the CFO of Apico Acquisitions.

Apico Acquisitions bought out Titanium Finance—which means Apico Acquisitions got executive authority over every single bank account associated with Titanium Finance.

Marco Van Sant is the only man in the whole company who's authorized to handle all those accounts—both Apico Acquisition accounts and Titanium Finance accounts.

Why the hell didn't I think of this before? The embezzlement accusation hinges on one thing. Samantha was the only person with access to both the accounts and the transactions where money disappeared—but she wasn't the only person with access. Marco did, too.

He's too smart to steal a bunch of money and hide it anywhere anyone might be able to find it. That would be too obvious.

So where did he put it? Where *could* he put it?

I have to stop myself from running back up to my office. I switch on my computer, but I don't look at the files the directors gave us. I already know there's nothing there.

The Board of Directors could only have gotten those files from Marco. He's the only other person besides Samantha who goes over them well enough to find the missing money.

How perfect would it be if he was the embezzler and sent those files to the directors so they could find the embezzlement?

Of course Marco heard the other Apico executives bad-mouthing Samantha. She was the perfect patsy to take the fall for him.

There was just one flaw in his plan. The money had to go somewhere. It has to be somewhere.

I switch over to the Apico internal financial records. It doesn't take me long to find what I'm looking for. All I have to do is narrow the search results to deposits made to Apico accounts from Titanium accounts.

It's all there in black and white. The son of a bitch hid the money in Apico's own bank accounts—the bank accounts Marco himself oversees. He could hide it there in plain sight and no one would ever see it because no one ever checks his work.

I shoot out of my seat real fast and rip out my phone on my way down the hall toward the elevator. I have to call Samantha. I have to tell her about this. She has to be the first person who finds out I caught the culprit.

The phone rings....and rings....and rings. Then it switches to voice-mail. Her voice tells me she isn't available and that, if I leave a message, she'll call me back as soon as possible. Damn it.

"Samantha!" I practically yell. Fortunately, I'm in the elevator and it's the middle of the night so no one can hear me. "I need you to call me immediately! It's a matter of life and death. I found out who the embezzler is. I know who it is! Call me!"

I hang up and navigate to Katrina's contact.

I pause with my thumb hanging over the button to call her. I should tell her and Casey about this, but something about leaving a message on Samantha's voicemail stops me from calling anyone else.

I've never left her a voicemail before—because she always picks up. I've called her at all hours about everything going on at Titanium Finance. We always talk about everything, big and small, and she always answers. Why not this time?

I get a very bad feeling about this, and right at that moment, the elevator doors open. I storm outside where Eddie stands with the limo door open. "Take me to the Titanium Finance building," I tell him, "and step on it."

# Chapter 45: Samantha

I strain my eyes at the spreadsheets in front of me. These aren't the documents I got from the Apico Board of Directors.

I've already taken twenty years off my life studying those. There's nothing in them.

Whoever the embezzler is, he covered his tracks too well. The files show the money leaving Titanium Finance bank accounts. These don't show where the money went.

The files don't show anything that might exonerate me. That would be too easy.

The embezzler must have given these files to the directors to frame me. That would be just perfect. Now all I have to do is find out who gave the directors these files.

But I don't look at those files. They're getting me nowhere.

Instead, I study different spreadsheets of transactions from different Titanium Finance departments. If I bury myself deeply enough in work, I might be able to forget that someone accused me of embezzlement.

I could never forget that. At least Casey, Katrina, and Lane are still helping and supporting me.

They can support me, but they can't help me because we have nothing—not a single shred of evidence that I didn't take the money.

Lane is working late tonight, too. He'll call or text me when he leaves the office. We'll ride in the limo to Lane's apartment where we'll meet back up with Casey and Katrina.

Then all of us will slave over this case until we're too exhausted to see straight. Then we'll crash and do it all again tomorrow. We'll keep getting nowhere and this case will go to the Police and the District Attorney so they can prosecute me.

I sigh. I really just need to leave the office and get some sleep. I've been burning the candle at both ends this past week. All four of us have.

I push back my chair to turn off my laptop, but right at that moment, I hear footsteps coming toward me down the hall outside. That's strange. Lane should have texted or called when he left the Apico building. He never shows up here without telling me first that he's on his way.

I don't know who to expect. My door swings open.

I wilt in relief when Marco Van Sant walks into my office. I start to smile at him. He's always nice to me.

"What are you doing out of bed at this hour?" I tease. "You should be on your way home."

"You don't need to worry about me and my sleep habits. You should be more worried about yourself."

I look up. "What do you mean? If it's the embezzlement case, we have to go over the...."

The words die on my lips when he pulls a gun out of his jacket pocket and aims it at me. "Sit still and don't make a sound," he murmurs under his breath. "I'm going to kill you anyway. If you make a sound, I'll kill you sooner. That's the only difference. If you keep quiet, you might live a few minutes longer."

I can't even gulp. I can't even blink. Marco Van Sant? Really?

He's the one person on the Apico executive board besides Lane who has been the nicest, the most supportive, and the most encouraging.

I sit glued to my seat and stare at him in disbelief. He can't be holding me at gunpoint. That isn't possible.

I'm too stunned to realize that Marco is only the second person ever to hold me at gunpoint. The other person who did that was the carjacker.

Marco watches me to make sure I don't move or make a sound. I'm too floored by this turn of events to move or make a sound.

He strides around my desk. The gun gets closer to my head. The charge of electricity crackling between the gun and my skull sets every nerve on end.

This is bad. This is just as bad or worse than the carjacking.

Marco just said he plans to kill me either way.

The carjacker may have been planning to kill me afterward, but he never came out and said so. He said he would kill me if I didn't cooperate. He didn't say he would kill me whether I cooperated or not.

Marco is calm, cold, collected, and deadly serious. I never doubt for an instant that he really will kill me no matter what.

He holds the gun an inch from my ear while he pulls a zip-tie around one of my wrists. He cinches it against the arm of my chair and then zip-ties the other wrist to the other arm.

He migrates around the desk back to the place he was standing when he first entered the room. "Now we wait," he tells me in the same calm undertone.

I take a chance. I have to do something to get out of this alive. I don't know what I'll do, but I better come up with something spectacular real quick.

The fact that he's being so calm gives me a chance to think. I won't just sit here and let him kill me. Hell no. Not after everything I've already gone through.

I try to keep my voice steady, but it winds up shaking anyway. "What are we waiting for?" I ask.

"We're waiting for Lane. Lane will come and find you here one way or the other. Then I'll kill you both, make it look like an accident, and I'll leave the country. It's that simple."

I allow myself to raise my eyebrows. "Accident? How will you make it look like an accident?"

"Someone is bound to find out I embezzled money from Titanium Finance. It's only a matter of time. So I'll make it look like Lane found out that you were the embezzler after all. He's head over heels for you, you know. So I'll make it look like he came over here to confront you. You two got into a heated lover's argument, you both pulled guns, and shot each other."

"With the same gun?" I snort at him. "That's going to be way too obvious."

"It won't matter because I'll be long gone out of the country before anyone puts it together that one gun killed both of you. I have a nice little nest egg stored up overseas. I'll move to a non-extradition treaty country and live happily ever after as they say."

He gives me a ghastly smile. What a disgusting creature he is.

Whatever fear I might have turns to fury. I can't let him get away with this. I have to warn Lane somehow, but I can't get to my phone while I'm tied up.

Marco glances around and spots the chairs opposite my desk. He sweeps his jacket inward, sits down in the chair, and straightens up so he can aim at me across the desk. He makes himself comfortable to wait for Lane to show up.

Marco's attitude pushes me over the edge. This dipshit is way too smug for his own good. I have to stop him if only to save myself and Lane. I can't let Marco kill both of us and then ride off into the sunset. I have to end this asshole right now—but how?

I get a sudden brainwave, throw all my weight against my chair, and hurl myself sideways onto the floor. Marco doesn't see in time.

He rockets to his feet and fires, but I'm already hiding behind the desk. He charges around the desk trying to get a clear shot at me, but I'm all done playing games.

The idiot left my feet and legs free. I can run just fine—and I can use my hands. They're just zip-tied to a chair.

I scramble onto my feet, but I have to crouch behind the desk and scuttle in circles to keep out of Marco's range.

He keeps firing again and again. One of his shots hits the chair behind me and pings off. I can't let him catch up with me again.

I make one last dive around the desk. I'm on the side facing the door, but I don't run for it. I could, but instead, I shoot to my feet, make a desperate grab for the desk, and snatch the letter opener sitting in my pen jar.

I have to duck for cover again as Marco opens fire. He bares his teeth and snarls at me in a rage. He doesn't even pretend to be his usually polite, distinctive self.

I lunge behind the desk and sprawl on the floor for protection, but I have to work hard to cut the zip-ties. It's kinda hard when I can't use my hands, so I use my mouth instead.

I jam the letter opener into one of the ties and twist just as Marco stalks around the other side of the desk.

The zip-tie gives way, but I don't have time to cut the other one. I yank the chair in front of me. I can't even stand up. I can only lie here on my back and hold the chair between him and me.

He barges around the desk and stands directly over me aiming the gun at my face. How much punishment can this chair take before a bullet punches through it and kills me?

He stops there grimacing down at me in pure murderous hatred. Why does he hate me so much? I only ever tried to do my job.

He raises the gun. His knuckles go white on the trigger. He tenses his whole arm to fire.

At that moment, Lane dives for Marco from the other side of the room. I don't even see Lane coming before he slams both hands down on Marco's jacket and rips him away.

Marco stumbles trying to catch his balance. He does his best to aim his gun at Lane, but Lane attacks too fast.

He keeps both hands locked on Marco's jacket and flings Marco staggering into my office window.

Lane yanks Marco away and smashes Marco's head into the glass again...and again. Marco struggles at first, but Lane overpowers him.

Marco's head leaves bloody splotches on the window and the glass shatters. Lane roars in fury, hauls Marco back, and sends him wheeling headfirst into the window for the last time.

The glass caves and Marco plunges out into the night forty floors above the ground.

# Chapter 46: Lane

I pace back and forth in the hospital waiting room. I've already given a million statements to Detective Beckett about what happened. Now I'm just waiting for word on Samantha. She's still in the back with Casey.

Katrina sits in the chairs nearby, but she doesn't try to talk to me or calm me down or reassure me. Nothing will be able to reassure me until I see for myself that Samantha is okay.

I don't even care that I killed Marco Van Sant. The cops say I killed him by crushing his head against the window. The forty-story fall ruined the rest of him, but he was already dead before he hit the ground.

Good. I'm glad. I would do it again. Anyone who aims a gun at Samantha can expect the same thing.

I jump a foot in the air when the Emergency Department doors swing open and Casey comes out looking equally murderous. Nothing better have happened to her, but I can't think of any other reason he would be so mad.

I have to find out the truth, even if it's bad. I walk over to him. "How is she? Is she okay?"

"Come over here, man." He takes hold of my arm and drags me into a corner of the room where no one will overhear us, not even Katrina. This must be really bad. Is Samantha dead back there?

She took a bullet in the side of her ribs. I was too busy stopping the bleeding to see how bad the wound was. The gunshot might have punctured a lung—or worse.

"Just give it to me straight," I tell Casey. "I can't take any more stress tonight. Is Samantha okay?"

He straightens up in front of me and levels me with that hard glare of his. "She's fine, man. The bullet barely grazed her ribs. They're going to let her out in a few minutes. I just wanted to tell you......she told me about the carjacking. I ...." He shuts his eyes tight. "I'm sorry. I'm sorry I was rude to you. I don't know how to make it up to you, but I'll find a way."

"Forget it," I tell him. "She's....."

Now it's my turn to falter. I have to get this out in the open between us now. I can't go another second without telling him where I stand.

"She's very special to me," I tell him. "I'm serious about her. I've never been more serious about any woman. I want to make it official—with your permission, of course. I just didn't know how to ask."

"Of course you have my permission. If you did all that for her.....I'd be honored. She needs a good man who takes care of her. Here. Take t his."

He pulls a notebook and a pen out of his inner jacket pocket and scribbles something on it. He tears off the page and hands it to me.

"This is my stepdad's address and phone number. You talk to him, but wait a few days until I talk to him first. Give me a chance to tell him about you. Then he'll be ready when you ask. He'll know what you two have gone through together. That will grease the wheels and

I'm sure he'll give you his permission, too. He's a good man. He'll be happy for you both."

I stare down at the slip of paper in my hand. "Thank you. This means a lot."

He claps me on the shoulder. "Not as much as everything you've done for her. I can't tell you how grateful I am. She's....she and Olivia are everything to me."

"I understand. My sister is everything to me, too. I would do anything to protect her. You didn't know anything about me. Don't think anything more about it."

"Thank you." He sticks out his hand. "Let me make it up to you now."

I clasp his hand tight and find myself grinning. "It's good to meet you."

He laughs. "Yeah. I'll go get her and we can all get the hell out of here. We all need some sleep after this week."

He goes back into the closed-off area behind the Emergency Department. The doors swing shut with him inside.

I stagger over to the chairs and collapse in the seat next to Katrina. The slip of paper burns a hole in my fingers. Did that conversation really happen?

I don't know why I'm surprised that Casey changed his attitude so radically. He actually gave me his blessing to marry Samantha. This is real. It's actually happening. Now I'm staring down at their stepdad's address and phone number in my hand.

The name on the paper reads, *Walt Agnew.* He's the man who raised, Casey, Olivia, and Samantha Mulholland as his own. Walt Agnew is the one who acted as a father to all three of them and raised them to be the outstanding people they are today.

I haven't met Olivia yet, but I'm sure she'll be as exceptional as Casey and Samantha. I can't imagine her being much different—which means Walt must be as good a man as everyone says he is.

I'll ask him next, but Casey will talk to Walt first. Walt will already know about me before I ask. If Casey is certain Walt will give his blessing, too, then nothing will stop me from marrying Samantha.

The doors swing open for the second time. I get to my feet when Casey comes out with Samantha this time.

She looks tired, but she walks on her own. He doesn't keep his arm around her nor does he have to support her.

She walks a little stooped over. She's still wearing the blouse she had on under her suit when Marco shot her.

Blood stains a torn hole in the fabric on the side above her ribs. I can see a big white bandage underneath covering the tear in her side, but other than that, she looks fine.

She smiles up at me. I can't keep away from her. I walk right up to her and put my arms around her. I don't have to worry anymore about Casey seeing.

I shut my eyes and let my face fall against her hair. "I was so worried about you!"

Her arms slip around me and she squeezes. "Thank you!" she whispers. "Thank you so much for coming for me."

"Of course. I'll always come for you." I push her back and gaze deep into those eyes. I can't stop petting her hair and cheeks. I want to smother her in kisses, but right now, I can just stand here and look.

She's so precious and beautiful.....and now she's mine. I'm going to take her home and no one will separate us again.

"Let's get out of here," Casey tells us. "I would suggest going out for some kind of celebration that the embezzlement case is over, but under the circumstances, I think all of us passing out for a week will be the best celebration."

I turn away and take Samantha's hand. He's right. None of us will be celebrating anything until we get some much-needed rest.

The four of us walk out of the hospital. I need to call Eddie to take us all home.

The four of us pause on the sidewalk to face each other. I don't want to leave just yet. I want to come up with a way to thank Casey and Katrina for helping clear Samantha's name.

*Thank you,* doesn't seem to cut it. Katrina smiles up at me. "Are you two gonna be okay?"

"We will be as soon as we get some sleep." I put my arms around her. "Thank you—for everything."

"Of course. You only have to ask."

She pulls away from me and turns to Samantha. "Thank you so much!" Samantha breathes when they hug. "I don't know how to thank you."

"Let's call it even for the parking lot," Katrina replies.

Samantha laughs. "Okay. It's a deal."

Casey takes a step toward me and holds out his hand. "Don't be a stranger,' he tells me. "I'll talk to you in a few days after I talk to my stepdad. Then you can take it from there."

"Thank you," I choke.

He nods and starts to say, "I'm the one who should be thanking you."

Right then, a deafening clang of breaking glass shatters somewhere up the block from us. Casey glances over his shoulder in that direction. Katrina, Samantha, and I all look over, too.

A sheet of window glass erupts onto the sidewalk twenty yards away. It scatters into the street and five guys in black ski masks jump through the window from inside the nearest building.

My world stops when I see all those guys carrying automatic rifles. They jump through the broken window onto the sidewalk to run away, but at the same moment, gunfire explodes from inside the building.

It scatters through the group of gunmen. They all spin backward and level their guns behind them to return fire.

Katrina, Samantha, Casey, and I stand rooted to the spot watching. This is like something out of a war zone. Gunfire hits one of the gunmen in the chest.

He pinwheels in all directions, spasms, and topples across the pavement. His four comrades try to back away, but they have to keep up a continuous spray of bullets through the window at whoever is shooting at them.

The whole battle is far enough away not to put us in danger, but I don't want to stand around waiting for something bad to happen.

I put out my arm to steer Katrina and Samantha away. At that moment, another blast of gunfire belches from inside the building and hits a second gunman.

He wheels in a complete circle as the bullets riddle his chest, but he doesn't stop shooting. His hand clamps on his weapon and he twirls in our direction still spraying bullets all over the street.

Katrina screams. She and Samantha dive out of the way. Casey whips around to rush us and help me get the two women away, but at that moment, a stray bullet pops into the back of his head and bursts out the other side.

Blood and torn flesh sprays all over me, Samantha, and Katrina. Casey's knees buckle and he sprawls across the pavement.

"CASEY!!" Samantha shrieks.

She rips herself out of my arms and dives for him, but he's already down. She tries to turn him over, but he's too heavy.

Gunfire keeps pounding across the street. I don't dare to stand up.

I pull Samantha away from Casey's body. I don't even try to do it gently. "GET INSIDE THE HOSPITAL!!" I bellow in her face. "Get in there, Samantha! I'll bring Casey inside. GO, SAMANTHA!! You have to tell them that I'm bringing him in. They'll be able to help h im!"

She blinks at me trying to understand. Katrina grabs her and tows her toward the Emergency Department entrance. We're still here outside the hospital after Marco attacked Samantha. We never even got a chance to go anywhere.

Katrina pulls Samantha away. Samantha wakes up enough at last and they take off running for the Emergency Department.

Now I have to carry Casey inside, but at least the gunmen are moving away somewhere else. I hear sirens in the distance, but that doesn't mean anything.

I roll Casey onto his back. I make an executive decision not to look at the damage to his head. He might be dead already and all of this is for nothing.

That doesn't matter. If there's even the smallest chance he might be alive, I have to help him. I have to get him to the people who will be able to fix this.

He's too big for me to lift. I heft him up and sling him over my shoulder in a fireman carry. Even that is asking a lot. He's a big guy—bigger than me.

Fortunately, I only have to stagger a few dozen yards into the Emergency Department. Katrina and Samantha must have convinced everyone that this was serious. A medical team meets me right inside the doors.

I lower Casey's body onto a stretcher—and then I lose sight of him when the medical team surrounds him and wheels him away into the back.

# Chapter 47: Samantha

I startle wide awake when a door slams somewhere. I look around in all directions before I remember where I am.

I'm sitting in the hospital waiting room—a different hospital waiting room. It's already been more than thirty hours since Casey got shot in the head. No one will tell us anything about his condition.

I sit up. I've fallen asleep on Lane's shoulder. He still has his arms around me. He has to let go so I can sit up and rub my eyes.

"You okay?" he murmurs.

I nod, but I'm not okay. I'll never be okay if Casey doesn't come out of this. I can't lose him.

I don't say that, though. Saying it would make it all too real.

It is real, though. Katrina, my sister Olivia, and my mom and step-dad slouch in the chairs nearby. They're all asleep, too.

Lane's phone buzzes on the seat next to him. He picks it up, checks it, and taps on it.

"What are you doing?" I ask.

"I've been talking to the Titanium Finance execs while we've been in here so you don't have to. I've been running all my businesses from my phone. They all know where we are and why—and they all send you their best wishes for Casey's recovery. They all insist that you stay as long as you want to and don't worry about the company." He gives me a very small smile on the side. "It's going to take a few days to repair your office window, so there's no point in you going back now anyway."

I should smile at him, but I don't feel like it. I want to curl up in a hole and stop existing until I hear that Casey is all right.

What if he isn't? What if he's permanently brain-damaged? What if he'll never be able to practice law again—or do anything else again? I don't know if I can live with that.

I look away feeling sick. Nothing will make this okay, not even having Lane here to take care of me—again.

My stepdad stirs across the waiting room. My mom fell asleep on his shoulder. He rests his head on top of hers with his eyes shut.

They and Olivia have all seen Lane sitting with his arms around me, running his fingers through my hair and down my cheeks, and talking to me non-stop about how everything is going to be okay.

My whole family knows now that Lane and I are together, but that doesn't help anything.

He rubs my back and squeezes my neck in a massaging motion. "I'm going down to the cafeteria to get everyone some coffee and something to eat. I'll bring everything back here. Will you be all right until I come back?"

I nod, but I can't feel anything. I look off in another direction when he leaves for the stairs.

My stepdad sits up and that rouses my mom. He says something to her and heads off toward the bathrooms. It's been like this for almost two days. Nothing ever changes.

I lose track of time. I don't even care anymore. I don't care about Titanium Finance or running the company. Nothing matters but Casey.

At least no one has come to tell us he's dead. I guess that means he's still alive.

Every passing hour shatters my nerves a little more. Every passing hour brings home the awful truth that whatever is wrong with him must be really serious.

My stepdad comes back and sits down next to my mom. Olivia wakes up and then Katrina stirs. They both spend a lot of time on their phones handling their own careers while we wait.

I can't resent Olivia for staying busy, but I can only sit here in shock. After everything that's happened, this is the worst.

Lane comes back carrying a big box loaded with sandwiches, snacks, drinks, fruit, and some packages of cookies.

He goes through the room delivering cups of coffee to everyone and asking them all what they want to eat. He gets more of a response from my parents and Katrina than from me and Olivia.

Olivia shakes her head and turns down all food except the coffee. Then she buries herself in her phone again. This must be her way of coping with the situation.

Lane sits down next to me and puts the box next to him. He hasn't even scratched the surface of what's in there. None of us will have to leave to go to the cafeteria again.

He places a cup of coffee in my hands. The heat radiates through my palms and warms me, but I don't want it to warm me. I just want to die.

"You don't have to eat anything, but at least drink this," he tells me. "You haven't eaten anything in three days."

I try to remember and realize he's right. I haven't eaten since the lunch I had before Marco shot me. Right now, today, this morning is the first time I've slept since then, too. No wonder I feel so rotten.

I take a sip of my coffee. I hate that it makes me feel better.

"Would you like a muffin or a sandwich?" he asks.

"Not really," I croak. "I'm sorry. I know I'm not very good company right now."

"Don't worry about it. You're always the best company no matter what's happening." He smiles at me and runs his fingertips from my forehead to my cheek again.

I want to look away, but I can't. He's the only one I trust to see me broken like this. He's the only thing that makes it okay.

"If we don't hear anything by noon, I'm going to take you home," he tells me. "We can't keep sitting around here or one of us is going to get sick and end up in the hospital. I'll take you home and Katrina can go home. I booked an apartment across the street so your parents can stay near the hospital to keep an eye on Casey, but we can't stay here. This has gone on long enough. It's time we all started taking care of ourselves again."

I stare at him trying to take all that in. He's right. Staying here like this—losing sleep and skipping meals—this is much worse for us than worrying about Casey. We could all cope with this much better if we actually had somewhere to stay—like home.

It sounds a lot like Lane has already made up his mind—because he has. He's making that decision for me—and for all of us. Someone has t o.

"If you don't want to eat anything, maybe you'd rather have this." He pulls a sealed white envelope out of his inner jacket pocket and hands it to me.

"What's this—my resignation letter?" I hear myself sneering at whatever he's trying to do. I shouldn't take this out on him.

He only smiles. "It's your promotion. I'd like you to take over as CEO of Titanium Finance."

I frown at him and then the envelope. "I don't understand. Why would I do that when I'm already calling the shots for the whole company?"

"I'm asking you to marry me, sweetheart," he breathes. "If you become CEO, we'll be equally ranked under the Apico Acquisitions Board of Directors. You won't be my subordinate anymore. There won't be any barrier to us getting married and still working together to run these companies. I already got your stepdad's permission and Casey's permission to propose to you."

"Casey.....Casey said......"

"I asked him right before the shooting. He said he'd be honored if I was the man who took care of you. Marry me, Samantha. I don't want to live without you ever again."

Tears well up in my eyes. I don't know if I'm happy or sad, but right then, two doctors in white lab coats come down the hall from somewhere else.

One of them is a young woman about my age. The other is an older man with salt-and-pepper hair and plenty of grey in his beard.

Their arrival sends a shockwave through everyone in the room. We all shoot to our feet and converge around the two doctors. "What's happening?" my mom stammers. "What's happening with Casey?"

"He's out of surgery. He's still in ICU," the female doctor tells us.

"How bad is it?" Lane asks. "He's been in surgery for so long."

"Actually, he's been out of surgery for about seven hours. We had a mass casualty incident with more than forty other patients, so no one has been able to come and talk to you before now. I apologize for the delay, but every other member of the hospital staff has been downstairs working this whole time to save as many lives as we can. Casey is going to make a full recovery."

"So.....there's no brain damage?" Olivia asks.

"The bullet shattered his skull and tore the outer membranes surrounding his brain, but the bullet didn't touch the brain itself. We spent several hours reconstructing his skull and installing plates in his skull to stabilize the broken bones. Other than that, he'll have a long scar on his scalp, but his hair will regrow and cover that. The tears in his cerebral membranes caused swelling in his brain, but that will all subside in a few months. After that, he should be back to full functioning. I'd be very surprised if he suffered any permanent damage from this at all."

My mom bursts into tears and falls apart on my stepdad's shoulder. He pats her on the back and blinks away tears. "He's going to be all right," my stepdad chokes. "He's going to be all right."

"You can come back and see him if you want to," the female doctor tells us. "He's still unconscious, but he should be awake and responsive in a few days. You can visit him for a few minutes, but after that, it's just a matter of waiting."

I can't move. The weight lifting off my shoulders leaves me dazed. Casey is going to be all right. I can't believe it. I don't want to believe it

.

I barely feel it when Lane puts his arm around me and guides me to the hall leading into the back.

My mom, stepdad, Katrina, and Olivia file down the hall and the doctors show us to Casey's room.

He lies flat on his back with tubes and wires going into his nose, mouth, and head. A giant bandage covers his skull. Black and blue bruises surround his eyes and he doesn't respond when my mom kisses him.

I can't go near him. I don't want to be near him until he comes back to us. I want to see him alive and well and sitting up and talking to us. I don't want to be around him when he's barely alive.

I shouldn't think that way, but I really need to get the hell out of here. I want to go home. I need sleep and a shower and....and an end to all this danger and chaos. I just need to go back to the one place in the world where I know everything will be all right.

That one place is Lane's apartment—the apartment where I've been living with him for the past week.

It seems like I've been living there for years. I can't imagine living anywhere else. He's right. I can't stand having anything between us—not even the question of what's going to happen between us.

I want all of that settled and taken care of so I don't have to think about it anymore. I want to know with absolute certainty that we're going to be together no matter what life throws at us.

Now I can do that. I can know that. I can marry him.

Katrina, Olivia, and I hang back while my mom makes a fuss over Casey, but of course he doesn't respond. My stepdad eventually has to pry her away from him.

Olivia waits until we get out into the hall before she politely takes her leave from us. "I can't stay here anymore. I need to go home."

"We all feel the same way," Lane replies. "I'm going to take Samantha home." He kisses Katrina on the cheek. "I'll call you later, okay?"

"Okay, bye." She hugs him and then me. "Take care of yourselves. Call me if you need anything."

Lane escorts me and my parents downstairs. He puts me in the limo while he takes my mom and stepdad across the street to the apartment he arranged for them.

I should go with them, but my brain isn't working well enough for that.

I curl up on the limo seat and shut my eyes while I wait. I'm more exhausted than I realized. I wake up when Lane opens the limo door.

"Don't move," he tells me. "You can stay there."

He sits down next to my head and runs his fingers through my hair while Eddie drives us home.

I must have drifted off again because I wake up again when Lane kisses me. "We're home, sweetheart. It's time to get up and go inside."

I pry myself off the seat. I'm almost completely unresponsive when I stagger out of the car and into the elevator.

Lane puts his arm around me and my head falls on his shoulder. I can't deal with this or anything else right now, but it's okay because he knows and understands. He doesn't expect me to function.

We stagger into the apartment—or I stagger into the apartment. He lets go of me so I can blunder upstairs to the bedroom.

I sink onto the mattress and bury my face in my hands. I can collapse here, now that it's all over.

Casey is going to be all right. My parents will stay in the apartment downtown across the street from the hospital.

They could be there for a while. Maybe they'll take Casey there while he recovers. He could be in rehab for a while after that before he fully gets back on his feet.

My mind ranges outward to my parents, my sister, Katrina, and wider than that to the Titanium Finance staff. Each of them calls me back to the life waiting for me out there, but I still have one more thing left. I can't move forward until I put it to rest.

Lane comes upstairs, sits down on the mattress next to me, and rubs my back. "How are you doing?" he murmurs low.

I look up at him….and our eyes meet. "Yes," I tell him.

He frowns. "What do you mean?"

"Yes," I repeat. "Yes, I'll marry you."

He bursts into a grin and kisses me, but this doesn't turn into a raging sex-fest. He slips his hand into my hair, falls back on the pillows, and pulls me down on his chest. My eyes close.

I could crawl on top of him and rip his clothes off.....or he could crawl on top of me and rip my clothes off.....or he could push me against the wall and make me scream.....or one of us could crawl between the other's legs to give them the greatest ecstasy of their lives.

All those pleasures and experiences wait for us in the future. Right now, we're just here, in our own home, in our own bed, together the way we should be.

The envelope with the paperwork making me CEO of Titanium Finance still stays hidden in his jacket pocket. All I have to do is sign the papers and it will be over.

Then the whole world will know that I'm Mrs. Lane Prince, keeper of his heart and the treasure chest of all he holds dear just as he is for me.

I can't think of anything better than that. Now that dream is coming true for us and everyone else who matters to us. It's going to be a wonderful future and it all starts right here, right now, right in this moment.

End of Book 1.

# Keep Reading

## T he Billionaires' Club Series: Book 2: Cruel Obsession

When billionaire investment tycoon Judah Hayes discovers his wife cheating on him in their own house, he decides to end it with a bang. He throws her out on the street stark naked in the middle of the night with nothing--not even a few dollars to call a cab.

Now he's going to need a really good divorce lawyer--a lawyer good enough to stop his psycho ex from robbing Judah of the empire he worked so hard to build. Of course he's going to hire the best--hotshot lawyer Piper Lagrange.

Piper and Judah develop an instant attraction, but their attorney-client relationship prevents them from taking it further. They'll just have to satisfy themselves by admiring each other from afar.

Judah's ex isn't satisfied with that, though. When she accuses Judah of cheating with Piper, the chain reaction could cost them both their lives, their fortunes, and everything else that makes life worth living. Can they at least salvage what's left of their relationship or will a murderous psychopath destroy that, too?

You can find it at your favorite book retailer.

# Get All of AE Moran's Free Books

S ign Up Once—Get all A.E. Moran's free books including brand new releases

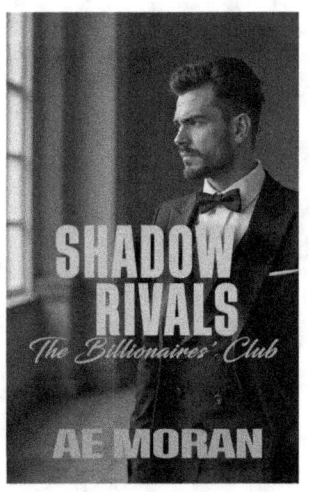

Holden Seager is hot, magnetic, and filthy, stinking, obscenely rich. He commands a room the minute he walks in the door. So what happens when meets another shark as powerful, as charismatic, and as successful as he is—not to mention ten years younger? When these two meet across the negotiating table, one of them will walk away the undisputed winner. The other will walk away with nothing.

Or so it seems.

Unless they're best friends.

When the business deal of a lifetime falls flat on its face and neither of these titans knows how to bring it back to life, this might be the opportunity Dayna Turner has been waiting for.

There's just one problem. She works as an assistant to one of these powerful men....and she's in love with the other. It's a recipe for disaster and heartbreak—unless Dayna can pull off an even bigger coup that will leave them all richer, happier, and more closely connected than ever. The alternative is the destruction of everything all three of them have worked so hard to build.

Sign up at www.authoraemoran.com to read it for free.

# About AE Moran

A .E Moran is the contemporary romance pen name for Theo Mann.

I write 70 books per year—and yes, before you ask, all these books are my original creative work. Nothing written under my name is AI-generated or ghostwritten because I write better than AI and any ghostwriter out there.

People don't read fiction for entertainment or to escape from reality. People read fiction to see their humanity reflected in another person's character and story.

This is my promise to you. When you read my books, you'll see your own humanity reflected in the characters and stories. I take this commitment to my readers very seriously. My books are an intimate form of communication between us. I would never disrespect my readers by turning that over to a machine or another writer. This is my bond between me and you as my reader.

I write 20,000 words per day as my daily work output. If anyone with a public platform would like to challenge me to prove this in a controlled environment, feel free to contact me on this website's contact page.

I worked as a professional ghostwriter for fifteen years. Now I'm going for the Guinness World Record by writing 700 books over the next ten years and 1400 books over the next twenty years, all originally written by me. See my website for the full book list.

I'm also the author of *Proof for the Existence of God* and the *Crimes Against Fiction* blog. You can find all my nonfiction work at www.crimes-against-fiction.com.

If you have a story idea, or if you would like me to explore a series in more depth, or if you'd like me to explore a character by writing a spinoff series about that character or world, leave me a message on my website's contact page. I answer all reader emails, so ask me anything, tell me what you liked and didn't like, and let me know where you'd like your favorite series to go. I would love to hear your ideas and find out what you'd like to read next.

You can find out more at www.theomann.com or at www.authoraemoran.com.

# Also by AE Moran (so far)